SoMa

KEMBLE SCOTT

KENSINGTON BOOKS
http://www.kensingtonbooks.com

KENSINGTON BOOKS are published by

Kensington Publishing Corp.
850 Third Avenue
New York, NY 10022

ISBN-13: 978-0-7582-1549-9
ISBN-10: 0-7582-1549-5

First Kensington Trade Paperback Printing: February 2007
10 9 8 7 6 5 4 3 2 1

SoMa

Jason,

I hope
Soma surprised
you ... a
least a little.

Best
Kemble

[1]so•ma

n.

An intoxicating or hallucinogenic beverage, used as an offering to gods and consumed by participants in ritual sacrifices.

[2]so•ma

n.

The body of an individual as contrasted with the mind or psyche.

[3]So•Ma

n.

South of Market. A neighborhood in San Francisco.

1

Raphe studied the wound in the palm of his hand. The hole still hadn't healed. The surgeon said it would take weeks—the blade had gone all the way through and out the other side. It was a miracle no nerves were severed. It still hurt a little, especially when he made a fist.

"Jesus." Raphe shook his head and laughed.

He didn't deserve it. His life was like a cruel joke.

All he ever did was love one too many. Where was the crime in that? Yet he'd been punished the same as if he'd committed unspeakable atrocities. He'd been pushed into poverty, faced a death sentence, and then *this*.

He looked up at the framed parchment hanging by a nail just above his computer. With his good hand he took it down. "To all men who are about to read this document, everlasting greetings of the Lord . . ." In pretentious Latin, no less. His diploma from Brown.

He tossed it in the trash, where it landed in a sea of bloodied bandages, the waste from the constant cleaning and redressing of the gash.

"Stupid fool."

Raphe took a tube of antibiotic cream and carefully dabbed the ointment on both sides of his hand. He awkwardly peeled two large adhesive bandages from their sterile packaging and nimbly covered each hole, being careful to avoid touching the centers. Then he grabbed one of the latex gloves the doctor had given him, advising him to completely cover the entire hand to prevent any risk of infection.

He held it up to the ceiling light. It was such a strange thing to behold—a hand encased in rubber. *Too weird* for what he had to do. Last time he went out with it on, people stared at him as if he were a freak. He didn't want people laughing at him. Not tonight.

He rummaged around the bottom drawer of his dresser until he found a pair of black leather gloves, the type race car drivers wore. He'd had them since high school when he thought they were so cool for driving his old, beat-up Camaro.

He slipped a leather glove over the latex. Much better. It added a certain air of mystery. He'd just wear the one.

He sprinkled a few pinches of shiny powder into a small glass of water and gulped it down. Not the best way, but he had to take the edge off.

The packed black bag sat on the floor. He peered inside to double-check and make sure he had everything he needed. The mask looked frightening, perfectly designed for secrecy and intimidation. He counted the tubes, all neatly sealed in their sterile packaging. Then there was the saline, and the needles. More than enough for what he had to do.

He tossed a pair of old sweatpants on top. He'd never be able to fit back into his jeans later. It would be too painful.

Before leaving, he sized himself up in his bedroom mirror. He needed to be sure he had his head on straight. *He could do this.* Others wouldn't understand, but in his own way this would be a night for payback. Fate had taken him on the strangest journey into worlds he never knew existed. He'd seen things, *done* things, that would make the old Raphe blush or run away. Funny how you can't be a fugitive from yourself. Where the hell would you go?

Now it was Mark Hazodo's turn to face his destiny. Raphe always thought they'd meet again—San Francisco was a small town that way. He just never expected it to happen so soon and under such bizarre circumstances. Still, this was his opening. Who knew if he'd get another chance like this one?

An old wisecrack popped into Raphe's mind:

Today I am handing out lollipops and ass-kickin's.
And I am all out of lollipops.

His thoughts pulsed with images. A flash of that beautiful, red hair. His baptism into that other world. The cleansing waters. The bizarre, purple house. He shook off the pictures that bombarded his brain. It was always like this when the powder first hit.

Some day he'd sort it all and write down what happened. Maybe even put it into a book. Of course, no one would believe him.

But it was all true.

One Year Earlier

SPRING

2

"Dr. Kaplan, Suite One?"

Raphe turned his head up from his book. The Dr. Kaplan question again. It was the third time so far that day. This time the query came from a blond man in his late twenties. Nice lean build, with too much tan on his face for April. Gotta be a surfer.

"I'm sorry," Raphe deadpanned from his stool behind the counter. He tugged on the small tuft of hair under his chin. "There's no one here by that name."

The blond looked around the room. He noted the dozens of built-in mailboxes affixed to the wall. It was clearly no doctor's office—just a mail drop. Shaking his head in disgust, the man quietly walked back out onto the street.

225 Folsom Street.

That's all the shop was called. No outdoor marquee or door sign that might even vaguely describe what the business offered. The name was just the street address, and vice versa. There were operations just like it peppered throughout the neighborhoods of San Francisco, their low-profile key to their success with certain seedy customers. Anonymous mailboxes, all transactions in cash, no questions asked.

Mr. Harrington owned the entire chain. At least he said his name was Harrington, though Raphe knew the moniker was as suspect as the shady business empire. Harrington was in his fifties with gray hair, streaked in occasional rows of black as if a dye job had started to leach out, all of it slicked back by pomade. He always sported one of dozens of different large-print, untucked Hawaiian shirts. Around his neck he wore a medallion of the Virgin Mary in gold, the size of an Olympic prize, studded with a circle of rubies. He was so clearly Mexican it pained him just to pronounce the name "Harrington," but even after six months he refused to drop the facade.

"What's with this Dr. Kaplan?" Raphe asked. "I keep getting all these guys coming in and asking to see him."

"Don't ax questions," Harrington replied. "What I tell you 'bout that?"

Raphe felt slightly foolish for his lapse. He knew Harrington would never share his secrets. He didn't have to. Within days of starting the job, Raphe figured out on his own that the shop was no mere mailbox drop. It was a safe haven for con artists of all sorts: diploma mills, magic-mushroom seed orders, herbal HGH. If there was a way to separate a loser from his money, then the "corporate headquarters" for such ventures inevitably seemed to be 225 Folsom. Raphe shrugged off Harrington's scolding and turned his head back down into his book, a translation of Georges Bataille's twisted *Story of the Eye*. It was amazing the sick shit people were into, even eighty years ago.

"I go to real post office now. You want tik bathroom break?"

"Uh, no. I'm okay," Raphe said. The office didn't have its own toilet, so Raphe used the McDonald's down the block. Not having a bathroom had to be some sort of code violation, but it seemed pointless to explain laws to a con man. Besides, Raphe had come to enjoy those moments when he could lock up, tape a "back in 5" sign to the glass door, and slip away to Ronald's world for respite.

Why complain? 225 Folsom existed on the fringe of legal, which is exactly where Raphe needed to be. He wasn't paid much, just five hundred dollars per week, but it was all in cash and under the table—an arrangement that wouldn't affect his unemployment benefits. He needed every dime to keep up with the payments on the condo. He couldn't risk losing that, even though it was an excessive throwback to better days. *The dot-com days.* Why did he go for the two bedroom? And at the height of the market! The mortgage payments would break him if it wasn't for 225 Folsom. These days he was like so many formerly upwardly mobile young men in The City, now betrayed and abandoned by the gone world of technology riches. *Metrosexuals without means.* How he hated that word.

At least señor Harrington only demanded a modicum of effort. Most of the time Raphe could just lean up against the counter and read. The solitude allowed him to ponder for the first time what Camus really meant. When Raphe felt ambitious, he jotted down a few notes for the outline of his interminably delayed book—the great American novel told through the eyes of a young adventurer making his way to the big city, living the dream of success until one day an epiphany strikes and he finds . . .

"Adios," Harrington said cheerfully, interrupting Raphe's mental doodling. Then, catching his slip, Harrington added soberly, "Uh, I mean gid-bye . . . old chap!"

Alone again. Sometimes hours would pass without a single customer. When Raphe took the job, the solitude seemed appealing. He didn't count on the paralyzing nature of boredom. He craved customers, even the creepy ones who patronized such a place. At the very least, they provided fodder—bits and pieces—for the still ill-conceived characters he wanted to populate his own pages with someday. Raphe quickly learned the types of people who ran scams were careful, nearly invisible. They purposefully let their correspondence accumulate for days. When they came to retrieve their latest pile of victims, they'd be in and out of the shop in less than thirty seconds. Even after six months, Raphe would have found it impossible to pick out a single face if forced to be a witness at a police line up. If there was business to be done at the counter, like paying up the next several weeks of the extortion-level fees that Harrington demanded, Raphe had been instructed never to make eye contact.

He could count on only two worthwhile distractions per day. At exactly 9:15 each morning the red-haired woman who lived somewhere upstairs would leave for work. She was stunning, in her twenties like himself, and would always smile at Raphe as she walked past the glass front of the shop. He would smile back. He hoped they'd graduate to exchanging little waves soon. In time, maybe they'd even say hello. He wished the smell of McDonald's hash browns would beckon her one morning. He'd jump in line behind her, finally giving himself the opportunity to converse. But she was never corrupted by the scent.

The other highlight of the day came when the mail arrived around ten each morning. Raphe would take the piles and sort them into the various boxes in the wall. Mindless drudgery, but at least it distracted from the tedium. It was in these moments of manual labor that his thoughts floated off into fanciful worlds and memories. He'd daydream about the red-haired woman from upstairs, contriving little scenes where he'd be so witty and charming, and she'd respond with raw animal lust. *Women.* It had been too long since his last date. Who'd want to go out with dot-com debris? Sorting the mail allowed his mind to escape to a fantasy parallel universe where there was no tech meltdown and Raphe was successful, wanted, and loved. Placing the envelopes in all the little mailboxes could be done in as little as twenty minutes, but on most days he would stretch the duty out for more than an hour.

At his last job at a big web site design firm he'd worked with his mind all day, leaving little brainpower left in the evenings when he planned to do his writing. At the height of the dot-com craze the work was frantic, the projects moronically ill-conceived. Not that it mattered. Since so much money was coming in, the CEO complained he was "going to need a pitchfork" to handle it all. Meanwhile, Raphe's frustrations with his own thwarted ambitions to write developed into ulcerative pains whenever he entered a bookstore, overwhelmed by the thousands of bound accomplishments that surrounded him while he remained unpublished.

He blamed dot-com. On the surface it all looked so frivolous and fun, with its casual bull pen atmosphere, roaming pets, and never-ending, free supply of caffeinated soda. But it wasn't all laughs for those few who actually did the work. From college economics Raphe remembered the classic 80/20 Principle—that 80 percent of the work is done by just 20 percent of the workforce. Like most employment concepts of the past, dot-com had turned that old theory on its head. In the web world, it was more like the 95/5 Principle, with Raphe stuck among the toiling few. His first big job, and Raphe was already bitter.

"It's a business that does systems analysis for corporations."

As he sorted the day's mail, Raphe remembered those fateful words from an attractive blonde venture capitalist looking to hire the firm. Was it two years ago? Spring 2000. It seemed like yesterday. "So we were thinking of AnalysisBusiness.com as the name for the site."

That's stupid, Raphe thought from his disgruntled corner of the packed conference room table.

"The problem is," the VC woman continued, "that name is already taken. Some virtual psychology site. So what we were thinking is shortening the title to something catchier. Just use the first four letters of 'analysis' and say 'bizz' instead of 'business.'"

Raphe already had four other projects to handle, and this was to be his fifth. The perky blonde's presentation hit him as the final straw. He already put in seventy hours a week, and now he was about to become the laughingstock of the office.

"You're shitting me!" Raphe burst out.

"Excuse me?" the woman said, straining to keep her relentless smile.

"You want to call this site '*Anal*Bizz'? '*Anal*Bizz'! Are you fucking serious?"

"It's not '*Anal*-bizz,'" she countered, now clearly flustered. "It's 'anaaahl-bizz.' As in 'analysis.' Not . . . 'anal.' It's 'anaaahl.'" She stretched out the pronunciation to try to make her point, but it was too late. She was humiliated, and Raphe would not let it go.

"It doesn't matter how *you* pronounce it. It's spelled '*anal*.' That's how people will see it. They're gonna think it's a site for butt plugs or something. We'll probably get porn traffic!"

"Well, hits are hits, right?" the woman said sheepishly. When no one else was looking, she stared across the table into Raphe's eyes. He knew what she was thinking. *Who the fuck do you think you are?*

When the tech bubble burst months later, and the gravy stopped flowing, Raphe was in the first round of layoffs. All the other dismissals were done by seniority, but his "bad attitude" pushed him to the front of the pink slip line. He'd been scrounging ever since.

"Excuse me."

The voice startled Raphe, so lost in his mail-sorting dotcom daydreams he never heard anyone come in. "Dr. Kaplan, Suite One?"

"What?"

"Dr. Kaplan, Suite One," the voice said again, much more determined and confident the second time. Raphe stood up from his sorting and turned. It was a young man this time. A teenager?

"There's no Dr. Kaplan here. I'm sorry. You have the wrong place."

"This is 225 Folsom, isn't it?"

"Yes."

"Well, Dr. Kaplan's office is at 225 Folsom, Suite One. You sure it's not here? Maybe on an upper floor? I really do need to see him. It's urgent."

Upstairs? Raphe thought of the red-haired woman. She was definitely not Dr. Kaplan. The young man seemed almost panicked, as if his life somehow depended on finding this doctor. Raphe had been told how to handle these situations his first day on the job. "Jus ax stipid," Harrington told him. Their customers paid for complete anonymity for their shams. If anyone came snooping, it was best to play ignorant. Besides, it would be a good defense if the police ever raided, or if a scam victim decided to show up for revenge.

The young man standing before him didn't look like the type Raphe figured fell for rip-offs like these. He always thought of them as double-wide trailer types, grifting for a way to make a quick buck in some scheme. If they got taken, then it was probably for the best—it proved Darwin was right. This guy was different. Just a kid. A college boy maybe, or even high school. He was certainly young enough, dressed in the Old Navy requirements of his middle-class generation. Raphe thought he saw tears forming in the young man's blue eyes.

"I really *need* to see him."

It wasn't Raphe's job to feel sorry for anyone, or teach a wayward teenager a lesson about life. He knew that. Still, there was something about this kid that got to him. Maybe it was the innocence of the boy's youth, or the fact that Raphe was so bored he was curious to see how it all would play out.

"Over there." Raphe pointed to the wall.

"What?" The young man's face filled with hope.

Raphe gestured again, and the kid walked across the room. He stared at the wall of mailboxes. "I don't understand."

Raphe walked over. "Welcome to Suite One," he said, placing his hand on mailbox number one.

"No, that can't be right," the young man said, now trying to act as if some perfectly reasonable mistake had been made. "I'm not looking for a mailbox. The address did not say PO Box One. It said Suite One. I'm obviously in the wrong building. Sorry I wasted your time."

Raphe shook his head and touched the young man's shoulder. "Does he owe you money?"

"What? No. I mean, of course not. He's a doctor. Why would he owe me money?"

"Did you send him money?"

"No. Look, I just came by hoping I could see the doctor. Or at least get an appointment. That's all."

Raphe took the master key out of his pocket and opened the box. It was stuffed with letters. He fished one out and held it up to the young man's face. The words were unmistakable, despite the messy cursive scrawl on the envelope: *Dr. Kaplan, 225 Folsom Street, Suite One.*

The teen became ashen, his youthful color completely drained as if he'd just taken a punch to the gut, unable to catch his breath. Without another word, he bolted from the shop.

It was always men who inquired about Dr. Kaplan, Raphe realized. Although once he remembered how a married couple came in and asked for "Suite One." The woman did all the talking, and Raphe recalled she was very aggressive. He worried at the time they were Feds working undercover, but they went away without incident.

The kid's emotional scene, however, made Raphe curious. What scam did this Dr. Kaplan have going that inspired so many people to come into The City in search of a personal appointment? He looked down at the letter in his hands and inspected the back. One corner of the flap was all that held the envelope closed. It would take little effort to peel it free and peek inside. He'd seal it all back up, and no one would be the wiser. What could be the harm?

He tore it open, creating a bit more of a sloppy edge than he intended. Inside he found a newspaper clipping. It was a small advertisement, the type found in the classified section of a weekly paper. The cheap ink easily smudged onto his fingers.

"DON'T BE ASHAMED ONE DAY LONGER!" the headline screamed. "Add one to three inches with Dr. Kaplan's patented system. Order your initial consultation kit now." Also inside the envelope was a check made out to Dr. Kaplan for $29.99.

The bigger penis scam. Anyone with e-mail got at least a few "add inches" spams per week. The electronic onslaught was so pervasive that a female coworker in dot-com once joked, "I never knew I had such a small cock until I joined AOL."

Poor kid. Probably only seventeen-years-old, and he's already worried about his shortcomings. It was about that age that Raphe himself became aware that size mattered. He'd never given it much thought until he and his high school girlfriend Judy ventured off to a nude beach. They couldn't have been more than sixteen at the time. Raphe spent most of the day lying on his stomach, trying to hide how easily he was aroused by the sight of all the naked bodies. He would pay later for his inability to control his passions, the sunburn on his behind made it excruciating to sit for days.

"*He's* the king of the beach," Judy sighed as she pointed to an obese man standing in the surf. The man was surrounded by a gaggle of six perpetually giggling, attractive women.

"The fat one?" Raphe asked, noticing how the man's back was so hairy it looked like a sweater.

"Yes."

"You know him?"

"No, I can just tell."

Raphe couldn't, at least not from the distance of their blanket set up against the dunes. When he was sure his excitement had been tamed for at least a few minutes, he headed down to the water to cool his already fiery backside. As he hit the waves, he saw why so many female admirers surrounded the portly man. His manhood was freakishly large, swinging like a pendulum, bouncing off his thighs as he walked.

It was the size of a baby's arm.

Raphe shuddered. He closed his eyes tight and squatted down into the cooling water. He reached down to examine himself for comparison. It was the first time Raphe realized there was a scale to such things. A pecking order of peckers.

That day he learned the differences could be enormous. Now Raphe wondered just how small the teenager was to be so vexed he would make his way to 225 Folsom—a part of SoMa not exactly on the tourist trail—in pursuit of the miraculous Dr. Kaplan and his mysterious cure. Raphe had seen the monstrosity on the man at the nude beach. The angst of the boy and Dr. Kaplan's scam made him wonder if there was another extreme—one at the other end of the size spectrum. Had the boy been stunted from becoming a man? How bad could it be?

Dr. Kaplan must have hit a nerve with a new marketing campaign. Over the next several weeks the foot traffic into 225 Folsom increased dramatically. Several men stopped by each day asking for "Suite One."

Raphe soon wished he'd never opened that envelope to discover the secret of Dr. Kaplan. The job had always been tedious, but at least it didn't cause anxiety. Now each time the door opened, he found himself in an awkward moment. The incident with the teenager had opened his eyes to this subculture of inadequacy, and he couldn't get the condition out of his mind. Not that he was worried about his own, since he was pretty sure he measured up OK. The crisis hit each time a guy came in and asked for "Suite One." Raphe could not prevent himself.

He looked.

Not that it was easy to tell. A casual glance didn't reveal very much, especially when pleated pants were involved. To get any sort of read on the situation took careful study. What might be a telltale bulge could actually be a large set of keys sunk to the bottom of a front pocket. Was that an embarrassing little acorn of manhood, or the bend of something pushed to the side? He thought blue jeans did the best job of exposing the truth, but even then he could not be completely sure.

Trying to determine the length and width of a man's nature soon turned into an obsession. No matter how hard Raphe tried to keep his eyes focused on a book, or even to look away in disinterest, his sight was automatically drawn to the crotch.

Clothing made it too difficult to see the truth, so Raphe began searching for other clues. He'd heard that foot size directly corresponded, but there was no consistency to the lengths of the feet of the men who walked in and asked for Dr. Kaplan. He expected to see dainty little shoes, like those worn by little boys going to church. Instead, all the men had regular size feet, with at least one sporting a size twelve. Foot size meant nothing—it was just a worthless old wives' tale.

Bald? Men with less hair were said to have more testosterone. Conversely, Raphe wondered if maybe men with lots of hair on their heads tended to be tiny down below. Over several weeks he carefully noted the fullness of the manes of the men who came to visit "Suite One." It quickly became apparent there was no pattern this way either. Just as many had thinning hair as bushy mops.

Fool! Nothing worked to provide an answer. Raphe felt his frustration burn, just as it did in the bad old dot-com days. Soon he began inspecting his own, becoming concerned that he too came up short. Then he found himself checking out men outside the shop. It was embarrassing and uncomfortable, and the guys inevitably felt the scrutiny of Raphe's glance. He knew he had sunk to a new low when he caught himself speculating about the size of Mr. Harrington's *pinga*.

He had to stop. He wasn't a gay—and he didn't want to be

one. Raphe figured it would be just a matter of time before one of the men clocked him for obviously staring. This was San Francisco, but not everyone was open-minded. An unhealthy seed was planted in his head that tore at any semblance of self-control. It was *sick* to obsess about such things. It reminded him of his friend Jeff's dog that impolitely and tenaciously sniffed the butt of everyone who visited. Soon people stopped coming over.

At first he wasn't sure how to rid himself of the obsession. He could quit working at 225 Folsom, of course, but he needed the money. He toyed with the idea of wearing sunglasses all day, so none of the men could be sure where his eyes inevitably wandered. At least they wouldn't know they were being so carefully studied.

No, Raphe agonized, those were just bandages aimed at quelling the symptoms of his disease. One day while sorting the mail his mind presented him with perfect clarity on the issue. The contents of mailbox number one had doomed him to a constant guessing game. The puzzle had to be solved, or he would fumble with the pieces forever. He would have to see firsthand what was tiny enough to cause such a big fuss.

On Thursday the next query came through the door.

"Can I help you?" Raphe asked.

"I'm looking for Dr. Kaplan, Suite One."

The man was tall, at least six foot two, and built like a runner. His face had boyish freckles, but a dark blue suit and polite mannerisms betrayed him as a product of the financial district, probably a broker. It was two in the afternoon, the typical quitting time for people working the West Coast version of Wall Street.

"No one by that name here," Raphe said, turning his face down into the pages of Salinger, forcing himself not to peek.

The man in the suit looked over to the wall of mailboxes.

"Oh." The man's tone revealed he understood. "Sorry for bothering you."

"No problem," mumbled Raphe.

"One more thing," the man asked. "You don't by any chance have a restroom I can use?"

"No," Raphe said, continuing to avoid eye contact. "We don't have one. Try the McDonald's down the block."

The bathroom. Of course!

As soon as the man left, Raphe practically leaped over the counter. He slapped the "back in 5" sign up, locked the door, and began the chase.

The pungent smell of french fries got stronger as he walked. Raphe slowed his pace, careful to stay at least twenty feet back to avoid being obvious. Once inside he didn't see the man. How could he lose him so quickly? He looked over to the dining area, but no one was there except a toothless bag lady gumming a spit-soaked cheeseburger. He glanced in the other direction just in time to see the door to the men's room swing shut.

Raphe took a deep breath to calm himself, then pushed his way into the room. There was the suit, standing at one of two urinals. Raphe moved up beside the man, unzipped and pulled out, as if he too needed to go. He looked down, first at his own, so not to arouse any suspicion. Then without turning his head, he let his eyes inch over to see the man. Finally, he would know what was considered such a horrendous, aggrieved appendage that it would require the enhancement services of Dr. Kaplan. How small was too small?

He expected to see something miniscule, like the sprout found on a newborn. It wasn't like that at all. Raphe couldn't say he was the most experienced judge of such things, but if forced to find a word to describe it, he would have to say *normal.* It was just about the size of his own. Maybe the man in the suit had ambitions to be as big as the man at the nude beach.

Raphe panicked—what if they were both puny compared to everyone else?

No, that wasn't it, Raphe reasoned. His wasn't small and neither was the man's. If anything, it looked even bigger than his own. In fact, in just the moments he'd been standing and gawking, Raphe could swear it was getting even larger.

Out of his periphery, he could tell the suit had turned his head and was staring back. If he had ever been undersized, it was impossible to tell now since Raphe's attention had stirred the man into full passion.

"Can I help *you*?" the man said, grinning while he tugged.

Raphe stumbled back, almost tripping over himself as he tried to zip and retreat. He bumped into the hand dryer as he fled from the room and back onto the street. He struggled to unlock the door at 225 Folsom, and once inside turned the deadbolt back into place. He kept the "back in 5" sign up and crawled behind the counter to sit on the floor, hoping that if the man walked past he would not see him through the windows.

3

"Whaddaya mean twelve bucks? The sign says seven!" Lauren screamed through the opening in the ticket window. The music from the club seemed as loud as the highest setting on her Bose, and they weren't even inside.

"Sliding scale," yelled back the sleepy-eyed attendant, scratching at the scab around her cheek-piercing. "It's seven if you're dressed according to the theme. Ten if you're in club clothes. Twelve for street clothes."

"I don't remember reading that on the web site." It wasn't a ton of money, but Lauren hated feeling cheated. The posting said seven, so there was no reason it should be anything other than seven.

"Sorry," the attendant yawned. "You coming in or what? You're holding up the line."

"This is our first time," Jessica said as she stepped up beside Lauren at the window. "What do you mean *according to the theme?*"

The attendant rattled off the list like a bored waiter reading the day's specials. "Leather, boots, teddies, whips, chains, tit clamps, vinyl, hoods, nudity, Goth. . . ."

"Nudity? People are *naked* in there?" Jessica gasped.

"Honey, this is Bondage-a-Go-Go. The less you wear, the

less you pay. You want something else, go try Bimbos in North Beach."

Lauren squinted. Who was this skanky bitch to act like they were in the wrong place? She knew it was Bondage-a-Go-Go. They drove in all the way from Concord for it! Lauren leaned over and whispered into her friend's ear.

"No way, Lolly," Jessica frowned. "I'm just gonna pay the extra five bucks."

"Fuck that, Jes. I'm not letting this bitch push us around."

"Lolly, I, uh . . ."

"Do it!"

Jessica shut her eyes, as if not witnessing the scene made it somehow OK. In unison, the two women lifted up their shirts. The attendant's eyes finally opened wide as she confronted two sets of firm, round breasts.

Lauren smiled, noting as always that hers were bigger—if Jes hadn't been such a nancy about surgery, she could have had the same.

Lauren shoved a twenty through the ticket window opening. "That'll be two for seven each, *please*."

As soon as they made their way past the thick, dark drape that obscured the door, they pulled their shirts back down. Jessica yelped, "Why do I let you talk me into this shit?"

"Relax, will ya?"

"Relax? Just what the hell are we doing here? We're not into this. And it's Wednesday night, for god's sake. We've got work in the morning!"

"Look, Jes. They only run this club one night a week. It's supposed to be the most bizarre in Frisco."

"So?"

"So? Let's put it this way. What are we supposed to do this Saturday night?"

"Uh, that party?"

"Right. And who will be the only two women there who have ever been to Bondage-a-Go-Go?"

"Us?"

"We'll have the undivided attention of every guy."

"I thought you said the boys back home were *boring*."

"Gotta keep 'em interested, Jes. Don't want any of my followers to stray."

Jessica grinned uneasily. She'd known Lauren to have boys wrapped around her finger ever since they were in junior high. When they were kids, Jessica wanted to be more like that, wishing a little of Lauren's brassy nature would rub off. She was hardly alone. Back then, Lauren was the envy of all the girls. Lately, Lauren snubbed the local guys. The more they wanted her, the less interested she seemed in them.

"Lolly, I just thought of something. What if someone wants to . . . you know . . . that whips and chains stuff."

"Fine by me. As long as we do the whipping," Lauren laughed.

The bartender smirked when the two pushed their way up through the three-deep crowd and asked for Cosmos. He filled their order, a heavy hand on the vodka. "Newbies," he whispered to the barback.

The barback sized up the two women. "Blonde. Pretty. Young. Think they're sisters?"

"Fuck if I know." The bartender rolled his eyes. "Chicks from the sticks. They all look alike."

Jessica glanced around the room as she took her first sip. It seemed like any other club, except most of the people looked like characters from an old Prince video. At the end of the room she noticed a ramp that led up to another doorway and what looked like a second large cavern in the back. She could see distant images of wild dancing, smoke, and lasers.

"Look over there," Lauren whispered as she tugged on Jessica's shirt. To the left side of the ramp a large crowd gathered in the corner.

"What is it?"

"I dunno. Whatever it is, people can't stop staring. Come on!"

Lauren spilled some of her drink on the buttcrack of a man in backless chaps as she pushed her way to the front of the mob. She yanked Jessica along by her sleeve. Without ever making a polite remark for their intrusion, the two managed to get up to a thick, black rope that sectioned off the corner like a boxing ring.

The space held a small group of women and men, all in various degrees of nudity or leather. A topless woman stood apart from the others, skillfully applying what appeared to be excruciatingly painful clamps on her nipples. Some in the crowd winced as the sharp metal teeth of the vice bit into the rose-colored flesh.

Beyond her a man stood with his back to the room, his forehead pressed against the wall. He was naked, except for black shorts dropped around his ankles. Beside him a woman wearing only panties and a garter belt took a big swing with a paddle to connect with the man's exposed behind. Snap!

"That must hurt," Lauren said as she raised her eyebrow at Jessica.

"Look at how red his ass is." Jessica grimaced.

An obese woman got down on all fours in front of them, while another came over and playfully brushed a cat-o'-nine-tails up and down her spine. She turned it around and took the knob of the handle and rubbed it between the woman's legs. When she moaned with pleasure, the dominatrix flipped the whip around and cracked it across the woman's back. The routine of teasing and punishing went on for several minutes.

Sitting on a stool just outside the rope stanchion was a man in his twenties, dressed in leather from head to toe. He wore a spiked dog collar around his neck, but his light brown hair was cut short, only slightly mussed. Lauren thought he looked like

Mel Gibson in *The Road Warrior.* He was the best looking guy in the place, even if he was a bit seedy.

"Hey you!" Even through the music, she spoke loudly enough to get him to turn and look. "How come you get the front row seat?"

"Well, missy, don't you see? I'm part of the show," he said with an unmistakably thick Texas accent.

"All I see is you sitting on your ass, instead of getting it beaten!" Lauren took a playful sip from her drink, already feeling the buzz.

"I play a very important role, darlin'."

"What's that?"

"I'm the recruiter."

"Recruiter? I got a news flash for you: this ain't exactly the army."

"Ah, but we are looking for a few good men. And especially a few good women," he said with a wide smile.

Lauren would find out later his name was Putt, short for Putnam, originally from Texas. "Midland, Texas, to be exact."

Putt brought Lauren and Jessica up the ramp and down a corridor across from the bathrooms. He unlocked a door that opened to a staircase up to an office, *his* office—assistant manager. When they got upstairs, Lauren took note of a large skylight that allowed anyone in the apartment building next door to see everything.

"You girls sure you want to do this?" Putt asked.

"Do what?" Jessica looked panicked. "Lolly, I never said. . . ."

"Not her, babe. Just me."

"Where you from?"

"Concord."

"Oh, a bridge-and-tunnel girl."

"Hmmm, I don't know about the bridge," Lauren giggled, now realizing she was already plastered after just one drink. How much vodka was in this?

"Just so you know, there are a few ground rules before you can get into that ring."

"Like?"

"I want to tell you, but those secrets are only for people who get on the other side of the black rope." Putt stared at Jessica.

"Lolly, I thought we came here to . . ."

"Don't worry, Jes. Putt and I are just gonna have a little chat. OK?"

"You sure?"

"I'm fine, honey."

"Well, then I'm going to get in line for the ladies' room. Meet you over at the ropes?"

"Sure thing, babe," Lauren said as she used the door to push Jessica out of the office. *Doesn't that girl know when she's not wanted?*

"My, my, my," Putt grinned. "Darlin', those are a beautiful pair of titties."

"Well, the ticket girl sure seemed impressed." Lauren pulled her shirt down, so it wrapped snug on her chest. Without a bra, the slight raise of her areolas emerged through the cotton. Lauren looked down at herself with approval. It was a nice rack.

Putt reached over and began to gently caress. "They're perfect," he said. "God doesn't make 'em this round in Texas."

"Well, *gawd* is not completely responsible." Lauren mimicked Putt's drawl.

"I do love you California girls. So adventurous with your bodies." Putt pinched the left nipple, making Lauren wince—a sensation of pain, yet somehow enjoyable. "You know, I've had a little reconstructive surgery of my own. Not at a plastic surgeon. Had it done over at The Gauntlet."

"What is it? A tattoo?"

"No, it's a little more personal than that."

"What is it? Lemme see!"

Putt leaned back against his desk and began the slow process of unbuttoning his black, leather pants. He never looked down, but kept his eyes on Lauren as she watched his hands at work. When he got to the final metal stud, he tugged at the two sides until a tuft of black hair surfaced. He shoved his hand down the opening and carefully pulled himself out.

Lauren stared, her fingers instinctually moving to cover her mouth. She'd heard of such things, of course, but had never actually seen one in person. The men back in Concord were too dull and conservative to even think of it. Through the head of Putt's penis was a metal loop, like the hoop of an earring. Dangling precariously from the ring was a small, precious little gold charm in the shape of Texas.

"It's called a P.A. Short for Prince Albert."

"I know what it is . . . I've just never come face-to-face with one." Lauren couldn't stop staring, fascinated by the decadence of it. "Does it hurt?"

"No way, girl. Just a pinch when it happened. It hurts a lot more to have a nipple pierced. Tit pain lasts for months."

"But . . . why?" Lauren thought the impracticality astonishing. Could you fuck with it? What about wearing a condom? Would it get stuck in your tonsils?

"Sensitivity. I feel things now that I never could have imagined before." He explained how the P.A. made even the most mundane motions intense by stimulating. Pulling up his trousers would almost always cause him to throb. He didn't dare put on tight-fitting underwear anymore. Once, while riding the crowded MUNI subway car, the constant stir of people brushing up against him caused him to climax and drench himself— it was over before he realized it had started.

"Can I . . . ?" Lauren paused. "Can I touch it?"

"I was hoping you would," Putt smirked.

Lauren got down on her knees, at first just tentatively tapping with her forefinger. It was odd, yet strangely beautiful.

She'd never dreamed that jewelry could be so *sleazy*. She remembered when she was eleven and had her ears pierced at the mall, without her parents' permission. Her father was so furious he slapped her across the face. *No child of mine is going to look like a slut!* The words still stung. They were just earrings, innocent little heart-shaped studs. Her father acted as if she'd been tainted, painted up like a prostitute, no longer a virginal child. Lauren stared at the loop and the little gold charm that seemed to hang by a thread. Dad didn't know anything. *This* was dangerous jewelry.

The touch was enough to stir a reaction, and Putt motioned for Lauren to bring her lips closer and take him inside. Within moments, he screamed, violently pulling her head until her face was pressed to his abdomen. Now all the way down her throat, she choked for air. After two brutal jolts, and one deep groan, he released her. Lauren gasped for air, annoyed she'd been forced to swallow. In Concord, she'd berate a guy for being so quick on the trigger and not meeting *her* needs. A damned two-pump bandit! Yet here, in this strange place, being taken so hard was weirdly erotic. That he climaxed so soon had to mean he thought she was hot, right? Raunchy, yes, but *exciting*. After a few awkward moments of small talk, Putt ushered Lauren back into the club.

It took Lauren a few minutes to figure out which song she was dancing to. Then it hit her. The tune was "Love to Love You Baby," but instead of Donna Summer this version featured a group of screaming men and blaring guitars tearing through a house music thump. Lauren liked the disco version better.

She and Jessica danced with each other for nearly two hours, in between rounds of drinks they had to buy for themselves. No guys ever approached to cut in. Instead, they were surrounded by a perpetual empty space of at least two feet that seemed to follow them wherever they went. They were alone in a crowded room, treated as outcasts in a world where leather and metal was the norm. J.Crew wasn't welcome here.

Fuck 'em, Lauren thought. None of *them* had been invited upstairs with Putt. Her mind drifted back to what happened. She knew if she ever told Jessica the details, her friend would say she'd been used. Lauren didn't feel used. Instead, it felt like a conquest to mess around with someone like Putt. So what if she barely knew him. Who knows? Maybe there could be more someday.

As the next song started to play, a rap metal version of "You Light Up My Life," Lauren felt suddenly nauseous. Must be cheap booze. She'd asked for top shelf, but in a dive like this she couldn't be sure what they actually poured. Maybe her stomach was upset from what happened with Putt. It was pretty abrupt.

"I feel like I'm going to yack," Lauren declared. "Let's split."

In the car headed up Harrison Street to the highway entrance, Jessica pointed out the open window. "Hey, isn't that Putt?"

Putt was on the opposite side of the street, walking back toward the club. He held a flimsy, white paper plate up to his mouth with both hands and munched a gooey slice of pizza. Lauren screeched her car into a mid-block U-turn on the one-way street, pulling onto the sidewalk facing the wrong direction. She narrowly missed hitting a young man in red leather on a neon pink Vespa. He cursed her, but she ignored him and left the lights on with the engine running as she jumped out of the car and raced up to Putt. "Hey, give me a bite of that," she said playfully.

"What?" Putt mumbled through a mouthful of pesto with sausage.

"Give me a bite of that."

"What are you talking about?"

"Putt, it's me—Lauren. From the club? Remember?"

"Yeah, I know who you are." He took another bite and spoke with his mouth full. "What do you want?"

"I want a bite of that pizza." Lauren smiled wide, still a little light-headed from the drinks. What a coincidence to run into Putt again. She didn't want to read too much into it, but—

"Fuck off." Putt kept walking.

Lauren caught up to him, suddenly jolted back into sobriety by anger. "What do you mean, *fuck off*?"

"I mean, get lost. I don't want your dirty mouth on my pizza."

"Dirty?" Lauren yelled. "It wasn't so dirty two hours ago! Now I can't even have a bite of your pizza!"

"Darling, it's what we did that made your mouth so dirty." Putt swallowed. "Can't hardly believe you're still hungry."

"Asshole!"

"Yeah, yeah. Go home to Concord. I reckon there must be a TGI Friday's or something there that's more your speed."

Lauren tried to scream again. Nothing came out. Suddenly she had an uncontrollable urge to spit. Her stomach. The nausea again. At first, little drops washed up. Then she hocked up thick phlegm from the back of her throat. The sudden confrontation on the street, mixed with too much booze—the contents of her stomach violently surged. But it was blocked. She hacked to the point of hyperventilation, then dropped to her knees and vomited.

"Stupid bitch. Gimme that back!" Putt knelt down next to the spill. He used two fingers to carefully reach into the puddle and fish out a small, shiny gold object.

It was the tiny Texas charm from his P.A.

The drive back to Concord went in silence until the two women got to Jessica's home. The whole trip Jessica tried to think of something to say to console her friend, but knew that anything would come out wrong. In Concord, nothing like this would ever happen. Men there *loved* Lauren. She was the one who dumped *them* when they'd served their purpose. Why couldn't she be content with a normal, nice guy? To Jessica, it seemed as if these days all Lauren wanted were men who would never work out. It was as if Lauren was on a mission to convert the hard-core cases, the ones who could never really be bent to her will. It made no sense. Jessica worried where these antics would lead her best friend. She silently vowed to keep an eye on Lauren, to intervene if she could. Much good it would do, she knew, since Lauren rarely—if ever—listened to others.

"Thanks honey," Jessica said as they pulled up to her apartment. She spoke softly as she opened the door, not wanting to wake her neighbors. "Try to cheer up, Lolly. Just think . . . we'll be the life of the party on Saturday when we tell people we've been to Bondage-a-Go-Go. For twelve bucks, it was an interesting place."

Lauren looked straight ahead, her face expressionless. "Seven, Jes. We paid seven."

4

Vacne. That was the word Raphe struggled to remember. Those tiny, red blotches of nascent pimples surrounding a guy's mouth. When a friend told Raphe the nickname for it, he laughed out loud. *Vagina* plus *acne* equals *vacne,* the minor outbreak caused by a man going down on a woman.

The man next to him on the BART platform definitely had vacne. He was average height, with black razor stubble. His hair was dark, with just enough gel to be kept professionally in place and defy the notorious downtown winds.

The man's pinstriped suit made Raphe's mind flash to the bathroom in the McDonald's. He always got a sick feeling whenever he remembered that moment. The embarrassment. How awful to be caught.

The incident had cured him of wandering eyes at 225 Folsom. To be sure of that, Raphe asked Mr. Harrington if he could bring his laptop to the shop, hoping to finally start writing his novel. What held him back, Raphe decided, was trying to scribble it all down by hand. Pen and pad was like using a chisel and rock. No wonder he wasn't making any progress. The laptop he kept from the dot-com—they didn't *ask* for it back—would be the answer to his writer's block.

"You use for kid porno?" Harrington asked.

"Well, uh, of course not!" The question caught Raphe off guard, forgetting for a moment Harrington's constant worry that no attention be brought upon the place.

"Okay. Sí." Harrington caught himself. "I mean, *yes*—you can use compiter."

That was two weeks ago, and Raphe still hadn't typed a word of his book. He'd get too distracted. First he'd check his e-mail. Then he had to get caught up on the latest news from SFGate.com. Next was a link from a friend to a hysterical story about online dating. "The odds are good, but the goods are odd." A spam brought him to a site called rotton.com, which led him to learning about a Japanese fetish called bukkake. Sick!

One day he went to craigslist.org to put up for sale the IKEA carpet he never really liked. He could use the money. While there he began to peruse the other classified ads, eyeing cars he would buy if he ever had money again. He checked the *Help Wanted* section, but didn't find anything even remotely worthwhile. Just a Pink Slip Party. He wasn't that desperate—at least not yet.

Then he hit the personal ads. He'd never explored them before. Why bother? There were a billion guys just like him in The City these days. Having a SoMa condo, tech stock options, and a degree from Brown once got a guy laid at places like the infamous meat market bar Elroy's. That place was long gone, the stock options worthless, and the degree meaningless until attached to a paycheck. At twenty-five, was he supposed to feel so washed up?

He turned to the *Casual Encounters* section of the web site: no strings attached sexual experiences for men and women. Maybe that would make him feel better. He hadn't had sex since Lisa, and that was nearly a year ago. He'd been on only one date since then, and she only wanted to cuddle. For hours Raphe read the listings, amazed at what people had the nerve to advertise. Three ways. Erotic massages. *K-9?*

A few times he answered the tamer ads, using a hotmail.com account he created to obscure his identity. To his surprise, many people answered back. But when they asked for a photograph he chickened out. Are there really women who like to do these things? Or are they just collecting photographs of idiots stupid enough to respond to their postings? He imagined girls huddled around a cubicle in an office somewhere giggling over which dorks had dared to send in the most revealing shots of themselves.

Then he found a listing with remarkably simple copy. The message contained just one word: "BART." He knew that stood for Bay Area Rapid Transit, the commuter train service that connected The City to the suburbs. What "casual encounter" could possibly happen in such a public place?

The word "BART" was tinted blue, meaning it was a hyperlink. With a click, Raphe found himself transported into a Yahoo group called "BARTM4M." M4M—men for men. A gay site. He quickly closed down the browser, ashamed that somewhere in his computer's memory would be a record that he visited such a web site.

As he closed the laptop, a sensation hit—that he was being watched. He looked up toward the front window, catching sight of the woman with red hair from upstairs. Raphe threw an animated smile in her direction, but she had already turned and the moment was lost. Had she been looking at him? If so, for how long? Is it possible she saw him looking at *that web site*? No, he chided himself. She wouldn't be able to see the screen from there. He was just being paranoid. Raphe continued to stare at the red-haired woman as she faded into the distance. How beautiful she was, even while walking away. She was wearing that pastel green pullover again, the one that showed off her athletic build. He loved that top. He knew it would be in her clothing rotation at least once a month.

Dammit. He wasn't *gay*. What was so bad about looking at

that web site? It made no sense for someone completely straight to feel threatened by such things. Besides, maybe he'd find material for his book. There was certainly nothing wrong with being curious. He'd never be a real writer if he didn't start to stretch his mind. BART was as good a place to start as any.

Raphe smiled to himself. She was checking him out—the red-haired woman from upstairs! He'd caught her. At least he thought he had.

Back on the web site, Raphe learned BARTM4M was a gathering place for men who enjoyed a specific sexual fetish, one intrinsically linked to the daily commute. At first, he wondered if it was a joke. But Yahoo counted more than three thousand registered members, leading Raphe to think it had to be real or one of the most elaborately staged hoaxes of all time.

If it was true, then it would make for a great story—a real shocker. The only way to find out would be to take the journey himself.

Raphe got into the underground BART station at the Embarcadero stop, uneasily walking past the loud, homeless contingent that sat on the park benches next to the entrance. He'd heard that people from the offices nearby cruelly referred to each of the decrepit men as a "Solitaire," since they never seemed to see each other, instead shouting nonstop at invisible demons who tormented them. Still, Raphe liked coming downtown to soak up the energy, and wondered why he didn't visit more often. After all, he lived only a few blocks away in SoMa. He could see the steel and glass monetary monuments from the windows of his high-rise condo, sometimes musing about the busy lives of the swarms inside those business hives. After his meltdown in dot-com, he figured he was never built for the life of a corporate drone, but envied the simplicity and camaraderie of it.

The BARTM4M web site said the trip from The City to the East Bay took seven minutes. Seven minutes under the floor of the bay. An amazing engineering feat, Raphe thought. Whoever figured this out were geniuses. Surely, they'd be stunned to learn their invention was now nicknamed "the tunnel of love."

The last BART train. Not the last of the day, but the final cabin at the tail end of any of the dozens of trains that made the trip. In another era it might have been called the caboose.

To get on the last car, Raphe waited at the far west end of the platform. As he stood, he sized up the man with the vacne. The man was definitely in the right spot for the BARTM4M fetish. He was clearly straight, and not just because of the telltale pimples. The way he walked. He was a handsome, ruggedly built Latino, somewhere around thirty, and devoid of any fey mannerisms. There was no way he was gay.

A train bound for the city of Fremont pulled up. Raphe got in and walked all the way to the back. It was the three-thirty train. Rush hour had yet to start. There was hardly a soul in the compartment.

Raphe sat in the final row, facing forward. He kept his sunglasses on, even though he wouldn't be seeing any sunlight for at least seven minutes. He felt more comfortable as an observer if it was impossible for others to see his eyes.

There were four benches in the back, each made to seat two passengers. They faced forward, two benches per row, with an aisle down the center. The brown, industrial fabric of the seats looked worn, and the matching carpet was faded and ripped in places. Still, Raphe thought it remarkably clean, seeing no trash or sordid stains. He noted how all the advertising on the walls had to do with AIDS. "HIV changed my life," proclaimed Magic Johnson, "but it doesn't keep me from living." Another poster pushed the next AIDS bike ride to Los Angeles, a charity fundraiser. Raphe saw them as warning signs and felt a slight twinge in his stomach. Maybe the managers of BART knew what goes on back here.

No one else sat in the entire back half of the compartment.

The Latino with the vacne must have gotten on a different train. The doors closed, and with a few hesitant nudges the train pulled away into the tunnel. Shortly after it picked up speed, a man from the far front rows walked to the back. Without ever looking at Raphe, he sat on the bench across the aisle. He immediately lifted a folded copy of the front section of the *San Francisco Chronicle* to his face.

Raphe felt an unexpected burst of flush. Did the man notice? He didn't seem to. He just sat in his nicely pressed khaki pants with open-necked blue dress shirt and stared straight into the day's headlines. Works in an office, Raphe figured. A brokerage, perhaps. Guys in that field really had to keep up with the news. So why was this guy glued to the front page of the *morning* newspaper? The man held that one article too close to his face. He must be vision impaired, or the slowest reader in the world. Why didn't he turn a page? Or flip it around?

Then Raphe noticed the man's other hand. In the moments since he'd sat down, the man had discreetly cupped himself. His legs were spread unnaturally wide. It was a position that could easily be interpreted as the body language of a slob. No, it could be more than that. Maybe this was the first signal for something to start.

Raphe repositioned himself, mimicking the same slouch. He scratched below his fly.

The man did the same.

Fascinated, Raphe pulled the front of his pants.

Instantly, the man repeated the motion. His eyes never seemed to leave the text of the newsprint, and yet somehow the man saw everything.

Suddenly it hit Raphe. The newspaper was just a clever prop to obscure the truth—a trick not revealed on the web site. The man had really been watching the entire time through the reflections of the windows. Once the train had entered the tunnel, the black of the outside turned the interior glass into a mirror, allowing for an unobstructed view into the row. One could see everything without directly looking.

Still, it was just spreading, scratching and pulling—not enough for Raphe to be convinced there was anything more going on than a couple of guys just coincidentally being guys. He needed a more concrete signal. Something to tell him it was safe to go further.

Without taking off his sunglasses or saying a word, Raphe offered the one gesture he figured would be interpreted as a sign that it was OK to proceed. He turned toward the man . . . and smiled.

The man smiled back, again without ever losing sight of the paper. With his free hand, he unzipped his fly. In a matter of seconds, he reached inside and tugged until he revealed himself.

The sight rattled Raphe more than he anticipated, a rush surged up his entire body. Would the man reach across the aisle and touch him?

No. Raphe knew that much from the web site. This was all about "showing off." Many of the men who told their tales on the site actually claimed to be straight. They just enjoyed "getting off with buddies." The web site said full circle jerks sometimes broke out, with as many as ten guys pretending to be strap hangers but really forming a wall to prevent anyone forward from knowing what was happening in the back. There was even a listing that said a woman often frequented those final rows, hiking her skirt to expose and please herself. She was a regular, accepted by the pack, even if some of the guys would rather have each other.

Except for the possibility of being arrested by the BART police, it was the ultimate in safe sex.

Raphe hesitantly undid his own pants and fumbled to bring himself to the surface. It was much harder to do sitting than he'd figured, and he needed both hands. The man with the paper was so skilled he never lost the pretense that he was just a guy in the back reading a newspaper.

Finally the newspaper came down, and the man looked over to Raphe. Blue eyes and boyishly handsome with mousy blond curls, slightly receding. Just as Raphe made eye contact, the man squinted, his face contorted as if someone had sneaked up behind and pinched him. But no one was there. Instead, there was a white splash onto the opened front page of the waiting newspaper. The splattered headline: BUSH A CROWD PLEASER.

In moments, the man composed himself and packaged everything back into his khakis. As if nothing had occurred, he got up and returned to the front of the compartment. Raphe frantically put himself in order, which was nearly impossible since he was still fully aroused. He wiped a few beads of sweat from his forehead with his sleeve. Seconds later the train emerged from the dark into dreary Port Oakland, past acres of empty cargo containers, stranded from the economic collapse. Going nowhere, Raphe thought. *Just like me.*

He couldn't get off at the first stop, his excitement refusing to subside in time to stand up. He waited until the train reached Lake Merritt, where he crossed the platform to the far end to again seek the final rows of the next inbound line. As he walked, he looked down at the ground, trying to avoid being seen. A familiar feeling of guilt hit, something that always happened whenever he experienced any type of sex—a shame that went back to the time when he was thirteen and reading a copy of *Penthouse* with his best friend Scott. The explicit photos and graphic stories had aroused both boys into pleasing themselves. Scott's father walked into the room, catching them with their pants down. He ordered them to get dressed and sent Raphe home.

For days Raphe feared his parents' phone would ring, and he would be destroyed. Both his mother and father were strict

and managed their emotions tightly around Raphe. Their lives
revolved around the many committees they served on at the
local Methodist church, setting a standard of behavior for the
family that bordered on pious. No son of theirs could be caught
with pornography. Worse, Scott's family attended the same
church, making his sin possible fodder for the entire congrega-
tion. Not just for reading pornography, but he was sure there
would be an accusation that he and Scott were caught having
sex, though they'd never even touched each other.

The devastating phone call from Scott's father never came.
Instead, there was something much worse. Silence. A sword of
impending doom dangled over Raphe's head for the rest of his
years in his hometown, worried each time he saw Scott's father
that his vice would be exposed to all. Sometimes he craved to
have it brought out in the open and to accept his punishment,
just to rid himself the anxiety of waiting. Raphe was too young
to understand the New England tradition of burying feelings
and secrets in order to avoid confrontation at all cost. An emotional scene would never erupt. Scott's father simply and sternly
told his son that he was never to be alone again with Raphe.
Ever.

As he got back on BART at the Lake Merritt station for the
return trip to The City, Raphe's heart raced. Guilty feelings
aside, he would take the trip again. On the next journey out to
the suburbs the train was sure to be packed, with rush hour hitting full swing. He wondered how that would change what the
BARTM4M followers did.

Raphe plunked down into the last section, this time on the
aisle, and shut his eyes. *Just relax,* he told himself. On the reverse
commute, the train would be empty, so he'd spend the time
making mental notes of what had already happened and commit them to memory—for the sake of his novel, of course.

It really would make a great story—a real shocker.

He heard steps coming toward him. Don't look. He felt the slight breeze of someone pass, and peeked in time to catch the glimpse of a man in dark clothes get into the window seat. The doors closed, and the train made its initial nudge. The man turned, looked over to Raphe, and grinned. They knew each other. The familiar pinstriped suit. Those rugged Latino good looks. The same dark hair, with just a bit of gel, and that same mouth, surrounded by the same telltale trail of vacne.

"Are you following me?" Raphe stammered.

"Would you let me?" the man asked.

5

"Sticky rice cooking here!"

Mark Hazodo had to admit it was a funny line. Tony used it on him when they bumped into each other Friday at Club Papi.

"Sticky rice?" Mark asked.

"Yeah—you know. A little rice on rice action."

Tony had passed thirty a few years back but still thought of himself as a twink, trying to keep current by adopting the latest lines of queer lingo between hits of *E*. Mark was younger, but even he had trouble keeping up. Just the other day he found himself spurned by a rugged looking tourist who explained he was in town for BOBO.

"Huh?"

"Bear On Bear Only."

Now *sticky rice. There's a category for everything*, Mark thought.

"You must be checking out the Filipino go-go boy," Mark yelled to Tony over the blasting techno beat. He gestured to a nearby riser where a beefed up young man gyrated his leather thong.

"No way, man. I am checking out *you*. Mark Hazodo, you are looking hot tonight! *You* should be up there dancing!" Tony took the cherry lollipop out of his mouth and playfully pointed and circled it in the direction of Mark's chest. "Why don't you take off that T so everyone can enjoy those firm pecs?"

Mark felt a small flush of embarrassment. They'd known each other for years, from when they both worked at the same video game company. Back then Mark was a star programmer and Tony was the snap diva of accounting. When they first crossed paths in the hallways, they gave each other knowing looks, as if they shared some sort of common bond as the company's only Asians. Later, when Tony spotted Mark out at a gay bar in SoMa, they discovered even more in common and became friends.

"Man, you know my rules." Mark worked up a smile to cover how Tony's advance made him uncomfortable.

"You mean the one where you won't sleep with anyone you know? I know—not with coworkers, and not with friends. I have only heard you say it a million times. But I gotta tell you that since you started working out, you are dangerously close to giving this boy wood."

Tony giggled. Then inspired by the *E*, he broke out in uncontrollable laughter. Somehow it defused the moment. They hit the floor together to dance, still just friends.

But the *sticky rice* line stuck with Mark. In the five years since moving to The City, he had never dated another Asian. Not even tricked with one. Instead, Mark would go to the same, mostly white bars where he'd always pick up Caucasians, more than he could remember. His routine had become so predictable that during nights of cruising he no longer asked himself *Would I?* when checking out a possible liaison. These days he wondered *Have I?*

Never a fellow Asian, though. And why? The question turned in his thoughts endlessly while on the treadmill at the gym. He just didn't find them attractive, with their hairless bodies. Like Tony, too many were girlish and fey. Mark was more drawn to white guys who dressed in blue-collar attire, with their burly, hairy chests. They were equally pulled to him. The experienced ones knew Asian men almost always assumed the dominant role in bed. Even a little queen like Tony was unequivocally a top. Maybe it was because Asian cultures demanded that men aggressively propagate their ancestral line.

It amused Mark to believe he carried such ethnic baggage. That wasn't *his* journey. He was a man of the modern world, making a fortune messing with people's minds. His new start-up game company NeverEnd was a huge hit, allowing users all over the globe to create characters and electronically coexist in wondrous little universes of their own design. The ultimate in escapism. The excitement they lacked in their dull real lives was quickly forgotten in Mark's online fantasy realm.

While he sold electronic adventures to others, in his own life he preferred to collect experiences of the flesh. Yet he had never coupled with one of his own race. Why? It was a quandary that kept going around and around in his mind, like the black rubber of the treadmill beneath his feet. He did his best thinking while working out, the hum of the equipment providing better counsel than most of his friends. In all of his A-gay circle, he didn't know any couples who were entirely Asian. Was it the need to fit in to what was still mostly a white man's world?

Mark loved The City in off hours. He would roll down the windows when taking a taxi home from a club at three in the morning, so he could fully absorb the emptiness of an over-crowded metropolis that had mostly succumbed to sleep without him. A puff of white steam above an isolated manhole cover, an ancient, faded advertisement on a brick wall for a long gone poultry market—details not noticed when the roads and side-walks were in full motion.

He couldn't remember the last time he was out on the streets walking at six in the morning, at least not at the start of the day. He'd seen 6:00 A.M. from the other side plenty of times. Today was special. A new experience.

His first time in the Bay to Breakers road race.

He'd looked forward to this moment for the past year, ever since stumbling home one Sunday morning to find himself confronted with the massive, colorful city-length race. He'd stood at the corner of Ninth and Howard, where a band rocked the runners as they passed. Ninety thousand people, including a handful of world-class athletes out for prize money, followed by amateurs in costumes. Many wore nothing at all.

He'd heard of the race, of course. He'd just never seen it, having been too consumed with his life of games. The games of dating men. The games of running his fledgling company. The intricate escapist games of his computer generated world. In all of that, he'd almost forgotten how he cherished the games of sports. How had he let that slip away? When he was in high school down in Manhattan Beach, he played soccer, relishing the times he battled the gritty L.A. metro squads. When he saw so many people running that Sunday morning through SoMa, he saw a void in his life that needed to be filled. He pledged to be in the race the next year, and increased his trips to the gym each week to prepare.

He didn't pass another soul as he walked from his loft on 11th up to the MUNI underground station at Van Ness. When he emerged down at the Embarcadero, Mark found himself crushed into a mass of thousands. His eyes consumed the various stages of nudity, the packs of runners dressed identically in politically-themed costumes, like a squadron of drag queen Monica Lewinsky clones in berets and heavily stained blue dresses.

He spotted several beer kegs on wheels. The density of the crowd reminded him of his trip to meet relatives in Kobe, though that wasn't nearly as interesting.

Mark was so far back in the pack neither he nor the others around him noticed when the race officially started. The eight o'clock gun was only really important to the small group of imported professional athletes who would complete the seven mile course in about thirty minutes. It would take nearly two hours just to get all the other participants past the starting line. He looked around to check out the runners in his own ranks. Instead of facing fierce adversaries, he found himself somewhere between a man dressed as a giant light bulb to protest greedy corporate power, and what looked like the perfect suburban couple pushing identical twins in a double stroller.

This would be a jog, Mark realized, not a race. Any fantasies of competition were dashed. He shrugged off the disappointment, realizing the challenge was in his decision to train and run. He'd made it this far, and the victory would be in crossing that finish line. For once he would be gaming only against himself.

The mob started to move. Mark felt a minor sense of accomplishment when he got past the starting line at Spear and Howard, taking note of the massive amount of equipment set up by television camera crews, and the noise of a helicopter hovering somewhere overhead.

"Hey." An unfamiliar voice came from his side.

"Hey," Mark said right back. Jogging beside him was a young man in a tight, green T-shirt. Mark guessed he was Chinese, probably in his thirties. Mark noted the man's sculptured physique, short black hair, and unusually bright green eyes reminiscent of jade stones hit by bolts of sunlight.

"Have you done this race before?" The man got so close his muscled shoulder brushed against Mark's.

"No. First time." Mark huffed. "You?"

"Me neither. And I *really* have to take a piss." The man caught his breath. "Drank too much water. Had no idea it would take so long to get moving. I'm not gonna make it up the Hayes Street hill if I don't get rid of it."

Mark laughed. "I looked at the map of the course. I think there's a Porta Potty set up just ahead in one of the alleys." Mark turned to look the man in the face. Handsome, he thought, for an Asian. "I'll go with you."

As they approached Ninth Street where the course turned north, Mark pointed for them to break through an opening in the line of cheering spectators. Once beyond the crowd, he gestured up to the right and tiny Washburn Alley. After turning they immediately noticed there was no bathroom. As if at the gym, both men kept jogging in place as they looked around. "What about over here?" Mark pointed to an area behind a gray wood and chain-link fence that protected a large air processing unit. A nearby dumpster kept the nook obscured from the throng of racers passing half a block away.

Finally they stopped moving, placed their legs far apart, and bent over into deep stretching sighs. They laughed at the coincidence. Their trainers had taught them well.

Mark was first to move over to the corner. He pulled up the leg of his black nylon shorts to part his briefs in a way that would allow discretion. Then he paused. A sudden urge went through his mind. Maybe it was time to answer the question that had rolled on that treadmill. *Why not sticky rice?* He didn't know if the man who jogged beside him would go for it, but that shouldn't deter. Like any game, victory only came when one was willing to take a risk. He had little to lose if the man ended up offended by a bold offense.

Mark took both hands and pulled down his shorts, allowing

them to fall to his ankles. His hairless, bare behind confronted the other man.

When the stream started to emerge, Mark carefully pointed away from the corner, instead veering slightly out in the street, hoping his fellow jogger would take a glimpse. But as Mark turned his head to the left, the man was not in his periphery. No one was there. Just an empty street, filled only with the sound of the dancing throng in the distance. The man was gone, probably scared off. Game over.

Then to his right Mark heard the unmistakable sound of water passing onto blacktop. The man had not bolted, but instead had quietly moved alongside, and let his shorts drop to the ground as well. His tight glute gently pressed back against Mark's as he aimed away in the other direction. What started as a loud gush rapidly turned into a slight trickle until the man said, "I can't go anymore."

Mark looked over and down. The man was gently stroking, too aroused now to urinate. He looked into Mark's eyes and grinned.

Mark swelled in his own grip. He motioned his head in the direction of the corner behind the dumpster. With their shorts still sunk to their sneakers, and palms confined to task, they hobbled over like two prisoners in leg irons.

The man dropped to his knees. The ground was dry, since they had so carefully avoided spraying that patch, as if they both knew it had to remain sacred. The excitement of the random, open air scene and possibility of exposure made Mark climax quickly. If the burst startled the man, he didn't show it, letting the rush pass into him like a stream traveling over a waterfall.

Barely taking enough time to catch his breath, Mark pulled the man up from the ground, and pushed him back against the wall. He looked over the solid, muscular physique—the large arms and pumped up runner's legs. The man was mostly hairless, his nose was small, and his features sharp. It was not the meretricious working class look that had attracted Mark so many times, but a man that mirrored an image similar to his own. His own race. His own kind. He finally saw the beauty of it, and got down in worship for the first time.

6

Raphe saw Troy each time he went to the bank.

It was Troy who signed him up for an account when he first came to The City. Those were the good times, when he'd go each week to deposit his inflated dot-com paycheck. It should have been a clue to the industry's ultimate demise that his high-tech employer was never competent enough to set up direct deposit.

Now he needed Troy's help. The afternoon was freakishly hot, an April day with temperatures in the nineties. Raphe wondered, *this is San Francisco*? Even though he'd arrived years earlier, he still struggled to figure out what to wear in the famously unpredictable weather.

Dressed too warmly in his lined L.L. Bean jacket, Raphe fumbled through his backpack trying to find all the necessary documents. He sat at Troy's desk with beads of sweat at his temples, the product of the heat combined with a latent fear of missing paperwork.

Troy wore an impeccable, dark gray suit, with the latest style of perfectly mismatched tie and pressed designer shirt. His dark black hair outlined rich olive skin and a boyish face. He was groomed with such precision there wasn't even a hint of razor stubble, as if he weren't yet old enough to shave, even though he was probably in his late twenties. His eyebrows were as dark as his hair, and his lashes thick and long enough to inspire poetry. Troy was that rare kind of man both men and women would describe with the word *beautiful*.

Raphe felt intimidated. It was odd a man should represent such loveliness. Raphe remembered reading about a scientific study of male beauty. The men considered the most handsome in the world are those whose faces have feminine traits. The small nose of Leonardo DiCaprio. The distinct cheekbones of Johnny Depp. Troy reminded Raphe of a Renaissance painting he'd seen at the Palace of the Legion of Honor museum. Just like that work of art, it was fine to look, but a crime to reach out and touch. Raphe would never dare. Stop staring so much.

"I need a loan," Raphe explained.

"Let's see if we can help you." Troy smiled, his teeth bright white and perfect.

Raphe told his tale of unemployment, carefully leaving out any parts that might make him look bad. He just wanted a second mortgage on his condo, enough to give him funds so he didn't feel like he was living on the edge. He was sure there was at least a hundred thousand dollars equity in his place.

"But you're not working?"

"Well, uh, not officially."

"What does that mean?"

"I'm collecting unemployment. And I try to pick up a few dollars on the side."

"I didn't hear that part about the few dollars," Troy grinned. "Still, I'm sure you know that unemployment benefits aren't enough to qualify for a loan."

Raphe rubbed his forehead, feeling a headache starting to emerge. The beautiful knight had failed to rescue him. Troy had fallen.

"We could try a 'No Doc,'" Troy offered matter-of-factly.

"What's that?" Raphe perked up.

"It's short for 'No Document.' Basically, it means we don't ask any official questions about your income. The rate is a little higher, but I think you qualify."

As Raphe left the bank, a sensation hit him that was oddly foreign, having been missing in his life for so long. *Joy.* He could put up with Harrington, unemployment, and all of his frustrations, now that a little money would finally be on the way.

The paperwork involved turned out to be daunting. So much for "No Doc." It seemed like new forms were needed each week, requiring Raphe to make endless return trips to the bank.

Still, Raphe enjoyed his little visits with Troy. He was always pleasant, keeping an appropriately friendly, professional distance. When not talking about the loan, their conversations would be limited to small talk about the weather or something equally banal. If they walked past each other on the street, it would be the same way, with Troy clearly struggling to recall the identity of a customer out of context. Raphe liked the wall that existed between them. It was comfortable. It felt safe.

Then Raphe saw *DMtv*.

DMtv stood for Dan and Marie Television, the name of a show that aired once a week on San Francisco public access cable. As far as Raphe could figure out, Dan and Marie got an hour each Saturday afternoon to air whatever video they shot with their home camera, along with non-stop commentary accompanying each clip. Dan was so flamboyantly gay he embodied stereotype. Marie looked like a fresh, young thing just off the bus from Idaho. While Dan did bitchy chatting through every frame of video, Marie simply responded with the occasional "yah," or "oh," or "I'll say so." She was the straight man of their act.

Raphe stumbled across the show one weekend, feeling too broke to do anything other than stretch out on his couch and channel surf. Dan and Marie had taken their camera to something called the "Queen's Ball," an annual event where all the biggest drag divas of The City gathered for an evening of gaudy runway walks and backstage back stabbing. Raphe never understood the allure of cross-dressing. If gay men were so attracted to other men, then why try to be anything other than men?

"And what's your name, honey?" Dan asked as he moved down the receiving line for interviews.

"Aurora Borealis, baby," the drag queen breathed heavily into the microphone. His costume involved thick makeup with a huge wig and a campy outer space motif.

"And where are you from?"

"The planet Uranus."

"Really?" Dan quipped. "We seem to have a lot of people from Uranus tonight, honey."

"Well, baby, a *few* people have been there."

"Who are you kidding, Aurora? You've had more ass than a public toilet seat!" They both laughed heavily at their exchange. The tape kept rolling until after the giggling subsided and an awkward silence stuck for a few seconds. The weird dead air had the two men's eyes darting off camera in a painful cry for an ending.

This show really needs some editing, Raphe thought.

For the next several minutes Raphe watched more badly-staged scenes of Dan interacting with caustic queens. Each tried to be more mordant than the previous one, with Dan straining to provoke a new reaction. Each time brought near identical jokes and insults. *Star Wars* was the theme for the event, so most of the men claimed to be from Uranus. Dan kept repeating the same one-liner in response. After the sixth time, even he struggled to smile through the entire repartee.

Raphe was about ready to start flipping channels again, when "Demi More Sex" entered the screen. Ha! He had to laugh out loud at that name.

"Demi More Sex, huh," said Dan. "I was just talking to Lotta Head. You two oughta get together and trade notes."

As the camera zoomed shakily into Demi's face, Raphe noticed the long, thick eyelashes. Pancake base doused the skin, and the lips shined with a deep red gloss. Even through all that camouflage, there was no mistaking him.

It was Troy from the bank.

Raphe stared at the television, his mouth slightly ajar. Troy? The handsome banker? A good-looking guy, yeah, but nothing to make you think of *this*. Raphe wondered if he'd missed some important clue. He vowed to check Troy's fingernails next time he went to the bank. That would be the dead giveaway. If the nails were too long, he'd take that as confirmation. Of course, he could just ask Troy if that was him on *DMtv*. If it really was, then he probably would be open about it. Maybe even laugh. Surely, it wouldn't be embarrassing to bring it up. After all, this *is* San Francisco.

Yet it didn't make sense. How could someone be so transformed? Gray suits by day, and then *this* at night. Troy was *beautiful* with his lush, dark lashes, but to straddle two such extreme worlds seemed inconceivable to Raphe, even frightening.

Raphe went to his bathroom and found the hand mirror that came with the clipper kit he used to trim his soul patch. Back on the couch, he watched *DMtv* while studying his own reflection. His eyelashes were puny, not as dramatic as Troy's. He noticed how some of the drag queens wore appliqués, clearly fake, with glitter over wondrous shades of neon blues and purples. Raphe wondered how they stuck on. Glue, he supposed. Must be very strong, with all the blinking they do. Raphe took his forefinger and ran it across his eyelid as he stared into the mirror. So sensitive, soft, and tender. The grasp of the glue must hurt when the false lashes are pulled free. . . .

Stop it! he scolded himself as he tossed the mirror onto the couch. What was he thinking? Maybe this drag queen simply looked like Troy, and was really someone else. If he brought up *DMtv*, and the banker didn't know what he was talking about, then he'd have to explain it. Besides, who was he to intrude in the guy's life? People have the right to be who they are, even if they blur the lines of straight and gay.

He tried to dismiss the whole idea, but for the next few days, Raphe couldn't get the image of Troy, or not Troy, out of his mind, and the questions it raised about the grays of sexuality. A man to the world, and a woman in secret. Of course Raphe had heard of such things, but it had never intruded in *his* life. By Wednesday, Raphe had clipped his own fingernails three times down to the nubs, causing his left pinkie to bleed. He worried how he would react next time he went to the bank. He hoped it wasn't Troy. Troy was so handsome as a man, but just remarkably average as a woman.

Raphe avoided the bank for a week. Late Friday his unemployment check arrived, and he knew he'd have to go to the branch the next morning.

Raphe set his plan. He wouldn't say anything at all. It was none of his business, really. If Troy was a drag queen, then that was his choice. It didn't affect Raphe's banking. It was silly to think it would. Besides, he might cause a scene and hurt his chances for getting the loan.

With money so tight, Raphe refused to use an ATM for deposits, fearing financial havoc if his check was somehow lost in the machine. The long line for a teller snaked by Troy's desk, and Raphe felt grateful for once to find the chair empty. Then Troy emerged from a back room. Saturday was "dress down" day, with everyone in jeans and short sleeve shirts. Even out of his suit, Troy looked the same. The boyish face and dark, manly hair didn't need any fashion designer's ornate pedestal, they were just as striking set upon street clothes. Raphe looked down at Troy's fingernails. Perfectly manicured. Not long like a woman's, but precisely crafted in the way of any budding, young banker. He looked at the way Troy walked across the room, trying to spy even the slightest feminine manner. Nothing.

Must have been my imagination, Raphe thought. It wasn't

really Troy. It was just someone who looked like him. Raphe laughed at his foolishness and moved up to the front of the line.

"Next!" the teller yelled.

"I'll need some cash, too," Raphe said after the teller finished depositing the check. "A hundred is fine."

The teller reached across the desktop and counted out five twenty-dollar bills, placing each on the counter in the shape of a fan, as if dealing poker cards. As Raphe looked down toward the money, he flinched. The teller, a tall, heavy man with thick glasses, had long, ladylike fingernails painted bright purple, with bits of gold glitter.

The startled look on Raphe's face must have been obvious, because when he glanced up the teller grinned widely, and his eyes darted to something across the room.

Raphe turned to catch Troy and the teller smirking and flitting their eyelashes to each other. It was an exchange Raphe recognized. That of two women throwing air kisses and pantomiming, *Hey girlfriend!*

Raphe grabbed the money and backed away from the counter, forgetting his receipt. He wondered if the two could see how embarrassed he was, or if the calm facade he tried to maintain was actually working. He didn't see the man standing behind him until it was too late and he had stumbled into the man's arms, sending them both crashing onto the bank floor.

The teller giggled.

"Shit, man. I'm sorry," Raphe managed to blurt out as he struggled to get up. "I really shoulda watched where I was going. You OK?"

"Better now," the man said, looking into Raphe's eyes with a knowing smile.

Raphe knew the man's face, though it was out of context in the bank. Normally, such a dramatic change of setting would temporarily paralyze Raphe while his mind flipped through its Rolodex, struggling to connect the stray facts and provide an identity. Not this time. Raphe immediately recognized who he was, as vivid as their first encounter. The short cropped dark hair, and thick, black razor stubble. The vacne, however, had cleared.

It was the Latino guy from BART.

"You?"

The man got up from the floor and stretched out his hand. "I'm afraid we haven't been formally introduced. I'm Baptiste." He took Raphe's hand in a firm grasp. "I hope you're not going to run away *this* time."

7

"Uh, I'm Raphe," he said, tugging the patch of hair under his lip. He tended to fidget with the tuft whenever he was nervous.

"Nice to see you again, Raphe. You bolted the other day before we got to talk."

"I . . . I had an appointment to catch."

"Actually, we were on a train," Baptiste grinned. "And it was at least seven minutes before the next stop."

The teller with the purple fingernails blurted out a girlish guffaw, then covered his mouth as if trying to muzzle a sneeze. Since their fall onto the bank floor, all the customers and employees had been staring at Baptiste and Raphe. The room was eerily silent as everyone waited to hear and see what would happen next.

"Let's get out of here," Baptiste whispered. Somewhere in the back of the room came a soft moan of disappointment. The show was over.

Baptiste led the way to a nearby coffee shop, where he insisted on treating Raphe to a latte. The Pick Me Up café at the corner of Ninth and Folsom was filled with its usual Saturday afternoon crowd, mostly locals who looked as if they were just greeting the day after too many hours spent at the all-night dance clubs. In line, Raphe stood next to a tattooed, older man whose disheveled hair pointed off wildly in different directions. Strong body odor revealed the man had not showered for at least a couple days. Such manly smells unnerved Raphe, and were typical of the customers who frequented the place. It was one of the reasons he tended to avoid the Pick Me Up—that and because the man who worked the counter was always too flirty.

"Look, I appreciate you being so nice," Raphe itched. "But I really have to get to work."

"On a Saturday? What do you do?"

Raphe thought for a moment. He didn't like being questioned about what he did for a living. It was such a non-San Francisco way to act. When he first moved to The City, he learned that lesson the hard way at a party when he asked a woman what her job was. "I am not defined by how I make my living," she snapped and walked off in a huff. "You must be from the East Coast!" Since then Raphe knew questions about work were taboo. You could be blunt and query to the dollar what someone paid for rent and where he lived. Discussing someone's sexual orientation was OK, even within the first few minutes of meeting. But no one ever pried about someone's employment. It was one of the quirks of The City Raphe had come to appreciate since being fired.

"You're pretty nosy," Raphe said as Baptiste ushered them over to a table near the front windows.

"Sorry about that. I'm a lawyer. Comes with the territory."

"A *lawyer?*"

"Yeah," Baptiste looked puzzled. "You seem surprised."

"Well, it's just that the other day on the train I got the impression that . . ."

"What?"

"That maybe you were looking to do something, well, you know . . . illegal."

Baptiste smiled. "Well, not anymore it isn't. Not since the Supreme Court decision."

Raphe remembered seeing something in the news about a law against sodomy being struck down by the court. *Sodomy.* Just the word made him squirm. "Look, I think I've given you the wrong impression."

"You're new, aren't you?"

"New? No. Not at all. I moved here more than three years ago."

Baptiste's expression turned serious. "I didn't mean new to town."

"I don't understand. What do you mean?"

"What did you say you did for a living?"

"I didn't."

"Well?"

Raphe squirmed in his chair. "I'm a writer."

"Wow! What do you write?"

"I'm working on a novel."

"What's it about?"

Raphe felt pressured, as if he was on the phone with his mother, always wanting to know what he was doing with his life. As far as she knew, he was still working at the dot-com. He didn't like lying to her, but it was better than trying to explain the truth. This guy Baptiste was relentless. He wasn't kidding when he said he was lawyer. A prosecutor? "Well, it's hard to put into words."

"You'd better figure it out."

"Why?"

"'Cuz you're the *writer*," Baptiste chuckled, gently patting Raphe on the shoulder.

As they drank their coffee, a bond started to grow between the two men. Raphe found Baptiste charming, once he got past the initial interrogation. It was refreshing to find someone so easy to talk to. He was funny, too. Raphe marveled at Baptiste's ability to effortlessly jump in and out of their conversation to drop witty one-liners about the crowd that passed by the café.

"There's a GQ."

"A GQ?"

"Yeah! Right there," Baptiste pointed. "Look quick, you're gonna miss it."

Raphe turned to see a person in jeans with a plaid lumberjack shirt and mullet walk past the window. "OK. I see. What's a GQ?"

"GQ. Gender question. Is that a man or a woman?"

Raphe looked again. A man. Definitely a man. He just had a bad haircut, and was probably visiting from some hick town. "That's a guy."

Baptiste cupped his hands over his mouth and made a sound like the loser buzzer on a game show. "Wrong! Minus two points for you. That's a woman."

"Really?"

"Yup. Kara Miller. Lives in Noe Valley. I helped her get a court order to have her neighbor's male dog neutered. Lesbians are big on getting the nuts cut off dogs."

"Man, you are vicious," Raphe snickered.

"Hey, *you're* the one who's laughing. Trust me—that dog wasn't!"

They talked for hours. Raphe was stunned when he looked at his TAG Heuer knockoff and realized they'd devoured the entire afternoon. It seemed like they'd just met moments ago, and at the same time known each other forever. Baptiste recommended they grab something to eat. His treat. They went to Bacar, one of the trendiest restaurants in SoMa, with a literal tower of wines that climbed three stories from the cozy basement to the upper loft dining area. The collection of rare vintages was among the most impressive in town, one that excited even the fussiest connoisseurs. Baptiste ordered an expensive Shiraz that went quickly to Raphe's head. He couldn't remember the last time he'd had such a delicious vintage—it went down so smoothly.

"The train the other day," Baptiste said tentatively.

"Yeah? What about it?"

"You were in the last row."

"So?" Raphe tried to sound nonchalant.

"Well, you know what that means, don't you?"

Raphe considered staging a long, convoluted protest about how he was just taking BART and didn't know what in the world Baptiste was going on about. Then it hit him. What was he hiding? He'd done nothing wrong.

"I was curious," Raphe said, his voice suddenly feeling scratchy.

"So you *do* know what it means?"

"I read about it online. I thought it would be a great story—a real shocker. You know, a chapter for my book."

"So you're not . . ." Baptiste paused. "You've never been with a man, have you?"

If it wasn't for the wine taking the edge off, Raphe might have reacted indignantly to such a probing question. He'd been hit on plenty of times since moving to The City, though never quite like this. It was usually unspoken, just done with stares. He didn't think of himself as particularly handsome, but his was the look of the moment. The *metrosexual*. Slightly disheveled, comfortable in a purposely untucked way—the *regular guy* type. He kept a decent physique without much effort, the product of favorable genes and youth. He wasn't beautiful like Troy, or ruggedly handsome like Baptiste, but he knew other men found him attractive. He'd always pushed their advances away with a mean look, like he'd been taught. *Damn queers*, a friend once said at Brown when they saw two men dancing together at a club in Providence. Raphe had played along. Now he felt ashamed of that.

"I'm not a homophobe," Raphe suddenly blurted out.

"I never said you were," assured Baptiste. "I mean, you know

I'm gay, and here you are having a perfectly wonderful dinner with me."

"Yeah, sure. I mean . . ." Raphe fumbled to find the right words. Some writer, he scolded himself. "Look, I have to admit something to you."

"Go ahead."

"You are the first gay I've ever really felt comfortable around."

Baptiste scoffed, "Oh, come on. I can't possibly be the first one you've spoken with since moving to San Francisco. We're all over the place here. You'd have to be hiding under a rock to miss us."

"No, that's not what I meant. I've met gay people before. It's just that somehow, I dunno, I feel like I can talk to you."

"Go ahead."

"What?"

"You want to ask me about it."

"I do. But it's so *strange*." Raphe suddenly felt flush. Emotions? What had Baptiste churned up with his questions? It wasn't like Raphe to become stirred into such a ferment. He was raised in a family with an emotional range that ran consistently at two on a scale of one hundred. No ups or downs, just a flat line, not moving a blip even in times of crisis. Like his grandfather's death. No crying allowed. It just wasn't seemly to express such a lack of composure, as if it were somehow in violation of the Methodist way. Baptiste's questions poked at him like a stick. His ears felt burning hot, and Raphe wondered if they were bright red with embarrassment, and if everyone in the restaurant could see. "I mean, I don't want to insult you by saying something wrong. I like you."

"I like you too. Ask."

Raphe took in a deep breath and held it for several moments. "How do you know?"

"That I like men?"

"Yeah."

Baptiste took a sip from his glass and relaxed in his chair. He looked into Raphe's eyes. "I didn't always go with men. Until just a few years ago I dated women."

"Really?" Raphe was surprised. Was it possible to love both?

"Sure. I love women. They're beautiful creatures. Then I had some experiences with men, and I knew it was a better fit. It felt more natural to me, like I finally found my place. Sex with men is different than sex with women."

"Duh," Raphe said, trying to use humor to distance himself from the strain of the conversation.

"No, I mean beyond the obvious. Look, we share common pleasure points women can't understand. Every man knows how to make himself climax, and he can work on another with an expertise women will never have."

"I hadn't thought of it that way."

"You're right-handed?"

"Yeah." Raphe nervously pulled on his soul patch.

"Ever try jerking off with your left hand? It's not easy, but you know what I mean. It can feel like another person is in the room with you. A slightly different hand, using a technique that might be only marginally dissimilar from what you do with the right. But that tiny variation! Well, you know. Now imagine you really do have another's hand there, one that knows all the intense places . . . when to bring you to the edge . . . when to bring you back . . . and finally when to bring you over."

Raphe swallowed hard. Not the wine, since he had none in his mouth. He digested the thought of what Baptiste described. It was overpowering. It had been months since he'd been with anyone other than himself. His heart beat faster, and he felt a surge of energy rise from below.

"The problem," Baptiste continued, sounding like he now had his audience hooked, "is our fathers."

Raphe visualized his father, dressed in his Sunday suit handing out church programs as a greeter. The thought jolted him back into the present. "What? What do our fathers have to do with anything?"

"Tell me about your relationship with your dad."

Raphe tried to gather his thoughts through the haze of the alcohol. He hadn't spoken to his father in at least two months. His mother always took his calls and monopolized the line, saying she would fill in everyone else later. "We have a normal relationship."

"Normal? Ah, yes. I know what that is. You don't talk much, unless it's about sports."

That was true, Raphe nodded.

"You probably shake hands when you see each other, instead of hugging."

True again.

"And he never says he loves you."

It was true. Raphe couldn't remember if his father ever expressed such feeling. He knew they loved one another. At least he thought he knew. But they never said it to each other. Are feelings genuine if no one ever expresses them? Maybe his father didn't really love him. His thoughts became smothered by a wave of sorrow. What had the wine done to him? What was Baptiste doing? Was that a tear he felt roll down his cheek?

"Hey, it's OK. I'm here," Baptiste consoled.

"I don't know why I am crying. You must think I'm a . . ."

"No. It's my fault. I get carried away sometimes, and ask questions I shouldn't. It's just that I was trying to make a point. We all grew up with dads who never told us they loved us. Instead, they were formal and taught us to be competitive—and look at other men as potential adversaries. Like we're back in the tribal days. As a result, we block out an entire gender when it comes to passion. We're raised to be rivals with our own kind. Women don't have these hang-ups."

"They don't?"

"No way. Haven't you ever noticed how women refer to

each other as girlfriends. They mess around with each other all the time."

"They do?" It seemed outrageous, but with the clarity of alcohol it made perfect sense to Raphe.

"Absolutely. They know they can please each other better than any man can. Let's face it. I fucked around with girls for ten years, and I never found that thing."

"What thing?"

"You know that *thing*. Fuck man, I looked and looked, and I never found it. But girls, they can reach down there and know exactly where it's hiding. The same with guys. We know how to push each other's buttons. We've just been raised to believe it's wrong."

Raphe wiped his eyes with his sleeve. "I don't want to be gay."

"You don't have to be. Just be yourself."

"And who is that?" Raphe studied Baptiste's eyes. He saw sincerity in the brown. Concern? They'd stumbled into each other as if by coincidence. Maybe it was more than that. At two moments when Raphe faced the question of sexuality, this handsome man appeared from nowhere. Was he providing a different answer? Those old feelings of guilt started to rise, but Raphe pushed them aside. A stronger urge hit. A desire to know.

"Let me help you find out," Baptiste said. He reached across the table and gently grasped Raphe's hand.

8

"This party is dee-oh-ay," Lauren complained, stretching the sound of each vowel.

"It's not *that* bad," said Jessica. "Uh, it's just a little, well, different." She turned up the corners of her mouth for a strained grin. After all, it was her idea to come to this thing. One of those biotech company parties her brother got her invited to.

"I want pizza. They don't have any pizza. What type of party doesn't have pizza?"

"Lolly, you only want pizza so you can go up to the nearest cute guy and ask him for a bite."

"It works!"

"Yeah, like it worked so well at that bondage club." As soon as the words came out of her mouth, Jessica regretted saying them. Lauren refused to react, instead looking away as if disinterested. Still, Jessica knew the memory of that awful night had to hurt. And what *was* that little piece of metal that Texas guy picked up from Lauren's puke? Jessica had never dared to ask, and wasn't sure she wanted to know how it got in her friend's stomach.

"What I meant to say," Jessica continued in a more diplomatic tone, "is that the pizza bite thing is *so September 10th*. It will scare the shit out of these geeks."

"You saying I need a new trick?" Lauren took a long gulp from her second Cosmo.

"I'm just saying that this is a more sophisticated crowd. Scientists, if you think about it. Smart guys. And my brother says the company is close to some new drug breakthrough. A bad breath cure or something really *important* like that. All these guys could become millionaires overnight."

Lauren surveyed the room. Only a couple of lookers in the entire bunch, most clearly hadn't had a date with anyone other than Rosie Palm in years. The stench of a bad lay permeated the air. "So that's why we're here," she said between gulps of her drink, grateful that at least the booze was free. "We came all the way into The City on a Thursday night because your brother is trying to set us up with rich guys."

"So what's wrong with that?"

"Boooooorrrrrrring!"

"You're not even trying. I mean, look at this place. There's nothing like this at home. Let's at least have some laughs."

There was no place like Virtuoso in Concord, or anywhere else. It was the latest in adult entertainment—a game center for grown-ups, complete with full bar and restaurant. Visionaries converted a huge, old billiards hall down near the waterfront in SoMa into a multi-level funhouse of odd-shaped rooms, each featuring a different challenge.

Unlike a video arcade, no game could be played alone. Teams formed to compete against each other in feats that forced instant camaraderie. "Throw the Virgin in the Volcano" required four people to pull on tethers to guide a magnet over a miniature tropical island, pick up metal-wearing Barbie dolls, then dump them into a papier-mâché smoldering peak. Few could accomplish such a complex task, especially when drunk. Instead the game routinely ended in fits of laughter, with all the virgins keeping their little plastic lives intact.

By day, Virtuoso was the perfect "team building" retreat

from corporate drudgery. At night it became a haven for singles to meet. The design forced strangers to mingle.

Lauren and Jessica looked over a balcony to watch four men try their luck at the giant pinball game. Instead of flippers, the men had to rock the entire table to get a cue ball to move into scoring holes. They ran around, pulled on grips, and shouted at each other until the surface tipped just enough to get the ball to tumble into a socket.

"Too much running," Lauren moaned.

Across the room a movie marquee lit up.

"Ladies and gentlemen!" An announcer shouted and waved his hands like a circus showman. "The 'Game Show' is about to begin! We need five teams of brave contestants down here in the main auditorium! Come on down!"

"Let's do that, Lolly. It sounds like fun."

Jessica tugged Lauren down the stairs, leaving splashes of pink cocktail in her wake. Inside the theater stood five podiums, each studded with large color-coded buttons. The stands were arranged in a semicircle under a ten-foot tall video screen. People fumbled into teams behind each control panel. The announcer, now transformed into the game show host, ran into the room. "Tonight's topic, 'Viva Las Vegas!'"

"Vegas? Shit. I don't know anything about Vegas," Lauren griped.

"That's OK. I've been a few times," said a guy wearing a Boston Red Sox hat. Lauren couldn't believe her luck. He seemed to come out of nowhere. He had bleached blond hair sticking out from under his cap, which had its visor dramatically rounded to embrace a boyish face. Wearing a mismatched sweat suit and sneakers in the party's sea of bland scientists, he stood out as hip.

"Hey, I'm Buzz."

"Buzz? That's a pretty cool name for a *biotech* guy."

"Hey, we're not all nerds."

"I'm Lauren. My friends call me Lolly. Like the pop."

Jessica rolled her eyes.

"And this is my best friend Jessica. And Buzz, I have to say something right up front."

"What?"

"I might not know anything about Vegas, but you are so good-looking I just know one of us is gonna get lucky tonight!"

Jessica cringed. Always the crass lingo from Lauren, ever since they were kids. Lauren chatted up boys with language that would embarrass a five-dollar whore. Where did that come from? Lauren's dad had walked out on the family, but half their friends' fathers had split. The other girls back in junior high didn't end up with mouths like prostitutes.

It was a shtick she only used around guys. With other girls, Lauren was still thirteen. As soon as a boy walked into the room, the subject immediately changed to sex. And the guys loved it, which only made it worse and pushed Lauren's raunchiness even further. Jessica figured Lauren said what other adolescent girls felt, but were too shy to express. Then came high school, and after that the two of them went to Mills College together. Now they were grown women, and Lauren still turned on the raunch every time a man was around. More than once Jessica had pleaded with Lauren to be more demure. Then a guy would come along, and Lauren would instantly hook him with one of her crude one-liners. She'd turn to Jessica and lift an eyebrow as if to say, "You don't know what you're talking about."

She's got to grow out of this, Jessica prayed. Until then, all she could do was watch her friend's back.

Buzz hooted, "Lolly, you're hot shit!" He shook hands with Jessica, then they all did introductions with the other people in their pod. Brad was in from Kansas City for the night, doing some consulting. He'd heard about Virtuoso and talked his way in, even though it was a private event. He fiddled with his wedding band as he leaned over and whispered loudly to Buzz that friends from home had told him it was an excellent spot to pick up some "easy pussy."

Then there was Michael, dressed neatly in striped Rolo pants and retro bowling shirt. He came as the guest of one of the biotech employees, who he somehow lost during the tag team scavenger hunt. Jessica thought the short brown professional haircut made Michael strikingly handsome. She chirped in a cheerful little "hi" as the game started.

Rapid-fire questions flew from the screen and the host's mouth. People raced to hit the colored buttons on their panels that corresponded with the correct answers from multiple choices on the screen. Buzz and Michael tore into the process like madmen, trying to outdo one another with their knowledge of The Strip. They nicknamed their team "The Bio Hazards."

"Tom Jones is the answer . . . not fuckin' Wayne Newton!"

"Everyone knows it's The Flamingo!"

The two guys playfully yelled back and forth, and bumped each other out of the way at the console. It was as if they were buddies from way back, even though they'd just met. Lauren and Jessica stepped aside, silently sipping their cocktails. Brad from Kansas City stood between them, trying to put his arms around them in a rallying cry for "the team." They pushed him off with stinging glares.

The game ended, and they all cheered as the host tallied the points and declared "The Bio Hazards" winners. As they received their round of applause, Buzz turned to Michael and said, "Hey buddy, let's bolt."

"Where to?"

"There's a bar on the top floor. Let's go hide out up there," said Buzz.

"What's the matter? Who are we hiding from?"

"That guy Brad from Kansas City." Buzz pulled Michael in closer. "You see him come over to me during the game?"

"Yeah," Michael smiled. "Wasn't he giving you all the answers?"

"Yeah, ha, ha, that's right—fuck you," Buzz laughed back. "No. All through the game he kept asking me where we could go to find some great snatch."

"He used the word 'snatch'?"

"Yup. You know what I think? I think the guy wants to blow me."

"He's definitely overcompensating for something," said Michael.

The game show host announced the prize for the winning team: a round of free drinks. Apparently no one had told him the event was already open bar. As the crowd moaned in disappointment, Michael and Buzz slipped out the back.

Jessica elbowed Brad after his palm found her behind during the victory cheer. "Where did the guys go?" she asked Lauren.

"Upstairs to play some more games," Lauren dismissed. "Boring, boring, boring."

"I thought they were cute," Jessica scolded. "Especially that guy Michael."

"He's OK. Buzz is hot. I wouldn't mind, well, you know . . ."

"Lolly!"

"It's my religion, Jes."

"You wanna go after 'em?"

"Sure, but let's grab a drink first and give 'em a little time to play," Lauren smirked. "Men are like dogs. Let them tire themselves out, then they'll be a bit more docile and ready for some heavy petting."

"You can pet my dog," Brad growled as he stuck his head between the two women to interrupt.

"Oh honey, this bitch in heat needs a Great Dane." Lauren made an obvious glance down to Brad's crotch. "Not a Chihuahua."

★ ★ ★

The upstairs bar sat empty. The bartender leaned on the counter aimlessly poking a lemon wedge with a small, plastic spear. She perked up as Buzz and Michael walked into the room.

"Wanna do a couple Daiquiri shooters?" she asked.

"I need a man's drink. Gimme a Jack, neat."

"Same," said Michael.

Chemistry between the two men came easily, no doubt helped along by the whiskey. Almost eerily they shared the same opinions about nearly everything. The City wasn't what it used to be. Lands End was hands down the best place to hike in town. Outbound Fell was the only street with true traffic light karma. After agreeing that Bonds was the most misunderstood man in baseball, they decided it was time to vacate their stools and do more exploring.

They picked up two Coronas with limes and wandered across the hall to a game called "The Buddy Test." The goal: to be blindfolded and have your partner talk you through a series of tasks inside a nearby room. The blindfold visor came equipped with a video camera and a bright light, which allowed the other partner to see what was in the room via television. They would talk to each other through headsets. The player outside the room sat in front of a video screen with a playbook describing each task that needed to be done to win. The game had a time limit of five minutes. Beating the clock was the trick.

A torpid female staffer explained the rules to the two men. Michael strapped on the gear and went inside the room, while Buzz guided him through each step. With the blindfold on, all Michael had were his senses of smell, taste, touch, and the sound of Buzz's mellow native Californian voice. The transmission in the headset was so clear he could hear even the slightest breath. The swig from a beer. The lick of lips after.

At first, Buzz asked Michael to turn 180 degrees for a full

visual sweep of the room to see where all the tasks were located. First stop: three steps forward to a gumball machine filled with jelly beans. "Feel the crank. Yeah, down to your left. That's it! Give it a turn. Pick up the jelly bean."

"Got it."

"Now put it in your mouth and suck it."

"You're shitting me."

"No man! Suck it! The next task you gotta press a button with the right flavor to win."

Buzz heard the candy swish around in Michael's mouth.

"Banana," he said with a slurp. "I'm pretty sure it's banana. I've tasted better."

Buzz talked Michael over four steps to the right to a board where he guided his hand to press the button labeled "Banana."

A bell went off.

"Congratulations. You have completed Step One," a computer voice said over the headsets.

The two remaining tasks involved finding a ball in the room, then tossing it into a chute to end the game. Their total time: four minutes and thirty-two seconds.

"Man, that was a fucking blast!" Michael said as he emerged from the room. The thick padding of the blindfold left small beads of sweat on his forehead.

"Yeah. It's like I was your eyes, able to tell you anything I wanted. You really trusted me not to mess you up."

The two men laughed. Buzz turned to the attendant and asked, "Can we do it again?"

"Yeah," the woman sighed. "Why not? No one else is around up here." She looked at her watch. "You guys seem to know what you're doing, and there ain't exactly a line. Mind if I shoot out back for a smoke?"

"No problem," said Michael.

This time Buzz got into the rigging, and Michael sat in

front of the TV monitor to hand out commands. As soon as the clock started, the staffer left.

"Can you hear me?"

"Yup buddy. I'm ready!"

"I was just thinking, man. This isn't fair, 'cuz you already know what the room looks like. I had to do this completely blind," Michael said.

"Yeah. So?"

"So I'm thinking of having you play a different game."

"I'm up for that, man. That girl gone?"

"Yup."

"Cool. So what do you want me to do?"

Michael paused. He wiped the moisture from his brow and brushed it on his shirt. He took a swig from a Corona, not knowing if it was his or Buzz's.

"Hey, man, the clock is ticking. What do you want me to do?"

Michael licked his lips. "I want you to look down. At your feet."

The image from the camera on the headset went from the dim sight of the room to the view of Buzz's body from the waist down lit brightly by the spotlight on the visor.

"OK. Now what do you want me to do?"

"I want you to hold out your right hand."

Buzz put his right hand out in front of the camera, palm side facing up. "Like that?"

"Yeah. Now I want you to take your hand and move it over to the fly of your pants."

Without the slightest hesitation, Buzz reached for his front.

"Pull down the fly, buddy."

Buzz obliged.

"Now I want you to reach inside. Find the top of your underwear and pull it down so your cock flops out. Yeah. That's it, man," Michael sighed. "That's a great dick you got there."

"What do you want me to do?" asked Buzz. In the moment of excitement, he looked up, as if searching for Michael's face.

"Hey, keep your head pointed at the floor! I gotta see it to tell you what to do with it man."

"No problem," said Buzz. By the time the camera was turned back down, Buzz was aroused. Outside the room, sitting in front of the screen, so was Michael.

"Take your right hand and bring it up to your mouth. I want you to spit on your fingers. Now I want you to take that wet hand and start moving it up and down the shaft of that beautiful cock. That's right. Get some more spit and get it nice and wet, so it glistens under the light." Michael could hear Buzz panting loudly through the amplification of the headset.

"Oh, man! This is so hot. I could nutt!"

Michael looked at the clock. Four minutes and counting.

"Then do it, buddy. Now!"

Buzz lost control. Effulgent white spasms hit the dark floor, their luminance exaggerated by the beam of the headset. Some landed on the hem of his pants. He moaned softly, then released a powerful breath. The time: four minutes and thirty-one seconds.

"Hey, bud, we beat our old record by one second!"

"That's not all you beat!" A muffled voice came from behind him. The attendant? Michael tore off the headset and turned so quickly he felt a sharp pain in his neck. It was Lauren, standing with Jessica, whose face was bright red. "You boys are beating all sorts of things up here!"

"Uh, Lolly, right? Hey, I'm sorry," Michael tried to choke out a few lame words. "You weren't supposed to see that."

"Really? No shit."

Buzz walked out of the dim room, stripping off his gear.

"And you! I thought all you science geeks were straight!"

"Who says I'm not?" Buzz said with a guilty smile.

"Lolly, let's get outta here," Jessica said, suddenly emerging from shock. "I wanna leave *now*."

Without another word, the two women stormed down the stairs and out the door, barely stopping long enough to get their jackets and stiff the coat-check guy his tip. Lauren lit a cigarette as they stepped into the parking lot.

"What's the whole world coming to? Aren't there any straight guys anymore? Geeks or gays! Now it's fucking geeks who are gay!" Lauren fumed.

"Lolly, calm down. It's just two guys. There are plenty more," Jessica tried to console.

"I didn't say I was giving up. Not without a fight." Lauren's voice changed to slow and sad. "I'm still in the game."

"Of course you are," Jessica said, taken aback by Lauren's sudden serious turn. It wasn't like Lauren to be so shaken. First Putt, now these guys. She hoped Lauren wasn't thinking the whole world of men was in some sort of revolt. If she'd kept to the normal guys back home and tried to act grown up, things like this wouldn't happen.

"Just promise me one thing, Jes."

"What?"

"That this is the last time we do virtual reality!"

9

Raphe and Baptiste walked along the darkened street just outside the huge Goodwill complex at the corner of Mission and
Van Ness. It was near midnight, and the sidewalks were mostly
deserted. By day this stretch would be packed with people and
traffic, the crossroads where residential neighborhoods met the
grand plazas of the Civic Center, both colliding with poorly
planned highway entrances. The nearby symphony had ended
more than an hour earlier. Now all that remained were a few
homeless addicts doing some fruitless begging. Across the street
two overweight men in leather smoked cigars outside a bar called
The Loading Dock.

It was cool enough for jackets, but Baptiste and Raphe wore
only white T-shirts and burrowed their hands in the front pockets of their jeans to keep warm. Baptiste said jackets would be a
nuisance where they were headed.

Raphe worried when he looked in the mirror before they
headed out. Blue jeans and a white T-shirt. Was this the official
gay uniform? He'd been with Baptiste for one week—had he
been converted in such a short time? It made him a bit more
comfortable to know he'd be venturing back into the straight
world for the night. At least it was mostly straight.

"You never told me about your first time," said Raphe. He

wanted to learn everything about Baptiste, this man who had emerged from their mysterious encounter on BART and so quickly became such an intimate part of his life. Since that first night, they'd barely been apart. It all happened so fast.

"With a guy?"

"No, I mean with a girl. You know. When did you lose your virginity?"

"When I was eighteen. I remember how important it was for me to have sex while I was still in high school. In the Mission, the idea of a guy still being a virgin at graduation made him a total loser."

"But you weren't attracted to women."

"Sure I was. I was a horny kid like anyone else."

"But you grew up in *San Francisco*?" Raphe was incredulous. "The Castro was only a few blocks away."

"You know, that's how everyone looks at this town. Because it's so famous as the home of the Summer of Love, and the world's Gay Mecca, people think everyone who grows up here must be a swinger. It's just not true. The Castro and all its temptations and opportunities were as far away from me as they were from you."

Raphe thought of his own youth, growing up in a tiny suburb of Boston. Even though the city was just forty-five minutes away by commuter train, he and his friends never went there. Their parents had done an excellent job instilling the same urban fears that bombarded any small town children. It wouldn't be until college that they'd learn that much of what they'd been told was wildly exaggerated for their protection.

"We had the same boy-girl scene you had growing up," said Baptiste. "Maybe even worse since I went to Catholic school, and my parents were first generation and very old-fashioned. Still, kids somehow invent their own rules. There was a lot of pressure to get laid."

"What happened?"

"Oh, man. It's a bad memory."

"Why?"

"Goo and toilet paper," Baptiste said shaking his head.

"Huh?"

"It was a week before graduation. One of my friends had an older brother who thought it would be fun to buy us some beer, get us wasted, and have a party at his apartment. We didn't drink back then, so in no time everyone was drunk. Then Nortita arrives. She was only sixteen years old, but she loved to fuck. She got drunk and decided to screw every guy at the party. So, one at a time, we each went into the bedroom and fucked her. It was all over so fast, I remember thinking—*hey, this is no big deal*. It felt good, but I wondered why losing your virginity was such a huge thing. Then a few days later, I noticed a little tingling feeling when I went to piss."

"Oh, shit."

"Then it got to be painful. I was too embarrassed to say anything to anyone, so I suffered in silence. I figured it would just go away. But it didn't. Soon I had huge gobs of puss coming out my dick. It got so bad, I crumpled up bunches of toilet paper and stuffed them in the front of my underwear to absorb all the goo."

"Jesus."

"I finally went to the doctor. I was still seeing a pediatrician at that point, and I was so nervous my parents would find out. But I went to the office and told the receptionist it was urgent. The doctor agreed to see me. So I'm standing there in the examination room, and he made me pull down my shorts. There was the wad of toilet paper covering my crotch. It was stuck there. The doc said, 'What's this?' I said, 'No!' But it was too late. He grabbed the paper and pulled it away. That's when a gigantic stream of puss burst out all over the doctor. His hand. His arm. A little on his glasses. The paper was like a dam, and when the doctor pulled on it, it just burst."

"Gross."

"I'll never forget that poor man's reaction. He jumped away in shock, like a vicious dog was trying to bite him on the hand."

"Gonorrhea?"

"Yup."

"If that girl had everyone at the party, then she and the rest of the guys must have been infected too."

"Suppose so. No one ever talked about it."

"What? That's unbelievable."

"Hey, it's a different culture. We kept our business to ourselves. Although the doctor asked for the girl's name and I gave it to him."

"That's awful, man. And your first time. I bet you didn't want to have sex again after that."

"No, I got over it. In fact, I did it again lots of times that summer."

"Well, I hope those were better."

"Nah. Not really. They were with the same girl."

74 Otis Street didn't look like much from the outside. It could have been an old warehouse or factory. Thick, white paint covered a brick facade, creating a kind of latex sheath. Large, red numbers cut out of plywood marked the low lit entrance. Baptiste and Raphe walked up to what looked like the reception of a modest hotel. They each paid ten dollars, and the clerk told them to write their names on the guest list. Baptiste signed in for both of them. Instead of putting down their own names, he signed them in with the signatures of others. One was the name of a guy he used to date, until a bitter falling out. He also forged the name of a pretentious colleague from the law firm who would "never be caught dead" at a place like 74 Otis Street. It was disgusting. Excessive. "A haven for disease." Baptiste thought about that as he signed in with the fake identities. He remembered how at the height of the AIDS panic clubs like these demanded people show their drivers' licenses, and the clerks would

take down names, addresses, and ID numbers. It was as if they were building a huge file of the possibly infected. Nobody built lists these days. You could write down any fake name you wanted, and no one would check.

Because Baptiste had been before, he knew to plunk down just ten dollars. That amount was like a declaration of orientation. *Gay.* Straight guys paid as much as seventy-five to get in. It was a pricing scheme that made Baptiste laugh—he relished the fact that people who emphatically claimed to be "breeders" were charged more. Who could be 100 percent straight and go to a place like this? Yet many men willingly paid extra, just for the ten-second privilege of declaring themselves heterosexual at the front desk. Only closeted guys would do such a thing, Baptiste thought, or those who grasped onto the thin myth that there was such a thing as bisexual. There's a price to pay for choosing that lie. Deceit bears deceit. Seventy-five dollars was the least of the price they'd pay. He wondered if any of them ever applied for a refund after getting topped in a dark corner.

The Power Exchange was the club's official name, sounding more like a Scientology center than a sex club. Inside stretched four floors of carnal excess displaying nearly every conceivable array and fetish. Patrons joined the exhibitions, or started their own. It was the hottest place in town for bachelor parties, curious locals, and tourists who'd had enough of cable car rides and discretely begged their hotel concierges for insider advice on where they could see "you know, the *real* Frisco."

Baptiste figured it was time to take Raphe, and let him witness the extremes of the straight world in case he had any intention of heading back to it. He'd perceived a growing nervousness in Raphe about their relationship. That always happened with guys who were new. It's what made them so desirable, although those feelings had to be managed.

It had been an incredible week, better than Baptiste imagined when he made his play. From the moment on the train, he was smitten. Raphe looked like something out of an Abercrombie & Fitch catalog, wholesome on one level and sexually charged on another. Raphe was at least ten years younger, but when they fell into each other's arms at the bank, Baptiste was captured by a sense of fate. He grew up listening to his grandmother's wonderful tales of old Mexico, magical little stories where "God's finger" intervened to prod two people into each other's lives through odd coincidences and circumstances. He loved Nana and missed her colorful fables now that she was gone, yet he'd never actually believed the tales. But when the man on the BART platform became the man on the train and then the man at the bank, he accepted the series of appearances as signs of something more meaningful. Maybe Nana was right after all, and God was the Almighty puppeteer. All Baptiste had to do was close the deal, a skill he'd spent his adult lifetime perfecting. Another coincidence?

He thought back to their first time. The night they left Bacar they went to Baptiste's apartment, conveniently located just around the corner. They were both still a little lit from the wine, but even that wasn't enough to completely assuage Raphe's anxieties. When Baptiste first touched Raphe's arm, he retracted it in a jolt as if struck by an electric shock.

"It's OK, man. Nothing is going to happen tonight unless you want it to." Baptiste spoke with all the sincerity of his psychoanalyst, borrowing the tone and inflections he'd learned to imitate after so many years of therapy. "I only want what's best for you."

He poured them both a glass of scotch, which Raphe refused at first and then gulped down all at once. Baptiste said he knew some massage techniques that would help Raphe relax. He got him to lie down on the carpet in the living room, knowing that suggesting the bedroom might have scuttled the whole thing. He caressed Raphe's back. His large, firm hands worked their magic, as they always did, allowing Baptiste to suggest that if Raphe took off his shirt, he'd be able to do an even better job. Unwrapped was the musculature of a naturally athletic form, his back peppered with occasional patches of short, dark hair. Far less hair than on Raphe's chest, but more than Baptiste had envisioned or wanted. He craved to caress smooth, hairless backs. This fur would need to be removed someday. For now, it was just one careful step at a time. Baptiste kissed the base of Raphe's spine.

He panicked he'd gone too far too quickly, but Raphe softly moaned.

"Turn over," he whispered to Raphe.

He got onto the floor beside him and gently traipsed his hand over Raphe's chest, barely touching the flesh. The brush of his hand was so slight, the connection was more energy than flesh. Raphe's nipples hardened as Baptiste hovered his hand above. Raphe sighed, even though there had been no actual contact.

"Close your eyes," Baptiste quietly instructed. He leaned over and kissed the edge of Raphe's mouth. His lips parted, searching. Baptiste held back.

He placed his hand softly on Raphe's chest and swirled it down over his abdomen to the top of his jeans. Baptiste's fingers crawled under, feeling the waistband and texture of boxers, just as he suspected he'd find. His hand went further. Raphe was hard. He flinched when Baptiste touched. He kept his hand there, just resting, until he saw Raphe's breathing return to normal. He brought his hand out and gingerly unzipped the pants, then nudged them down with the boxers until Raphe was exposed.

Baptiste smiled at the eagerness of Raphe's body. He took him into his grasp. He pulled and stroked until he felt Raphe was so hard he'd burst. Then Baptiste relented and waited for Raphe to calm. Baptiste caressed again, concentrating on the places and techniques he knew would make Raphe writhe.

When he felt the pressure under his fingers near explosion, he pulled back until the moment subsided. He knew how to edge a man like this for what could seem like an eternity. After a few more advances and retreats, he could see the agony in Raphe. His body begged to be satiated. Baptiste brought Raphe over. He convulsed and climaxed.

So fast. It was clear he had no experience with men.

"Keep your eyes closed," Baptiste said. He leaned over and parted Raphe's lips with his own.

Each day since, Baptiste taught Raphe something new. From touch they went to taste. He wondered if Raphe would hesitate at taking him into his mouth. He tried teasing, by only allowing a little at a time past the lips. Raphe's thirst to know caused him to gag for taking too much at once. His eyes watered. Baptiste patiently revealed the subtle ways of the mouth. He was surprised at how quickly his student learned, and claimed he was caught off guard when he erupted into Raphe's mouth. In truth, he wanted him to have it. To fuse with his new lover. To stake his claim.

On Thursday, Baptiste took his conquest completely for the first time, needing two hours of foreplay to quell the apprehension. The sensation overwhelmed Raphe, and his body shook in spasms after only a few seconds. Baptiste waited patiently before starting again, this time bringing them both over simultaneously.

The new feelings were almost too much for Raphe to comprehend, Baptiste could tell. Such complete bodily enjoyment inevitably led men to question whether they were really men any longer. Untrained to understand their own emotions, they confused being brought to the physical edge with being submissive and weak. It always happened like this with the new ones.

Baptiste knew tonight's adventure at 74 Otis Street would give Raphe a new perspective. The club had four floors and

more than forty thousand square feet of play space. The basement and the ground level were mixed, while the second and
third floors were for men only.

The main floor appeared to be like any other club, a large,
long comfortable room with couches, chairs, and a snack bar. It
was the only well-lit space in the entire building. Very few people hung out there, not wanting to be seen, or not wishing to
witness the true features of their liaisons. They walked past the
snack bar into a corridor of black walls, mirrors, and strobe
lights, conjuring up for Raphe childhood memories of the run-
down Fun House ride at the annual traveling carnival in his
hometown of Medford, Massachusetts. It always stank of aging
vomit, and its worn attractions provided little amusement or
thrill. Here the odor was different: a musky, dank smell with the
hint of some sort of cleaning chemical mixed with the remnants
of marijuana.

At the end of the hallway, a cavernous, dark room opened to
the right. Large jail cells lined the walls. Inside one chamber a
man prowled around alone, pacing back and forth like a tiger in
a zoo, eyeing Raphe and Baptiste as if they were prey. Next
door, a man in a latex hood playfully whipped a blonde in a
leather corset with a cat-o'-nine-tails. In another cage, two men
and two women leaned up against the bars, sizing each other up
and talking dirty. Shocked tourists gawked and safely kept their
distance. Beyond the cells emerged a maze of fantasy-themed
chambers. The Egyptian room allowed couples to pretend to be
archeologists having sex in a mummy's tomb. Another space featured the decor of a gothic mansion. There was even a mini
Paris motif, complete with a replica of a dingy walk-up, reminding Raphe of the kind of place Henry Miller and Anaïs Nin
might have used for a rendezvous. Each area had at least one
bed, semi-private spaces for others to watch or play, and hard-
core porn pumped in on video.

"This is boring," said Baptiste. "Let's go downstairs to the dungeon."

On the stairs to the basement they passed a man in his early thirties in a preppy, blue sport coat holding hands with a young, pretty woman in a white Laura Ashley dress.

"First date?" Baptiste joked.

The dungeon had more jail cells and more theme rooms. The "Operation Iraqi Freedom" area allowed people to have sex amid camouflage. A beaded curtain opened into a little room reminiscent of a turn-of-the-century New Orleans bordello. Inside a man sat with his pants around his ankles as a transvestite performed fellatio. "Chicks with dicks," Baptiste scoffed.

There was a re-creation of Frankenstein's laboratory, complete with electromagnetic gadgets. On the monster's slab lay an overweight naked man in his fifties. A dominatrix circled him, swatting at his legs and stomach with a narrow paddle. The man winced each time he was struck, then smiled and stroked his erection.

At each turn, the scenes became more bizarre. In one room two obese black lesbians licked each other in an awkward sixty-nine atop a jiggling bed. One dipped a celery stalk in the other's vagina and ate it.

"Thank God they're not on the Atkins diet," Baptiste joked.

Down the hall in a dark area to the side a woman stretched out on a weight lifter's bench. One man held her wrists, while another took what looked like a stun gun and shot blue volts through the air to sting her labia. Genital assault. Raphe put his hand on his stomach and thought he might become ill.

In The Sling Room six malleable leather chairs hung from chains bolted into the ceiling in a motif that eerily evoked a child's playground. Each saddle was occupied, with several people leaned up against the walls waiting their turns.

In one sling was a particularly stunning woman. Her face revealed maturity, but not age. She might have been in her early forties, but she had a striking beauty that transcended any years. Her body was exceptionally fit, one any younger woman would covet. A handsome, muscled blond man hovered above her, holding onto the metal chains and thrusting into her with violent enthusiasm. For fifteen minutes, Raphe and Baptiste stood mesmerized, hypnotized by the movements of the penetration. Although older, the woman had red hair, reminding Raphe of the girl who lived upstairs at 225 Folsom. Was that world dead to him? Now that he had been with men, what woman would ever want him? He wondered if he could ever be thrilled by such things again, now that he'd been shown where secret pleasures dwelled. Part of him felt like damaged goods, as if he had somehow given up his manhood. He thought of the people he'd seen so far in the club—the pain the men and women inflicted on each other in the pursuit of their desires. It held no appeal for him. He had felt no such agony with Baptiste. Maybe theirs was his true destiny, his true nature.

The man continued to pummel the woman in the sling until she let out a series of screams. To Raphe, the guttural yelps evoked an awful torment, as if being stabbed repeatedly. Was it just an act? *She must be a hooker*, he thought. No, that didn't make sense. Wouldn't a guy like this have his pick of women? Maybe they were both pros, hired by the club for the night to entertain the crowds. When the man finally pulled out and burst onto the woman's stomach, the back of Raphe's neck turned scarlet red—not out of desire, just embarrassment.

"Now we can finally say we've seen everything," Baptiste said, his voice scratchy and unsure, sounding as if he had just climaxed himself. "Let's go upstairs."

They left the mixed floors and ventured up to the levels that allowed only men. They wandered through The Electrified Forest, a huge room made to look like a campground. Dozens of tents with bedding inside were scattered across the floor, mixed in with artificial trees. Black lights made everyone's jeans appear a light shade of neon purple. On the top floor was a disco with pulsating lights. Off the dance floor lurked a maze of shadowy hallways, littered with beds and more slings. At the far end of the room stood a series of freestanding walls and gloryholes, followed by a video room with a large screen projection TV of gay porn, featuring the most perfect male bodies Raphe had ever witnessed.

Other than the campground motif, there were no other fantasy settings—no bizarre kink, just an endless journey of gratification expressed for all to see or join. Raphe and Baptiste watched for a while as a beautiful, brown Latino and a freckled, white young man fucked on a raised mattress covered in black leather.

"Typical bean and potato combination," Baptiste mused.

Raphe signaled to Baptiste that they didn't need to wait for the climax. He wanted to explore. He felt a kind of kinship here that didn't exist below on the straight floors. No pain or abuse up here, only sex. Or was it love? He felt a strange rush—a brief epiphany that maybe now he was among his own kind. It was a thought he tried to suppress. How could he have a crush on the red-haired woman upstairs and *also* be attracted to *this*? It was too confusing. All he knew for sure was that he was here, he was aroused, and there would be little thrill in merely watching.

Baptiste grinned. He took Raphe by the hand and led him through a doorway into a dark maze. They stopped in a corner and Baptiste unbuttoned Raphe's jeans, dropping them to his ankles, followed by his boxers.

"The hole," Baptiste said. "Stick it in the hole."

Raphe looked down. Level with his crotch was an oval opening in the black, plywood wall of the maze. It was dark on the other side, but he could make out something moving. A mouth surrounded by a short dark beard.

"But I'm with you," Raphe said.

Baptiste turned his pupil toward the hole. He hugged Raphe

from behind and nudged him close to the opening. "You're still with me," he whispered into Raphe's ear.

The sensation of Baptiste's breath tingled his skin just as Raphe was swallowed by the mouth on the other side.

"In our world, we have the freedom to distinguish between flesh and love," Baptiste breathed into Raphe's ear. "You deserve to have all your needs met, yes?"

Raphe felt a hand on his behind. But Baptiste's were still wrapped around him. He turned to see that another man had come into their corner of the maze. His caress felt good.

"It's OK," Baptiste said as he pressed his mouth into Raphe's ear. The sound of his voice filled Raphe's head, blotting out all thoughts and anxieties. "I want you to know pleasure."

More hands. Then lips. And tongues. He hadn't seen their faces. Where did they all come from? Who were they?

So many sensations from all directions. Baptiste continued to whisper. Soon Raphe could only pick out random words. *Joy. Us. Love. Deserve.* The music from the disco muted. The world outside disappeared. His body shook uncontrollably, unable to hold back a moment longer.

10

Mark Hazodo looked around the expanse of the room. Typical straight bar, he dismissed, a place trying too hard to look upscale. He noted the worn leather on the bar stools, the scuffs in the carpet, and the brown fringe on the leaves of a dying palm near the door. The place had been designed to have the motif of an aging, French *boîte de nuit* in colonial Vietnam. At least they got the stink of old beer right.

He recognized some of the guys. He'd seen them around—at the gym, the clubs, the cafés. San Francisco was like a small town in that way—you were always bumping into the same faces. Mark was pretty sure he'd tricked with at least a couple of the men, although he couldn't remember their names. Even if he had fucked them, that didn't mean he knew them well enough to strike up a conversation.

Especially at an event like this. These boys were the Best in Show, the beauties. In such a crowd the game would be to check each other out silently, quickly casting judgment. Speaking to one another—that was out of the question.

"He's really very handsome," Meg said to Porsche and Devina. She referred to Mark in the third person, as if he wasn't standing with them. Meg reached over and took the lapel of

Mark's dark Armani suit to feel the silky fabric with her fingers. "Cleans up nice, too. Where in the world did you find him?"

"Yes, Mark *is* quite the catch," Porsche said as she took the last sip from her wine. "We got him at the gym."

Mark was silent and smiled. He knew he was not allowed to speak unless spoken to. For now, he was just to pose while the ladies jabbered on about him.

"What do you mean, *we?*" Porsche's partner Devina jumped in. She put her arm over Mark's shoulder, forcing Meg to step back. "*I'm* the one who saw him on the treadmill. He was wearing one of those muscle shirts that revealed these beefy arms. When I chatted him up, he said he was training for the Bay to Breakers. I immediately knew he would be the one."

"Which gym?" Meg asked.

"Gold's on Brannan, of course. If you want to find good ones, they all hang out there."

On any other Saturday night, hundreds on the prowl would pack the upstairs bar at Le Colonial. Single men and women at play. The music was always too loud, providing a shield for pretty girls to pretend that they could not hear if an unattractive guy tried hitting on them. It was a large space compared to most San Francisco bars, but it never seemed that way because it was always jammed beyond capacity.

Not this night. Patrons who arrived were stunned to be turned away and told the club was closed for a private party. It was invitation-only with an unusual mix of women and men. Two women for every one man. Precisely.

"Well, we found Andrew at The Café nightclub on Market," Meg offered, despite the fact no one had asked. She didn't acknowledge Andrew, even though he stood beside her. "We spotted him as he sat on the balcony smoking a cigarette. He was watching the crowd do its evening stroll through the Castro. We actually debated approaching him for a while. You know how Carly feels about smoking."

"Did you get him to quit?" Porsche asked. The tone in her voice revealed her disinterest in the conversation. Instead, her eyes darted around the room to the other men.

"We sent him to one of those hypnotists," Meg went on about Andrew, again acting as if he weren't there. His only reaction was to pick a stray umber hair off the front of his blue Versace jacket. "I was skeptical at first, but it really worked. I have to admit I agree with Carly. No one wants a smoker. Even if he doesn't do it in front of you, it gets in his breath, and it seems to end up all over you."

"Does he still do meth?" Devina asked.

"Oh, sure. But that's different. Crystal doesn't smell as bad."

Mark wondered if anyone in the room knew who he was. Apparently not. So far no one had approached him, even though the place teemed with players from the business world. He recognized many of *them*—it was like a Who's Who of The City's richest and most successful women. Some had famously cashed in on the dot-com boom at its height. Others made their way up through the corporate world. Banking. Medicine. Biotech. All the major fields of The City's financial elite. The longer Mark stared, the more he realized there was something else at play. Something all the women had in common. What was it? Mark had seen many of the women profiled in local newspapers and magazines. He thought back to the stories, trying to decipher their common thread. Then it struck him. Each woman had struggled and fought to attain her status. There was not a dime of inherited wealth on the floor.

Under other circumstances, they might know him, too. His videogame empire was one of the few success stories to come out of SoMa in the past two years. Tonight, however, they looked right at him, scrutinizing every inch, but failed to see who he was. *Hide in plain sight,* Mark laughed to himself. He was simply out of context here. For this cocktail party he was destined to be just another handsome face, known only by his first name. The women said they liked it that way. It kept things in their proper place.

Mark relished the anonymity of the moment. Free of who he really was, it would make it so much easier to submerge himself into the intensity of the events ahead.

His mind flashed back to the moment he first met Porsche and Devina at the gym.

"Yes, Porsche. Spelled just like the car. My father had a thing for expensive rides."

He heard their offer.

"Are you serious?" he'd asked. "Is this some type of game?"

They seemed to know just what to say to tease him, cleverly holding back the details. They'd explain it all over dinner, Devina said.

"No strings, as you boys like to say," Porsche assured.

At the time, Mark wondered if it was a practical joke put on by one of his friends. What would two women want with *him*? He had to admit he was intrigued. He'd never submitted to the whims of women before. At the very least, it would be a new experience to accumulate. That's what life was all about. Do everything, see everything, feel everything.

When they met for dinner, Mark was struck by how beautiful the two women were. Everything was perfect. The private dining room at Gary Danko. The best wines, trendy American paddlefish roe, and bluefin tuna sushi flown in from Nova Scotia that morning. The scent of dozens of candles made the women seem even lovelier. Lilac? His mother's favorite.

Porsche wore an elegant, cream-colored sheer silk dress that cascaded in a provocative deep plunge down her chest. She donned no jewelry—nothing to distract from the intense, bright blue of her eyes, sitting under the nave of her long, blonde pinned-up hair. Mark had never seen eyes that looked more like gems.

Devina went for the classic short black dress. Simple, but Mark immediately recognized it as the work of a very expensive designer, the kind of dress that sells for several thousand dollars. Not only did it worship Devina's petite, dark features, but it spelled out class in a way Mark appreciated. It was one thing to have money. It was another to use it to truly enjoy the finest.

He figured they must be in their late thirties, but their style and beauty made them seem so much younger. The fact they had found each other charmed the small sentimental side of Mark, happy to know such lovely couples really existed.

Then they revealed the details of their proposal.

Mark knew all along some sort of game was in play—the idea of a scheme had lured him this far. Still, what they offered was shocking, even for him. Mark thought of staging a mock drama and storming out of the restaurant. That would test their mettle. He searched their eyes for a few moments and realized it was no joke. They were serious. They wanted *him*. Not as Mark Hazodo, rising entrepreneur, the man others desired for their greedy agendas. Porsche and Devina clearly didn't know anything about that part of his life. They wanted him just for his flesh.

And a little piece of his soul.

"In exchange for being a part of this, we will shower you in wealth," Porsche explained. "You will travel to the best places, eat the best food, and be dressed in the finest clothes. You can live in one of the condos we own at the Four Seasons. It has maid service and anything else you could want."

"We'll get you a personal trainer to help you stay in shape," Devina jumped in. "You'll be pampered with the best grooming—massages, haircuts, manicures. We have an arrangement with a salon on Maiden Lane. You'll get to use it as much as you want."

Five years ago, when he first arrived in The City, Mark

would have jumped at their offer. He'd seen plenty of kept boys. An older man walking down the street arm in arm with a younger guy with wandering eyes—it was almost a stereotype in The City's gay world. Once at Café Flore a man in his fifties sat beside Mark, bathed him in compliments, and talked about the spare, empty room in his Victorian on Henry Street. At the time Mark was just another Stanford CS student trying to make ends meet. It was a nice offer, but nothing like this.

"And you would pay me?" Mark asked.

"No. Absolutely not." Devina acted repulsed by the suggestion. "It's not prostitution. The very idea of that is, well, offensive."

"So I would be . . . what?"

"In our group we've always liked the term *Boy Toy*," Porsche grinned.

They went on to explain that the cocktail party would be once a month. Personal sessions with the women would happen at least once a week. Mark would have to be flexible about which nights, since both women traveled often for business. Still, he'd get plenty of notice, so he could plan his own personal life. They had no problem with him seeing others, as long as he never mentioned their arrangement.

Mark had heard of such games, but never with women running the show. Wealthy, old gay men had Gamma Mu, a so-called fraternity that used handsome young men in much the same way. The idea of being the plaything of some perverted geezer repulsed Mark. He didn't need the tokens of attention and wealth they'd throw his way. He didn't need what Porsche and Devina offered either. But the thought of being *their* property—it was a sensation Mark had never experienced. *Submission*. Now that the opportunity dangled within his reach, he craved to know how it would feel. In all aspects of his life, Mark considered himself as the man on top, the ruler. What better way to perfect that role than to fully understand what it's like to be on the other side? Even if only as a game.

Mark agreed to be their Boy Toy.

Porsche and Devina hugged each other in delight and ordered champagne to seal the deal.

"If you don't mind, we'd like to start as early as tonight," said Porche. "I mean, if you are in the mood. I know that some guys like to, uh, prep first."

It amazed Mark to think that the dinner and deal had happened only two hours earlier. Now he was standing in Le Colonial being paraded around in front of the others like a new prize—just as Porsche and Devina said he would. He was like a fashion model on a catwalk.

"We really should be leaving," Porsche said to Meg.

"So soon?" Meg moaned. "I was really enjoying your new one. He's very pretty to look at."

"True. He's a beauty. We'd love to stay all night and make the other girls jealous," said Devina. "But we have a big night ahead."

They left the bar and took a limo up to Devina's immense home on Telegraph Hill. Mark was surprised to discover the two women didn't live together as a couple.

"We really do spend most of our time with each other," Porsche explained. "Separate residences are nice investments . . . and bigger tax breaks."

The bed was already turned down and dim lighting created a romantic mood. A jazz CD played softly in the background. Mark wondered if the women always lived like this or if the room had been prepared for his arrival. Were they so confident he'd succumb to their plan?

Slowly the expensive clothes came off, and Mark found himself the center of attention. The women caressed his smooth body and gently ran their fingers through his thick, black hair. They kissed his lips, neck and cheeks, but never once wandered to the parts of him that actually made him a man. That was OK, he reasoned. He probably wouldn't get aroused. They were beautiful, but women just didn't do it for him.

Then the moment came. He knew what they wanted to do. They had explained it during dinner. In a way, Mark looked forward to it. Being shown off at parties as the prized bull was just the surface. He thought back to Le Colonial and the room full of successful women. He remembered their faces, their stories, and what they all had in common. He thought of the brutalities they all had likely endured to rise to the top in professions dominated by men.

Devina instructed him to get on his knees. Mark was usually the one who did the driving, worried that taking the passenger seat might make him less of a man. Still, he wasn't a virgin to it. Besides, he reasoned, these were *women*. Not men. When all was done, he'd still be the only real man in the bedroom. Still the king. He was ultimately in control of what was about to happen. Let the women believe what they want. He could simply walk out at any time.

No, he calmed himself, this was about gaining a new experience. Another checkmark on his list. What was it like to be dominated by women? He supposed he could have asked any henpecked husband. With Porsche and Devina he would *learn* how total submission felt.

Porsche strapped on the harness. The phallus was larger than Mark imagined it would be.

Then it went in. It wasn't so bad. He knew this wasn't supposed to be about *his* pleasure, at least not the physical kind. He winced as each violent thrust seemed to go deeper and deeper. He recalled how a friend once told him that Fortune 500 executives regularly subjected themselves to degradation to help them keep their edge. King on the Streets, Queen in the Sheets was the old expression. They used sessions like these to drain any submissive tendencies from their bodies, so they could do battle without the danger of weakness emerging. All vulnerability was to be expelled, by appointment.

The pounding started to hurt. Nothing he couldn't handle. The verbal abuse, however, was another thing. It bugged him. Did they really need to say that? *Payback* . . . for what? He'd just have to learn to block it out of his mind.

He wondered if Devina would go easier on him.

SUMMER

11

"Is this a straight bar or a gay bar?"

The man was tall, clean-shaven, about thirty, and very clearly drunk.

"What?" Phil asked from behind the bar.

"Is this a gay bar?"

Phil looked around. It was a Saturday night in late July in San Francisco, with forty-eight degree temps and bitter winds that made it feel freezing outside. The bar, his bar, died on nights like these, and now at 1:30 A.M. it was nearly empty. He wondered how the other SoMa bars were doing. The only people in the place were four stragglers he'd spent the evening filling with strong drinks. Four guys he was pretty sure were gay. Didn't the Latino say something earlier about *felching*?

Phil looked at the four men at the bar, then looked down at his own chest, and laughed to the tall man, "It's all gay right now, buddy."

The tall man pounded his fists on the bar. "Geesh!" He walked out.

"What the fuck was that all about?" Raphe slurred his words, the result of his fourth Sidecar, a brandy Margarita with sugar on the rim instead of salt. When he was straight, no one ever told him such a delicious drink existed. The gays sure knew great cocktails. *The* gays. He'd have to stop referring to them in the third person, now that he'd become one. He was gay now, wasn't he?

"He was too drunk and too big of an asshole," said Phil as he wiped the counter.

"That is so awesome, man. I mean, it's not like you're filled with customers tonight. He was cash, even if he was a jerk." Raphe took another gulp from his drink. For the past hour he'd been on autopilot, ordering one after another, even though they were so strong. He was gone after the first.

Baptiste's friends—Raphe's *new* friends—Steve and Jeremy sat stewed on their stools next to Raphe. Even drunk they made for an exceptionally handsome couple, with Steve's rugged goatee and cultivated blue-collar veneer contrasting Jeremy's black skin and clean-cut Ralph Lauren style. Raphe imagined what it would be like to watch the two of them together, a delicious swirl of white and dark chocolates.

Jeremy was the first African-American to befriend Raphe in all the years he'd lived in The City. It always struck Raphe as odd that in a place so revered for its liberal politics and tolerance, black people were still mostly relegated to live in the outer neighborhoods, or banished to Oakland. Only when their paths crossed through the queer world were their lives able to mesh, otherwise they'd likely never know each other. Sexual orientation threw so many disparate people together. America's true melting pot, as long as everyone in it sucks cock.

"I thought this *was* a straight bar?" Jeremy suddenly blurted in a dramatically delayed reaction.

More than anything, Scotch and Soda was a SoMa pioneer, moving into a part of The City where few restaurants dared. Located across from the Hall of Justice courthouse, the bar sat on narrow Harriett Street, squeezed between bail bonds storefronts. It wasn't unusual for first-time customers to think twice before opening the door, worried they'd find themselves in a room full of felons' families and their car titles.

Once inside they found a hidden treasure. An old cop bar called the "Inn Justice" transformed into a sleek eatery. As the name implied, the bar was stocked with just about every type of scotch known to man. The area was the latest in SoMa to face gentrification. Across the block a fleet of new loft apartments readied for sail, and with them Phil's hope that his investment would soon pay better dividends.

"It's mostly a straight bar," Phil smiled, his teeth slightly yellowed from years of too much coffee and the occasional joint. "Then you guys walked in."

"Straight or gay, I think it's fantastic, and we wouldn't have found it if it wasn't for Baptiste." Raphe gave Baptiste an elbow, which barely registered through a Dewar's haze. "Go on, man. Tell Phil how we found his place."

Baptiste reached into the front pocket of his blue plaid buttoned-down shirt and pulled out a crumpled sheet of paper. He spread it out on the bar and began smoothing out the creases with meticulous, slow detail.

"Give me that!" Raphe impatiently snatched the note. He playfully smiled at Phil as he shook the paper into the air like a magician preparing his handkerchief for a trick.

"We'd just been to another good-bye party," Raphe explained. "Stu and Erica this time. I met Stu at my old dot-com job. Their building is suddenly going T.I.C. Uh, that means Tenants in Common. You know, where a bunch of people buy a building and get to kick everyone out."

"I know what it means," nodded Phil.

"OK. So they're getting evicted, and they don't have jobs. So that means they are leaving The City and headed back to Albany."

"Albany sucks," said Steve, his first words in nearly an hour. Jeremy nodded his head in agreement.

"Anyway, it was a good party," Raphe continued. "An afternoon thing. Eviction parties can be wild, especially if they're at night, and everyone gets drunk and takes out their anger on the building. But Stu and Erica are so nice, they didn't want to do that. They just wanted to mourn."

"OK." Phil wondered when Raphe would finally get to the piece of paper he flailed.

"You know, I'm starting to develop a theory about San Francisco," Raphe continued. "I say people only last here three years, and then they're gone. At least the regular people. They put in their time, struggle with high rents and low wages, finally get fed up, and leave. Three years. That's all they can take. I've been here more than that, so I'm really pushing it. Did I tell you I'm a writer?" Raphe took a gulp to drain his glass. "Do you have a boyfriend?"

"The paper? You were going to tell me about the paper." Phil's grin had grown into a chuckle. This Raphe guy was a trip, Phil thought, the type he wouldn't mind for a little after hours fun. He'd never done that in the bar—no one ever hit on him there. At just over six feet with his razor-stubbled shaved head, trimmed goatee and deep voice, he was always assumed to be straight. His recalcitrant slight stomach bulge in a land of six-pack abs also threw people off.

"Oh, yeah. The paper," Raphe said as he pushed his empty glass toward Phil and smirked. "Can I have another?"

"I'll pour, you talk."

"Well, the eviction party got us talking about things we haven't done yet. I mean, how much longer do any of us have here? In a way, you just never know when it's gonna end. Just like for Stu and Erica. So Baptiste came up with a great idea. Let's hit the worst skank hole bars of The City."

"Yeah, skank holes," Baptiste burped.

"Uh, thanks," Phil put on an exaggerated grimace.

"I didn't mean *this* place." Raphe smoothed out the paper

on the bar. "Look here. We went on the internet and printed out a list of dives for us to visit. When we got to Lucky 13, the bartender there turned out to be a friend of Baptiste's. He said we should stop by here—that your place was new and worth the trip."

Phil now looked at the list on the wrinkled page. Sure enough, there was Lucky 13. He'd been there and swore it drew a crowd of chain-smoking Vietnam War veteran amputees. And Annie's Lounge, frequented by bike messengers during the day and bail bonds customers at night.

"Jezebel's Joint?" Phil asked. He'd heard it was the unofficial watering hole of people who worked in The City's sex trade. "What was that place like?"

"Never got there," said Raphe. "We started at eight. Now it's nearly two, and we only made it to three places."

"I'm honored to make the cut." Phil rinsed off a glass he picked out of a sink of soapy water and began to dry it. Almost closing time. Maybe he could get this guy Raphe to stick around and go face down on the bar. He'd wanted to do that ever since he bought the place, and this guy was hot and maybe even drunk enough to do it. Wasn't Raphe with the Latino? It didn't matter. He'd be more than happy to fill them both. Maybe he could get the two others to play. This crappy night could turn out to be . . .

"Is there still time for me to have a nightcap?" The words came from a man down at the darker end of the bar near the door. No one had seen or heard him come in. The voice startled the others.

"Sure thing, man. Sorry I didn't see you down there. I'm Phil. What can I get you?"

"I'm Mark." He reached across the bar to shake. Phil noticed the thick, silver band ring on the middle finger of the right hand, and the soft feel of Mark's palm and fingers. It was a firm handshake, not limp or feminine, but the skin was remarkably gentle to the touch. After so many years working as a bartender before he finally bought his own joint, Phil knew how to use a handshake to size up a customer. The guy was money.

"Well, you certainly have a lot of choices when it comes to scotch. Let's see. I think a Lagavulin, on the rocks."

"Nice choice," Raphe said, though he had no idea what Lagavulin was. He figured from the look on Phil's face it had to be something expensive.

Mark just smiled back, subtly leaning forward on his stool to take in a full sweep of the guy with the soul patch. *Not bad,* he thought. Handsome, masculine, nice body. Even with just the two words he'd heard, Mark thought he caught a slight New England accent. Definitely worthy of pursuit.

Mark Hazodo had never been to Scotch and Soda before, but he'd heard it was the new straight bar in SoMa. He'd spent much of the night down at the Midnight Sun video bar in the Castro, taking in the same routine he'd witnessed far too many times. The club would put a mix of music videos and comedy clips up on large TVs. Men then pushed their way through the jammed crowd while everyone kept his eyes aimed up at the screens, pretending to watch the programming. Instead, those navigating the pack were actually doing a ritualistic dance of sorts. *Excuse me. Oh, excuse me. Coming through.* The zigzag through the mob had no real destination. The idea was to touch as many guys as possible, subtly checking out the details under their clothes with tactile determination. If they liked what they felt, they'd make a play for the guy. Mark nicknamed the game "The Fat Frisk." Inevitably when they got to Mark, guys would feel his firm torso and pause. The more brazen would come right out with some catchy, queeny line like, "Oh my, you're so hard I thought I had bumped into a table." For Mark, getting laid at the Midnight Sun was as easy as shooting fish in a barrel.

He went there because he thought that's what he wanted tonight. Just simple release. He might even let someone service him in the bathroom. The stalls didn't have doors, but he'd done it before. The other men seemed to get a kick out of watching.

But when he got there, he saw how predictable the evening would be. He supposed it was like a great amusement park ride—so intense at first, but after taking the trip so many times it was bound to become boring.

He needed a challenge. A game. He thought of calling Devina and Porsche for a session with them, but even that was starting to get old. Being submissive was exciting at first, but he'd learned all he was going to from that experience. He looked forward to the moment he would break it off and tell them the truth, that it was all just a game. He had never truly relinquished his role as the man. How would they react when he told them he was the one really in control the whole time? It would certainly make their man-hating rants and abuse seem silly and pointless. He'd played them. Maybe he'd even offer *them* money to be *his* sexual subservient.

On second thought, Mark cringed, there was nothing worse than head from a woman.

He was driving around SoMa looking for something new when he spotted the sign for Scotch and Soda. Almost closing time. And a straight bar. He'd have only twenty minutes to try and close a deal. Could he make it happen?

He looked at the guy at the bar, admiring the little tuft of hair under his lip. One of those metrosexuals, no doubt. Handsome, clearly straight, and completely wasted. A good candidate for a fuck and dump.

"What's your name?" Mark asked.

"Raphe."

"Raphe? That's an unusual name. Like that actor?"

"Ralph Fiennes? It sounds the same—like waif—but I spell it different. It's my mother's maiden name turned into my first."

"I'm Mark. Mark Hazodo." Mark looked over to the other three men at the bar. They all had their heads down resting on their arms on the counter, as if they were elementary school students all ordered to nap at their desks. "You with these guys?"

Raphe looked over at his snoozing friends. "Yeah. But with one big difference. I'm still conscious!"

"It looks like the end of the night for them."

Phil finally chirped in. "It's closing time." He could tell from the way Mark looked at Raphe that his fantasy of sex on the bar would have to wait for another time. "Can I get anyone a cab?"

Baptiste raised his hand in a gesture of surrender. He looked over to Raphe. "You coming?"

Raphe thought of their night at The Power Exchange and the intense scene in the maze. Later Baptiste said Raphe should "branch out" whenever the opportunity hit. Monogamy, Baptiste insisted, was an emotional state, not a physical one. Their bond could not be threatened by experiences of the flesh. The way Baptiste reasoned, being gay meant they had an obligation to rewrite the definition of relationships, since much of the so-called normal world refused to recognize theirs. "We don't have to play by the straight rules."

Raphe learned that night, and in the weeks to come, what Baptiste meant. The rulebook of sexual limits was rewritten for the gay world. There was no dating, dinner, and a movie first. Often people never even bothered to exchange names. Obtaining gratification was a common and accepted practice, with no shame assigned even to the most extreme behavior. Dating and relationships were the anomaly. Instead, many men developed sexual specialties, their appetites for particular acts evolving into astonishing expertise. A man might be interested in doing only one thing, and therefore be too limited for a full partnership, but for that one act he had few peers. Baptiste introduced Raphe to guys so talented that just one meeting taught Raphe remarkable techniques he likely would never have learned in a lifetime of loving just one person. Baptiste explained that for the sake of their relationship, Raphe was expected to embrace this education, and bring back his new knowledge to their bed.

Baptiste, of course, would do the same. It's just the way things worked between men.

Now here was Mark, a handsome, apparently wealthy Asian man. Raphe wondered what he would be taught this time.

"I know an after hours spot if you wanna hit it," Mark offered.

Baptiste raised his head again off the bar. "Go ahead, man. We're worthless." Steve and Jeremy kept their heads face down, but both lifted their hands simultaneously and waved good-bye.

The after hours spot Mark had in mind turned out to be his loft in the heart of SoMa's nightclub district at 11th and Folsom. Mark owned the entire third floor of an old brewery building that had been converted into spectacular dwellings. What impressed Raphe most was that the key-operated elevator opened directly into Mark's home. No hallway. No one else living on the floor. Just Mark's vast, open space—the size of a small gymnasium.

The decor was dramatically minimalist, with black leather furnishings placed carefully to draw attention to the wide-open feel of the massive room. Huge two-story arched windows offered panoramic views of The City on three sides. Against the back wall a staircase snaked up to an open bedroom that seemed to hover in midair. Raphe had never seen anything like it. Most of his friends lived in dreary three-bedroom flats in aging Victorians, where the walls had more scrapes than paint. Even his own condo, something he was so proud of when he bought it, was a cookie-cutter motel room by comparison. He thought of asking Mark how much the place cost. Instead, he looked up in awe, mesmerized by the thirty-foot ceiling.

Mark came up from behind, put his arms around, and nuzzled. There was no reason to feel presumptuous. Any man who agreed to go to another's home at this time of night could only want one thing. "You are so handsome. Would you like to go up to see my bedroom?"

"That feels nice," Raphe said as he closed his eyes and gently hummed.

By the time they reached the top of the stairs, they had groped and pulled each other's clothes off. Raphe loved seeing the shirts and pants fly over the bedroom's balcony railing down to the hardwoods below. They tumbled onto the black lacquered king. Soon Raphe's face was buried into the matching black comforter, held down by a hand pressed brutally between his shoulder blades.

Even sooner it was over. Mark had entered. No condom. Not even lubricant. A sharp pain, like a knife. Did Mark come inside him? Before Raphe could utter a word of protest, Mark fled to the shower. Raphe stayed prone on the bed, numb and only beginning to comprehend what had happened. After a few minutes Mark emerged from the bathroom. He had one large, plush black towel wrapped around his waist, while using another to dry his hair.

"You're still here?"

"Well, uh, what just happened?"

"Look, I'm tired. I really have to get some sleep now. I have an appointment later today to look at some property. I need to crash."

"Well, come over here into bed. You don't have to do anything. Let's just doze off together."

"No, I don't want to do that. I hate sleeping with anyone. Besides, I don't really know you all that well, and I feel funny about having you stay overnight. You should just leave."

Stunned, Raphe didn't know what to say. He quietly retraced his steps and gathered up his clothes and put himself back together. Mark stood on the ledge of the bedroom looking down as Raphe stepped into the elevator, never saying good-bye or another word, just watching intensely as if to make sure nothing got taken.

As he hit the street, Raphe felt a wetness drip down the inside of his leg. Sheer terror raced through his mind. Mark had climaxed inside him. He turned to return to the elevator and head back up to the loft to confront the man who assaulted him in such a dangerous way. The door had locked behind him. He couldn't find any intercom system to ring for Mark to let him back inside.

He looked around the desolate streets. An hour earlier he knew this block would have been teeming with people leaving the clubs. Now there was not a cab to be seen, and the subway system didn't have overnight service. It was at least a dozen blocks back to his condo, and he had no jacket. He'd have to make his way back on foot, in the bitter cold of a San Francisco summer night, across the vast, gritty blocks of SoMa. With each step the wind bit his ears. Even that couldn't distract him from the horror of the enigmatic moisture he felt below. Was it the elixir of death? Two words kept pounding in his head. He purposely kept repeating them in his mind so he would never forget them:

Mark Hazodo.
Mark Hazodo.
Mark Hazodo.
I hate that guy.

12

"We're going to a bar called My Place," Lauren said, her spiked black heels making determined taps on the filthy sidewalk. "I think it's just a little further."

"Lolly, we left 11th Street blocks ago. I don't like this area." Jessica tugged to close her pink cashmere sweater as they walked past a leatherman who leaned against the wall of an Indian restaurant. She whispered, "It's too gay."

"It's not *all* gay. The 1015 is just down the street. And up there on the left is where we went to that bondage club."

"Yeah, and after that night I can't believe we're back to another SoMa dive."

The determination in Lauren's face evaporated, replaced by annoyance. "Look, Jes. At least I am *trying* to hook us up with cool guys."

"I'm trying, too!"

"With what? Those virtual reality boys? Uh, no thanks. I'd like some *real* men if you don't mind."

"Fine. Then let's go to the Bubble Lounge. Or North Beach. No! We have to crash a gay bar!"

Lauren stopped walking and turned to confront her friend. Ever since they were kids, she'd put up with Jessica's tagging along. Most of the time it was fine to have a follower, safety in numbers and all that. Why was she such a drag lately? This was not the moment to abandon the quest. If anything, these were urgent times.

"I am only going to explain this once more. The bar is *usually* gay, but tonight is a special event. It's The Cocktail Club, one of the coolest inner circles in The City."

"Do you know *any* of these people?"

"No. But that's the point, isn't it?"

Lauren had read all about it in a local magazine. The Cocktail Club wasn't a place. It was a concept. "A burst of electrons through cyberspace turned into flesh and blood reality," the article called it. People joined the club through a web site, agreeing to show up once a month at some unsuspecting bar en masse. The bar could be a famous city landmark, or a disgusting dump. It didn't matter. When the Evite went out to the clique—hitting computers, PDAs and text-message cellphones—hundreds of people followed the order to invade the chosen destination. *A flash mob.* Regular patrons would sit in awe of the club's instant surge of humanity, or scurry away.

A mysterious man named Thorpe created the club. He only went by his last name, having dropped his first several years ago. Thorpe said his goal was to form a community that would draw people from all walks where their only common bond was technology—those anonymous electronic marching orders. He envisioned a convergence of humanity, a new definition of instant society. Lauren loved the idea that with the stroke of a key, hundreds would follow a command. She only wished that she was the one giving those orders.

"Jes, I had the shit scared out of me the other day," said Lauren, restarting her trot.

"What?"

"I went to Safeway and noticed the expiration date on the milk in the cooler. The August milk has arrived!"

"So?"

"I don't know. For some reason, it hit me like a fucking rock. It seemed like just yesterday I was buying June milk. Now August milk is already here! I don't even remember July milk. It was a total wake-up call. Our lives are slipping away. Just like the June milk. We've gotta move or expire on the shelf."

Jessica looked concerned. "Lolly, it's just frickin' milk!"

A few more steps down Folsom was the dirty, dark awning of the My Place bar. A blue and white PT Cruiser cab pulled up, and two giggling young women jumped out and went for the door. They pushed open the metal-studded black leather sheath that hung down over the entrance to prevent streetlight and any stray eyes from wandering inside. The cowhide curtain was so thick and heavy it took both of the thin, small girls to shove the flap open. Even ten feet away, Lauren and Jessica heard the cheers and squeals of the crowd inside. The noise comforted them. They were at the right place.

Jessica picked a stray blonde hair off the shoulder of Lauren's black four-button, three-quarter length Kenneth Cole jacket. Lauren sniffed her friend's neck to see if the Glow by J.Lo was still potent. It was. They nodded to each other and headed for the leather curtain, a bit nervous about the adventure on the other side.

Thorpe sat anonymously at the bar and watched the crowd arrive. When he spotted Lauren and Jessica, he sighed in disgust. Two more fucking blondes. Probably from the burbs. Just the two latest examples of how his utopian vision had been corrupted. Instead of the e-society he imagined, The Cocktail Club had become a fad that attracted the wealthy, young privileged types he despised.

He thought back to the night three hundred of them

crashed the Tonga Room at the snooty Fairmont Hotel. He dreamed of bringing a burst of energy into the aging San Francisco legend, but the mob made sure the blue hairs and tourists knew they were not welcome to stay. A bratty clique had replaced the mix of humanity Thorpe envisioned.

Thorpe hated the mob that he'd created.

That's why he picked the My Place bar for their latest adventure. He knew the locals here wouldn't be so easily run off. They'd give the spoiled brats a good fight for the turf.

On any other day, when the doors opened at noon, My Place was a bar where men went to have sex. They'd play in the long, narrow urinal trough room, where the stench of piss was so strong it made eyes water. When it got too crowded there, they would grope each other at the bar, surrounded by eager observers. If a man went to the dimly lit area in the back past the pool table, he knew what he was getting into—most likely someone's mouth.

Thorpe looked around the room and grinned. The brats will finally be chased off tonight. The Cocktail Club will once again be his.

"I'll have a Cosmo," Lauren yelled over to the bartender. When she leaned on the counter, she stuck her hand in something moist and sticky that felt thicker than just water.

"We don't usually serve those here," the man said. He had curly, dark hair and wore unbuttoned bluejeans with the fly down half an inch. He worked shirtless, revealing a tattoo near his nipple in the shape of a supermarket bar code. "We don't get much call for them."

"Oh, *please*," Jessica flirted. Her eyes followed the slight trickle of dark hair from the bartender's belly to his parted fly. "It's the only thing we drink."

The man sighed and turned to make the cocktails, leaving Lauren to scope out the room for the first time. The walls were black and scuffed, and everything from the pool table to the three pinball machines appeared worn. The ceiling was draped in hundreds of strands of white icicle holiday lights. The thousands of tiny bulbs reminded Lauren of Christmas. Her father always took Lauren and her brother to Aspen during the holidays, his attempt to make amends after the divorce. It would take more than ice and snow to do that, Lauren always grumbled. Still, ever since those days, winter scenes stirred pleasant feelings. Even the faux luminescence of the bar's tacky icicle lights brought comfort and somehow transformed a dank watering hole into a place with mystical appeal.

"You girls look like five-and-dimers." A rough-looking woman laughed and pushed her way between the two women. She took a swig from a bottle of Miller.

"What's a 'five-and-dimer'?" Jessica asked.

"You know. Five and dime. Five. One. O. Like your area code?"

"Haven't heard that one before," Lauren said. "Yeah, we're from the East Bay. Concord. That's 9-2-5."

"Well, well, well. You must be here for The Cocktail Club. I'm Sue," the woman said, gesturing her arm in a sweep like a master of ceremonies. "Your local tour guide."

Sue introduced herself as a My Place regular. As she explained, it didn't matter that she had a vagina and almost none of the usual patrons had been in one since birth. She lived around the corner in the same flat above a grocery store that she'd been renting since the early eighties, long before SoMa was "kewl with a K and filled with fuckin' dot-communism." She was well into her forties with badly bleached hair over skin yellowed from decades of smoking Kents. Lauren sipped her Cosmo and stared, wondering if this is what she would look like if she expired before getting off the milk shelf.

"It was a real fucked thing you kids did, invading this place tonight without warning. There must be two hundred people in here—and they're still coming!"

"We're not involved with the organizing," said Jessica meekly. "This is our first time at one of these."

"Who's in charge?" Sue demanded.

"Some guy named Thorpe," Lauren explained. "He sets it all up through e-mail and text messages. I have no idea what he even looks like. I don't know if anyone does."

Thorpe sat two stools over. He wasn't listening to the conversation, but once his name was mentioned, it was as if his mind was able to rewind the moment and hone in on the whole reference. Of course no one knew who he was! How disappointed these hipsters would be if they learned the man behind their latest fad was really just a poor, balding, freelance graphic artist who lived in the Mission. Having hit his late thirties, his looks were beginning to fade. As each year went by, he seemed to become less mainstream and more fringe.

He sized up Lauren and Jessica. Rich girls. They weren't *his* people. While he struggled to pay his rent, he bet most of their angst came from waiting for the next checks to arrive from mommy and daddy.

"Let me show you girls around," Sue barked as she took the women deeper into the room. Lauren noticed how the further back they went the icicle lights became less frequent until they disappeared completely, leaving the farthest corner of the room mostly lit from the glow of the front. The magical feeling created by the thousands of lights was replaced by sporadic sections of wall made mostly of steel rods. It reminded Lauren of a jail cell.

"Normally back here the guys would be going at it, if you know what I mean," Sue said as she pointed to an especially dark corner. Lauren squinted and could make out movements and what appeared to be a tight huddle of men, but it was too dim to see details. "But with all you kids around taking up space, they can't do much tonight."

Sue pushed her way through until they got to another leather flap. Jessica looked scared and grabbed Lauren's shoulder. "Don't worry, hon'. They don't bite. At least not women." Sue explained they would only be able to peek inside, since the room was too crowded for another soul to fit. "But it's worth it. You'll never see anything like this again."

She pulled back the curtain. The urinal trough room. A dozen men gratified each other, with one older man stretched out in the ceramic tub as others washed him down with their streams. One spout went directly into the senior's eager, open mouth.

Jessica cringed.

"Goddamn it!" Lauren screamed. She grabbed Jessica and headed back toward the relative safety of the front of the room. "Fucking old bitch! She did that on purpose!"

Sue laughed so hard she had to bend over to catch her breath.

For about an hour Lauren and Jessica tried their hand at small talk with guys in the clique, being sure to avoid going anywhere near the dark back of the bar again. One hour, three Cosmos, and countless rejections later, Lauren was pissed, in more ways than one.

"How about that guy over there?" Jessica gestured her head toward Thorpe, who sat at the other end of the bar. "He's weird looking, but he's been smiling at us the whole night."

"Really?" Lauren looked over to Thorpe. Bald. A bit older than she liked. But he had that alternative edge. What the hell, why not? For a moment they made eye contact. Thorpe grinned. Lauren smiled back. Still, before she did anything, she needed to tend to some private business.

"Do you have a bathroom here that *doesn't* have an old guy drinking piss in it?" Lauren demanded an answer from the bartender.

"Over there next to the pinball machine. One room. One toilet."

Lauren wasn't the only one who had a full bladder and privacy concerns. When she got to the front of the line, she ordered Jessica to guard the door.

Once inside Lauren grabbed her nose to mute the stench. It had to be the filthiest bathroom she'd ever seen, and that included the puke-tainted stalls at the country club on prom night. The plywood floor was drenched in liquid, and the once-white bowl was beige inside and out. The walls peeled their paint like dandruff, and the ceiling tiles reeked from brown stains that could have only come from an overflowed toilet somewhere on an upper floor. Where there should have been at least a door handle, and maybe a lock, there was a hole that had long since abandoned its mechanisms. Lauren wondered why this was the only spot in the entire place that was well lit enough to see every detail. She spotted what appeared to be a fresh roll of paper and with drunken bravery decided to attempt the squatting-but-not-touching trick she learned from her mom so long ago. It was going to take the flexibility of a contortionist to figure out.

"I bet you girls don't even know how to give decent head, do ya?"

It was Sue. Just the sound of her voice brought back the image in Jessica's mind of the man lying in the tub of pee. Sue was now barely coherent and stank of cheap beer.

"Please leave us alone," Jessica pleaded.

"I'm just trying to tell you young ones something I learned a long time ago," Sue mumbled.

Jessica gave Sue a mean stare. It had no effect.

"In the eighties us girls had to deal with something called cocaine cock. You see, back then we all did a lot of coke. And for guys that meant they had trouble, you know." Sue raised her hand to make her outreached forefinger drop and droop. "So us girls had to learn to give really great blow jobs. I mean, if you wanted to get laid, you had to get the little guy back up at attention. I used to do this trick. I'd beat on the head of his cock with the tip of my tongue, jabbing like a boxer, punishing and punching . . ."

Sue stuck out her tongue and thrust it back and forth into Jessica's face.

"You are disgusting!" Jessica's eyes started to tear.

With Sue's distraction, Jessica never noticed the man who slipped behind her and cut the line, pushing everyone out of his way in a rage of need. It was the old man from the trough. After all he had consumed, now it was his turn to relieve himself. His kidneys were apparently too shy to perform in front of others.

It happened too quickly for Lauren to dive out of the way from her elaborate squat. To avoid wetting herself by splattering the seat, she had stared down with iron concentration to make sure everything got into the bowl. She never saw the man burst into the room. By the time she started screaming, she was already soaked in a powerful torrent from the man. He'd never opened his eyes, not seeing Lauren there until he heard her shriek. Then it was too late to clamp the surge midstream.

"You were supposed to be guarding the door!" Lauren yelled at Jessica as she bolted from the bathroom, her face, hair, and black jacket drenched. The members of The Cocktail Club all seemed to turn at once, observe the scene for a few moments, then murmur and giggle to themselves before getting back to their conversations.

"Lolly, what happened?" Jessica looked at her friend in horror. Lauren's eye makeup dripped down her cheek. She smelled like the zoo. "Did a pipe burst? You're all wet . . ."

"A pipe burst! You're fucking kidding! Let's get out of this goddamn dump!"

"What about that guy?" Jessica looked over to Thorpe.

"Jessica, for fuck's sake, I'm covered in *piss!*"

Lauren violently yanked Jessica through the crowd and toward the door, shoving members of the clique aside as if they were weeds. As they passed by Thorpe, he looked down from his barstool throne and laughed.

Two down. So many more to go.

13

Harrington acted more suspicious than usual, his eyes constantly darting around 225 Folsom. Each time a customer entered, his stomach made a loud growling noise.

"You see anything not proper?" he asked Raphe.

"Not proper? What do you mean, not proper?"

For several weeks Harrington had carried around a copy of *A Tale of Two Cities*, and Raphe noticed a sheet of paper sticking out—a homework assignment from City College's ESL, English as a Second Language class. All of a sudden it began to make sense why Harrington strangely peppered his speech with words like "proper," "chap," and "cheerio." *Those poor people*, Raphe thought. They come all the way to America, and then go to school to learn English so they can fit in, and some pretentious bureaucrat of a teacher throws the classics at them as a way to learn contemporary conversation. He imagined a whole misguided league of people from third world countries running around The City saying "Hello governah!"

"You know. People coming in, axing questions."

"Just the usual," Raphe deadpanned. He'd grown to like Harrington, and thought of offering to help improve the man's English. But even after nine months together, Harrington had yet to drop any of the pretense that he was Irish and admit to his true identity and obvious Mexican ethnicity. As the owner of a chain of mailbox drops for con artists, Harrington wasn't in the trust business, but lately he was on edge more than usual, always interrogating Raphe with questions about activities in and around the store. Much to Raphe's boredom, there was nothing new to report. Nothing had changed.

The side door to the building creaked open, and the red-haired woman from upstairs walked out. This time she turned and looked into the shop. Spotting Harrington, she flashed a bright smile and gave a friendly wave. He gestured back, just as enthusiastically.

"You know each other?" Raphe marveled.

"Si. Miss Julie. She live upstairs."

"Yeah, I know. I see her every morning. She's a beautiful woman."

"You lick her?" Harrington asked. Raphe knew the man actually meant *like*, but gay or not, a lick wouldn't be too bad. "We both on tenant board of building together. I ax her in sometime so you meet."

Raphe mused over the thought of finally exchanging words with the woman from upstairs. Now he knew her name. *Julie.* He thought of the character of Julia in Orwell's *1984*. It was never one of his favorite novels, but that could change. He would be Smith, and together they would take on the world. . . .

Why not? Maybe it was time to go back to women. The men thing had taken far too many tough turns. He thought back to that night with Mark—*Mark Hazodo, I hate that guy*—and the drama of when he told Baptiste what happened.

"You let him cum in your ass!" Baptiste was livid. It was the first time Raphe had seen the always charming man angry.

"I didn't *let* him. It just happened. He forced me."

"He *forced* you to go back to his apartment?"

"Well, no."

"He *forced* you to take off your clothes?"

"No."

"He *forced* you to get into his bed?"

"No."

"OK. I'm struggling to see now where the so-called *force* comes into play."

"Hey, don't be a lawyer with me!" Raphe snapped. He'd never been cross with Baptiste before. Since they'd met, much of Raphe's old bitterness had evaporated. He didn't like being back in that splenetic zone. He nervously pulled on his soul patch. "What am I going to do?"

"You have to get tested. Right away."

"I'm sorry about all this," Raphe said, walking to Baptiste. He needed to feel the embrace of those muscular arms.

Baptiste stepped back. "Don't touch me. You could be infected."

"But . . ."

"Look," Baptiste paused, "I thought you knew the rules."

"You don't have to lecture me. I've been using condoms my whole life. I know about safe sex. It was just a stupid mistake."

"With guys, it can be a *deadly* mistake."

"Yeah? Well, why do they do it? I don't get it."

"Shit. I keep forgetting. You're new," Baptiste sighed. "It's called barebacking. Or breeding. Some say seeding. Fucking without a condom. It's very common these days."

"Why? AIDS is still out there. People are still dying. Why would anyone take that risk?"

"Some guys who bareback already have it," Baptiste explained. "They figure anyone who agrees to bareback must have it too, otherwise they wouldn't. Then there are the new drugs. Some people mistakenly believe they are a cure, and it doesn't really matter if they catch it. Others do it, but only as tops, since they think they can't catch it that way. Low risk, but it's like playing roulette."

A feeling of dread swept over Raphe. Not just because of

the fear he'd been exposed. He saw an expression in Baptiste's face that hit hard. Disappointment.

"Who knows?" Baptiste continued. "Maybe after twenty years of having sex with each other wearing the equivalent of a plastic trash bag over our dicks, some of us crave real intimacy—the type of feeling that only comes with flesh to flesh contact. I know I want that someday. I was hoping to have that . . . with you."

Intimacy. Raphe knew that's what Baptiste wanted emotionally. Physically, too? As in monogamy? It seemed so contrary to the lifestyle he'd pushed Raphe toward, the decadence and sexual experimentation.

Is this what it meant to be gay? On one level you were supposed to embrace an open sexuality, eager to experience pleasure from many others. At the same time, the goal was to be with just one. The two ideas seemed in complete conflict, yet he was unable to simply dismiss them as nonsense. There was an appeal to the idea, even if it didn't make sense. Perhaps he wasn't sophisticated or smart enough to be gay.

It was all too much to figure out right now. At least it seemed Baptiste still wanted him. Raphe liked the feeling of being wanted. He grasped onto that thought to help distract him during the drive to the clinic.

When they got there, the nurse drew blood and gave Raphe an ID number so his identity would be anonymous. She told them to come back in a week. For seven days Baptiste kept his distance. They didn't have sex. They barely spoke. Raphe found himself constantly staring at the number he'd been given by the clinic. This is what he'd been reduced to? Number 18. Just two digits that could add up to life . . . or death.

There was no excitement when the day finally came to return for the results. The two men sat silently in the waiting room. Raphe wondered how much time he'd have left and whether to tell his parents or just wander away and die.

"Number 18!" A nurse walked out from the exam rooms. Raphe meekly raised his hand. "Negative. You can go."

"Number 9!" An elderly man looked toward the nurse. "I need to see *you* inside." The nurse turned and went back through the door, holding it open for the shell-shocked man. He was shaking, as if he could collapse at any moment.

"That was cruel," Raphe said.

"That could have been you," Baptiste dismissed.

How could he survive in the gay world, Raphe wondered, when the rules were so confusing and the stakes so high? After the day of the results, Raphe looked for excuses to avoid sleeping over at Baptiste's. He needed a break from the gay world. He felt like he'd dodged a deadly bullet and could use some time apart to reflect.

Besides, who said his life with women had to be over forever? Relationships with women were glacial compared to the frenetic sexual pace of men. In his decade of dating women, multiple partners happened over the course of years. With men, he'd had as many encounters in a weekend. Or a busy Saturday morning. Pursuing a woman took patience, time, and finesse, all of which felt like the pace he needed now. The rape, the AIDS test, the scolding from Baptiste—it had been the most horrific week of his life.

He never faced such anxiety with the women he dated since moving to The City. The last was Lisa, with her crooked, quirky smile that Raphe cherished from the first time they'd met at the Starbucks near South Park. She worked behind the counter running the noisy espresso machine. It took Raphe weeks to muster the courage to engage her in anything more than small talk. In a quiet moment between the shrill of the milk steaming, he formally introduced himself. With contact finally made, he invited her to stop by his nearby dot-com office for one of the company's weekly Friday beer bashes. He'd rehearsed the conversation the night before to be sure his tone would be appropriately nonchalant, giving Lisa the option to hear the request as one of either friendship or affection. No pressure, Raphe figured. If she doesn't see me as date material, we can still be buddies.

He was thrilled when she arrived at the office that Friday. She'd changed out of her coffee uniform into jeans and a white silk blouse—a good sign that she intended to be more than just a comrade looking to blow off steam at the end of another workweek. Their mutual dance of coy advances would go on for nearly a month before they wound up in bed. Raphe missed Lisa and the touch of her soft flesh against his when they would wake up together on lazy Saturday mornings. They'd walk along the Embarcadero down to the farmer's market, holding hands while taking in the breathtaking view of the bay. They might still be together, if not for the economic collapse of The City. The days were gone when a liberal arts graduate could make cappuccinos one day, and become a dot-com project manager the next. Like so many lured to town who suddenly found it impossible to break into decent jobs, Lisa went back to get her Masters. Michigan was too far away and too cold for Raphe.

His life had changed so much since then. After all the manic sex, his brush with death, and the contretemps with Baptiste, Raphe longed for those slower times. The Lisa times. The pleasure was not as intense, but at this moment he found new appreciation for the leisure of it. Despite all that had happened, he realized *that* life—the straight life—was not out of his grasp forever. Maybe love is more complex. It wasn't just about choosing one or the other. Perhaps you can have both. Want both. Love both.

He was about to finally meet the red-haired woman from upstairs.

Julie.

Mark Hazodo.

He thought of the two extremes.

"It was the best of times, it was the worst of times," he heard himself mumble aloud.

"I know dat!" Harrington said excitedly. "Deekins! Charles Deekins! I know dat one!"

"Of course you do," Raphe smirked. "Any good Irishman like yourself would."

14

As far as Lauren was concerned, it was not the best address in The City. Main and Bryant. The South of Market boondocks.

Once a desolate land known for its homeless encampments, these days the settlements were of a different kind. The eastern-most part of SoMa flourished under the more upscale name South Beach. On one edge was the Giants stadium, praised as the most beautiful ballpark in the world. Close to the water-front, new modern high-rise housing continuously sprouted.

At the water's edge The City installed public art, a giant cupid's bow and arrow four stories tall. The first time she saw it, Lauren snickered to herself. How appropriate for today. Now on her third pass, she was not at all amused. She was lost in the maze of one-way and "wrong way" streets, unable to find her destination. For a moment, she wished Jessica was with her. That girl was always so smart and practical, she would have gone to mapquest.com ahead of time to plot a course. Today, however, Jessica was not invited.

Finally, there it was. The Bryant. With its severe steel-and-glass exterior, it was the kind of building Lauren admired. She paused on the sidewalk for a moment to take note of the awesome size and strength of the structure. It took up an entire city block, home to at least a hundred different apartments, each with that touch of glamour that comes from being new.

Even from the outside she could tell the views would be breathtaking. The neighborhood still had a dirty, unkempt feeling, but most of San Francisco did these days. Regardless, she could definitely live here—it was so much better than Concord. The suburbs were for losers.

She unfolded the printout with the instructions "3pm. Apartment 919. Enter code #1228 on the keypad to the right of the main entrance."

"Who is it?" Despite the electronic distortion of the speaker, the voice sounded deep and masculine. *Thank God,* Lauren thought. *This one's not gay.*

"Uh? It's Lolly? I'm here about the room for rent?" She scolded herself for ending each of her sentences in question marks, something she tended to do when rattled. She vowed on the drive over not to be jumpy. It was her first time trying the craigslist room4rent scheme, but she'd read all about it on the internet. She knew what to do. There was nothing to be so jittery about.

After what seemed like an endless pause, the voice from the speaker squawked again. "Sure. Come on up. I've been expecting you."

When she got to the door, it swung open before she even knocked. The motion caught her off guard, but it took only a moment to feel at ease. Perfect, she thought, after her first glimpse. All the trappings of a regular guy. Her nose caught a faint musk smell, possibly the manly aura of a recently finished workout.

The view was spectacular, just as she imagined. The exterior wall was all glass. The Bay Bridge seemed close enough to touch. The sky was clear and sunny, so lovely even dumpy Oakland sparkled like a gem on the other side of the water. Miles beyond that was home—Concord—but it was too far away to see with anything other than her imagination.

She sized up the space. The living room had a gleaming pine floor, peppered with modern but tasteful furnishings. Pottery Barn? No, IKEA was more likely—and that rug needs to go. The opposite end held a first-class kitchen, filled with stainless steel appliances.

"I'm Raphe. The guy you spoke to on the phone."

"Lolly," she said as she stretched out her hand to shake. She'd decided ahead of time to use her nickname, rather than her real one, in case things went badly. Raphe's grasp was firm, his palm slightly callused. She imagined it was from working out on the machines at the gym. He had that type of athletic body, topped by a messy crop of chestnut hair and one of those cute little flavor savers just under his lip. She liked those on a guy, they looked so *bad boy* and always felt so awesome.

"Well, uh, this is the place," Raphe stammered, not completely sure how to proceed. He hadn't expected her to be so beautiful. He thought the women who answered his ad would be older and somehow hardened by The City.

"It's incredible," Lauren gushed. "I've always wondered what one of these looked like from the inside. I think I understand why people love it down here."

"You've never been in one before?"

"No. I'm over in the Marina," she lied. Why give any extra clues to her real identity if it didn't work out? Besides, she'd learned the hard way that just mentioning Concord was an automatic buzz kill with city guys. "A typical old flat. Three of us share the place. The landlord doesn't put any money into the building because of rent control. So nothing really works, you know, perfectly. I can see that wouldn't be a problem here."

"Yeah, not these places." Raphe became more comfortable, his nerves now abated by the ability to talk about a subject he knew. "They have everything. State-of-the-art heating, air, appliances—we even have fiber and satellite TV wired into the outlets in every single room."

"I knew it would be spectacular, just from the way you described it in your ad on craigslist."

"Yeah . . . craigslist. I love that site. It's really the best way to do this."

Raphe posted the ad the evening he got the call from Troy at the bank. The "no doc" loan turned out to be a "no go." His application based on the equity in his condo was rejected. Raphe was incensed. The process had dragged on for months with endless trips to the bank to turn in a growing mound of paperwork. All that, and he was turned down—even though an appraiser reasoned the condo was worth $150,000 more than Raphe paid for it.

"Why?" Raphe had asked Troy over the phone, bitterly wondering in the back of his mind if the drag queen had somehow screwed up. The guy couldn't even keep Raphe's name straight. Perhaps if he spent less time wearing tiaras and put more effort into . . .

"It's *you*, actually," Troy explained. "You've gone through some changes in the past few months that really threw up a red flag."

Changes? Did the bank somehow track that he'd gone gay. *I'm not completely queer!* Raphe wanted to shout. Maybe somehow they found out about the HIV test. Was that enough to scare them off? Well, it was *negative*. They aren't supposed to know any of that, are they? They told me it was confidential . . . and anonymous. I even got a number, instead of using my name. His head was spinning.

"Yeah. You should have told me about the big American Express balance. And in just the last month you took out that loan to buy an Audi A6. Your credit report has you maxed out."

"What? I don't even have an American Express card," Raphe gasped. "Or an Audi A6, for that matter. What in the world are you talking about?"

"I have the documents right here in front of me. The bank

also didn't like to see you keeping two mailing addresses. That's a big no-no. If you ask me, I can't understand why you would live in a high-rise condo in South Beach, and also keep a place in the Haight. Isn't that a bit excessive?"

"I don't have a place in the Haight." Raphe asked for the address. His heart sank. It was the street address of one of Harrington's other mailbox scam centers. From everything Troy had told him, it appeared his financial identity had been hijacked and a huge tab run up. Making matters worse, his own under-the-table employer was connected. Probably just a weird coincidence, Raphe concluded. Harrington didn't actually know the details of the scams run out of his shops. It was set up that way to create a defense of plausible deniability.

"What can I do?" Raphe asked Troy.

"I am so sorry. I hate to say it, but we see so much of this these days. Of course, we take it very seriously, and we will launch an immediate investigation. I'll do everything I can to help. But I'm not going to lie to you, Mr. Raphe . . ."

"Uh, it's just Raphe. Raphe is my first name."

"Oh, yes, that's right. Sorry 'bout that. Raphe. Got it." It sounded like Troy scribbled something down, then continued. "Anyway, I need to warn you up front that these things take a long time to sort out. Up to six months. And in the meantime, there's no way anyone is going to process your loan."

The ad for a roommate went onto craigslist.org that night. Raphe figured he could get as much as a thousand for the room, though he'd settle for five hundred. Anything to make him feel a step back from teetering on the financial edge. A handful of people responded to the posting, but Raphe decided only to invite women over to interview. Maybe having a woman sleeping across the hallway would bring a feeling of balance back into his life.

Lauren's eyes crawled over to a wall of bookshelves. She recognized some of the titles as novels she went out of her way to avoid reading while in college. *Atlas Shrugged*. *Finnegan's Wake*. *Mrs. Dalloway*. Too hard. This guy sure reads a lot, she thought, hoping he wouldn't be too much of an egghead. Eggheads tended to overthink, making them remarkably inept when it mattered.

"Bedrooms over there?"

"Yeah, there's two of 'em. Each with its own bathroom. One used to be my office, but I've cleaned it out."

"Can I see it?"

"Uh, yeah. Of course," Raphe fumbled his words again, tugging on his chin tuft. Lolly was just so unexpectedly attractive. Her blonde hair reminded him of Lisa, but with a much more voluptuous body. It was almost too curvy, and for a moment he wondered if it was all real.

The bedroom for rent was empty except for the tan Berber carpet. Raphe had taken his office contents and stuffed them into his room, cramming his computer and workstation up next to his bed. The hum of the machine actually helped lull him to sleep each night. Lauren walked around the vacated space, peeking into the closets. She paused again to take in the remarkable view.

Raphe gave her a tour of the rest of the apartment, including his own room. Along the way, they talked about their lives. Raphe spoke of his work in dot-com, omitting the fact that the company had gone out of business. If things got that far, he'd tell this girl Lolly his entire life story. Right now he didn't want to say anything that might spike the deal.

Lauren made up a fib about being a recruiter for one of the big firms downtown. She felt it important to create the image of herself as powerful and take-charge, attributes that would be useful later.

"This is an awesome computer," Lauren marveled. "That's one of the biggest screens I've ever seen—like a wide-screen TV. It must have cost a fortune."

A fortune easily afforded in better times, Raphe thought.

"Yes, it's a nice one. One of the largest made by Apple. You can even watch wide-screen DVDs on it."

"And what's this? You afraid someone's gonna break in here at night?" Lauren picked up by the handle what looked like a long tribal knife, something possibly from the remotest regions of Africa.

It was a letter opener, a piece of promotional schwag used as part of a lame campaign Raphe's old company contrived to launch an e-mail service called Uganda. "Uganda get it," was the web site's moronic motto. It was yet another sign of how tech was destined to collapse under the weight of its own silliness—sending letter openers to call attention to a technology that's supposed to make paper mail obsolete. These days Raphe used the knife to flick pebbles out from the grips of his sneakers.

"Oh, that's just a toy," he said, carefully removing it from Lolly's fingers to place it back onto the desk. It was a foolish artifact, but it was still remarkably sharp. They must have spent a fortune on them, the negative thought suddenly burned in Raphe's mind, money that could have gone to keeping him on the payroll longer.

Lauren sat down on the edge of Raphe's bed. "Come. Sit down." She patted the mattress. "I'd love to ask you a few questions."

"Shoot," Raphe said as he sat beside her. His anxiousness started to soften into an eagerness to be close. It felt nice to be on a bed with a girl again.

"Well, you'll have to tell me if I am getting too nosy. So I'm just going to ask. If you think I'm being too personal, then you should just tell me."

"No problem. Go ahead." For a second, Raphe panicked. Could she tell he'd been with a man? Was he walking differently? He'd heard that could happen. Would she ask if he was gay?

"Well, this is an awesome place. Anyone would love to live

here. I guess I just don't understand why you're looking for a roommate."

"What do you mean?"

"Well, clearly you have the money to afford this place all on your own. I mean, dot-com! That's very impressive. Why rent out a room? Wouldn't you prefer to have the apartment all to yourself?"

"Oh, that," Raphe said, his worry evaporating. He chided himself for thinking she was going to ask the gay question. Of course she wouldn't. He hadn't become a big queen like Troy. He didn't fit into that world. No, he was still fully a man. And Lolly, she was a woman. A beautiful one. Was it his imagination, or did she seem attracted to him? Raphe thought he felt that vibe. It had been so long since a woman flirted with him— maybe he was misreading the signals. If anything was going to happen, she'd have to make the first move. He wouldn't mind if she did. Maybe he needed to show he was open to it.

Raphe reclined onto the bed, crossing his arms behind his head like a child in a field looking up to study the clouds. "I guess you could say I'm the type of guy who likes to be around people."

Lauren took Raphe's cue and joined him stretched back onto the bed.

"You get lonely?"

"Yeah. The whole idea of living alone doesn't do it for me."

"And living with a girl? What do you think about having a girl as a roommate?"

"Well, I like girls. I like girls . . ." He looked over to her with a slightly overcompensating smile and tone, ". . . a lot."

Lauren turned on her elbow, taking in Raphe's handsome face. She stared into his dark, brown eyes and smiled back. "That's good. Because I like boys."

She leaned over and kissed him. It wasn't a tentative little peck on the cheek. She went straight for his mouth, her lips lifting his apart so her tongue could explore. Raphe was surprised by the aggressive move, but he lunged back with the same intense passion.

In just moments they removed each other's clothes. She took him into her mouth, bringing him to the edge of release. He did the same for her, until her moaning and moisture told him she was ready. Under the veil of anonymity, they committed playful little acts of brutality with each other. He rode her hard, throwing out small verbal assaults. She made him submit as she used her wet finger to force him to feel the intrusion and pleasure of invasion. Unlike other guys, Lauren noticed Raphe didn't flinch.

After two hours they collapsed onto each other, sticking and sliding from their own sweat and fluids.

They showered and dressed, barely speaking a word to one another until Raphe escorted Lauren back to the entrance.

"Are you missing a tooth?" she asked.

"What?"

"A tooth. When I was kissing you, I . . ."

"No, not at all." Raphe grinned and pulled down his lower lip with his finger.

On the left side of his mouth was something Lauren had never seen before. A perfect baby tooth, still intact.

"It's called a retained deciduous. There was never a grown-up tooth to push it out, so it decided to stick around." Funny, Raphe thought. Baptiste never noticed or mentioned it. That's one thing he definitely missed about women. They noticed the little things, and cherished them. With men, it was all about getting it done. Hunters versus gatherers. It was so wonderful to be with a woman again. He hadn't gone completely gay, after all.

"I'll let you know about the room," Lauren said as she left, knowing she would never actually rent it. She felt a moment of regret about that, glancing before the door shut to grab one more glimpse of that incredible view. It was a great apartment. What a shame she really never had any plans to move. But she had to admit, using the craigslist room rental ads to hook up worked just as well as she was told it would. Amazing what people do to get laid these days.

Screw that guy Putt, Lauren thought as she headed down the hall to the elevator. *Fuck those queer boys at the virtual reality party. And those faggots at the creepy Cocktail Club.* She hadn't lost her touch. She had finally bagged a real city guy. Clean. No mess.

Score. She was still in the game.

15

"It's a game, man. You know how I love games."

Bill Soileau was the fifth guy Mark Hazodo had approached with his pitch. All the others turned him down. He'd never had so much trouble closing a deal. For a moment, he wondered if he was losing his powers of persuasion.

"Sounds like the stakes are too high for this game," said Bill. Sometimes he didn't know if Mark was joking. Bill knew Mark loved risk, everything from snowboarding to scaling cliffs—the stories of his thrill seeking were infamous. Just last year Mark cashed in his company stock and quit his lucrative, cushy job to launch his own game company, something no one else had dared to do since the dot-com bubble burst. Where did the virtual end and the reality begin?

"Nice jacket. New?" Bill asked. The jacket looked like something the cartoon character Speed Racer would wear, with yellow sport stripes highlighting green satin. The perfect match to his black jeans and matching green Fluevog buckle shoes.

Mark frowned. "You're changing the subject, man."

"I just can't believe it's for real."

"It is *so* real, guy."

"Explain it again."

"OK, look. It's this Saturday night at my loft. I've got a

bunch of guys coming over. Hot guys. All the furniture is pushed up against the walls so we have the entire middle of the room."

"An orgy," Bill said flatly.

"Yeah. So?"

It wasn't the first time Bill had been invited to one since moving to The City. He was thirty with clean-cut looks and polite Louisiana manners. Men cruised him everywhere—walking down the street, filling his car at the gas station, even shopping at the supermarket. More than once guys jerked off in the showers at the gym while staring into his stall. In a weird way, it was always what he thought life in San Francisco would be after moving from Baton Rouge. Still, what Mark proposed went too far.

"But not just any orgy," Bill scolded. "This is like Russian roulette."

"Exactly! Eleven guys. All hot. All naked. All fucking each others' brains out. No condoms. No bug-killing lube. No protection," Mark explained.

"And . . ."

"And one of the guys is HIV positive, man. *Only no one knows exactly who.*"

"Except you, of course."

"Yeah, well, I'm the host."

"I can't believe people are doing this. Don't they know how dangerous it is? It could be a death sentence."

"And that's what makes it the ultimate rush."

"It's sick."

"Bill Soileau, when did you lose your edge?" Mark loved saying Bill's full name out loud. Soileau was Louisiana Acadian and pronounced "swallow." The perfect dig from one gay man to another.

"Don't try to play me, Mark. I'm not one of your idiot employees."

Mark knew Bill was smarter than most of his friends. He worked as a petrochemical engineer over at the big refinery in Martinez. They'd met at a party, and Mark was instantly impressed. In a sea of queens chatting about celebrities and boys, he'd stumbled onto a man comfortable discussing politics and international affairs. Bill could not only find Japan on a map, but he'd actually been to Kobe, and talked more intelligently about Mark's heritage than he could.

Mark also marveled over Bill's complexity. He considered his friend a type of puzzle box, comprised of endless compartments filled with secrets. In the South, Bill once explained, good gossip was more valuable than money, mysteries the most prized currency of the modern confederacy. "If a man has no intrigue, he has nothing at all."

It became a philosophy Mark learned to embrace. He apportioned his own life into compartments, revealing only the pieces needed for each situation. To his parents, he was the dutiful, responsible son pursuing a career in technology to provide a decent, stable living for him and his family. His mother and father had no idea how remarkably wealthy their son was at such a young age. Mark knew if he told them, they would frown and give him a lecture on modesty and some silly, ancient Japanese wisdom about candles burning too brightly. They never came up from Los Angeles to visit, so his contrived image to them was easily manageable by phone.

The fact that his parents were old in so many ways embarrassed Mark. They were of a different era, having spent their youngest years in the awful internment camps of the war. What little their families had achieved was taken away and never given back, making them emotionally scarred about the nature of possessions. They tried to pass that baggage onto Mark, along with their avowed Japanese cultural traditions. "They took everything, except our beliefs." As the only child, conceived late in life, Mark was to be the patriarch destined to revitalize the fam-

ily line. He would never tell them he was gay. Instead, he cultivated a straight facade in any of the compartments of his life his
parents might visit.

Mark admired how Bill Soileau also managed his compartments. If things were different, Bill would be a worthy partner.
As it was, he could only be a player in Mark's latest game.

"One of the dudes is into fisting, man."

Bill raised an eyebrow in disbelief. "For real?"

"And he says he'll take on all hands," Mark goaded.

"I guess that means you'll have to change the rules and
allow people to use lube."

"No way, man. What do you Southern boys always say? 'Spit
and shove or it ain't love.'"

"I don't think you can do fisting without lube. I saw a video
on it."

Mark had found Bill's weak spot. Bill was a player. He described his passions as vanilla, but in truth he loved to see the
extremes of others. Just like the Southern tradition, he desired
to know the secrets of strangers.

"Crisco, dude. *Crisco*. That reminds me, I better get something to cover the floor."

"I still don't know if I can do it."

"You can't back out, man. You can't!" Mark affected a whine,
acting as if Bill had previously committed and was about to be
dishonorable by reneging. Yet another trick to corner a South-
erner.

Silence. Mark counted the moments. One, two, three, four,
five . . . The silence meant Bill was seriously thinking about it.
He'd hooked him.

"Fisting, dude. I know you want to see it." Mark's voice
lifted in exaggerated temptation. "It won't be the same if you're
not there. I can't play this game without you."

"What time does it start?"

★ ★ ★

When the night came, Bill was the first to arrive just after nine.

"Where is everyone?" He could smell the remnants of cooking done earlier in the evening. It was some sort of Asian dish, although he couldn't make out exactly which one. Maybe it was the stink of that freeze-dried seaweed Mark liked to munch on like candy.

"Don't worry, they'll be here."

"Hmmm," Bill grinned. "Orgy etiquette, I guess. Never be the first one to come."

"Very funny, very funny. Now get over here and help me."

Mark designated the huge main floor for the orgy. They pushed all the pricey furniture from SoMa SoFa up against the walls.

Bill sat on the pine floor and rubbed his butt back and forth. "I don't know, Mark. This is so hard it hurts just to sit. You gonna give out knee pads?"

"Better than that, buddy." Mark ran up to the bedroom. Large black pillows began to rain down on Bill. "I got forty of 'em. Cheap. From over at Pier One. We can do anything on them, then just toss 'em in the trash!"

"Mark," Bill said. "I have to ask you something before all this starts. . . ."

"Sounds serious." Mark paused the pillow tossing.

"With this orgy. I'm really uncomfortable with the idea of you and me . . ." Bill looked down to the floor. He knew Mark was a smart guy who didn't need it spelled out, but what if? "It's just that . . . you know . . . when people are having sex, sometimes things can get out of control. They get lost in the moment."

"Don't worry about it, Bill Soileau," Mark cut him off, then threw another cushion over the rail. "You know I never have sex with anyone I know. And I am always in control."

★　★　★

There was still a line to get into the Cat's Alley Club on Folsom as Bill walked by. One in the morning. The bar would stop serving alcohol at 1:45 A.M., and bouncers would confiscate and dump any remaining drinks at two. It didn't matter. All the club kids would just drop *E* and dance until five. Tweakers.

Bill rubbed the outside of his front jeans' pocket. Yup, they were still there. It was almost time.

He was the first to leave Mark's orgy. Coming four times in just three hours was the best he'd done since he was a teenager jerking off in his parents' bathroom. Mark was right. The men were hot. And they all seemed remarkably grateful to meet a top.

Even as the others started to arrive, Bill wasn't convinced he could go through with it. Then as the men began to take off their clothes, he noticed how thin so many of them were, with pale faces drained of their natural color. Meth heads. He should have known that's who Mark would get to show up. Roulette sex was just their latest game, the next extreme. Not a death wish, but the added thrill of mortal risk. A man might receive his death sentence that night, or be coupling inches away from someone who did. They all went in knowing the dangers, craving them. Bill saw how the proximity to sexual homicide aroused Mark, inspiring him to passionately mount man after man. Always on top. And as promised, Mark kept his distance from Bill. Mark was, after all, the master puppeteer.

The fisting was a letdown. It looked the same as on video, but a television screen could never transmit the most distinctive part of the ritual. Hours later, he could still pick up traces of the smell in his nostrils if he concentrated.

Ahmed's Market was open. He headed to the back and bought a small bottle of water, some brand he didn't recognize. He twisted it open when he got back on the street and reached into his pocket to pull out a small handful of pills. Three different kinds, three different shapes and colors. He shoved them all in his mouth and swallowed with just one swig. His choke mechanism had disappeared years ago.

Some cocktail, he thought. Every eight hours. Will there ever be a cure?

16

The local branch of the Internal Department of Labor and Employment looked ominous even from three blocks away, imposing itself over its Townsend Street surroundings. Raphe's unemployment checks came from somewhere inside the stark twenty-floor tower of metal-and-black tinted glass. When he got a letter demanding he appear at a hearing at ten on Tuesday morning, he was struck with terror.

He arrived at nine-thirty, figuring his promptness would be noted with favor. It didn't matter. A dense crowd packed Room 101, all scheduled for the same hearing. The room was so full that new arrivals couldn't reach the closed up receptionist's window to tap and try to get attention or information. The scene reminded Raphe of a nature documentary where drone ants piled tightly into each other, all waiting for their chance to serve the queen.

There were far too many people for the nineteen seats he counted scattered throughout the bullpen-sized room. He had no option but to stand. He pulled out of his backpack a second-hand copy of *What Color is My Parachute?* He hastily picked it up the day before, hoping a caseworker might spot him reading it, and it would look as if he'd been trying hard to find employment. At exactly twenty past ten, he took note on his watch, the bolts on the shutters were undone, and the receptionist's window opened. The room fell silent in anticipation of some sort of announcement, but the capacious middle-aged woman at the desk just sat expressionless, allowing the phone next to her to ring unanswered. Finally, a balding man in an orange BIG-WORDS.com T-shirt approached the receptionist.

"Excuse me, ma'am."

"Ma'am?"

"Yes, uh, hello. I was just wondering," the man spoke nervously. "I mean *we* were all just wondering . . ."

"Ma'am?"

"Yes, uh . . ."

"I am not a ma'am," the clerk said indignantly. "My name is *Frank.* You can call me *sir,* if you'd prefer."

He's dead, Raphe thought, relieved he had not been the one to dare approach the glassed-in cage. The clerk explained, loud enough for everyone to hear, that people would have to take a number and only come up to the window when that number was called. A wave of panic swept over the room. *A number? Did you see any numbers? Where are the numbers?* People whispered timidly to each other, not wanting to risk the same wrath that had befallen the bald man.

Sensing something was wrong, the clerk stood up and leaned out from his perch to look at the table near the entrance. It was empty, except for a copy of the *Economist* from March 1999. The clerk rolled his eyes, sighed, and then reached into a drawer in his desk. He picked out a stack of small, reusable plastic cards, each with a pre-printed number. Taking note of the density of the mob, and apparently not wishing to traverse it, he took the rubber band off the stack and tossed the cards over the heads of the crowd. The numbers littered down like confetti. It took only moments for people to realize their fates for that day were showering down on their heads. In a scene worse than any bridal bouquet toss Raphe had ever witnessed, the frantic assemblage lunged at the flittering plastic tabs, hysterically rampaging into one another like a swarm of rabid animals. Raphe shoved his way into the fray, elbowing a heavyset man in the breast, and scarfed a ticket off the floor.

Number 57.

At three o'clock he was summoned into the back. The crowd hadn't thinned very much in the passing hours, so Raphe felt a certain sense of accomplishment that he'd been called and wouldn't have to put in another day of waiting. The hefty clerk pointed him down a hallway to the office of Mrs. Nadia Buendia.

"I'm just about ready to go home, mister. . . ." She paused and pointed to a piece of paper that sat in a manila folder on her desk. "How do you pronounce this name?"

"Uh, that's Raphe. Rhymes with waif," he said as he peered down at the document, noting how his name was out of order. "And actually that's my first name."

"How unusual. What does it mean?"

"Mean? I'm not sure. It's a family name. It belonged to my mother. . . ."

"That's a nice story, I'm sure. Can't we save it for another time?"

"Uh, yeah. Of course." Raphe continued to stand. Buendia never offered him a seat. There was no chair in the room except her own.

"It says here that you've been on unemployment now for eighteen months, and that you'd like to extend that for another six months."

Raphe had to think for a moment. Had it been that long already? He remembered how after he got over the initial anger of being fired, and those first awful weeks of applying for government assistance, he made peace with himself by pledging to use the time to finally pursue his life's calling and write his novel. A year and a half later, he was still staring at blank screens, unable to even come up with a chapter outline.

"Hello? Did you hear what I said?" Mrs. Buendia sounded annoyed.

"Yes, I'm sorry. I guess I was just surprised to hear it's been that long."

"We're not made of money," she said, acting as if the funds were coming out of her own purse. Raphe noted the exaggerated length and painted intricacies of the woman's fingernails, wondering how in the world she ever got any work done.

"I know," Raphe looked down. Maybe if he appeared ashamed she would have sympathy for him. "It's just that I can't find any work in my field. I used to be in dot-com. . . ."

"You and a billion others," she snapped. "Ever think that maybe it's time to move on to something else?"

Yes! A million times a day! Raphe thought, but kept to himself. "Well, it was my major in college," he lied. At Brown, students were allowed to make up their own majors, and everything was taken pass/fail. Even failing didn't count for much, since an "F" was automatically removed from every transcript. It was the Ivy League school known mostly as a haven for lazy children from wealthy families, celebrity offspring, and Eurotrash. Raphe had gotten in on a scholarship, but that hadn't stopped him from taking advantage of the school's lack of academic rigor. His own contrived major was "Cultural Electronica," or as his friends joked, "Internet porn with a minor in Madonna."

The university wasn't a complete joke. He loved his literature courses and embraced the work of the masters under the guidance of several especially bright and caring faculty. At graduation he realized he'd worked harder than most of his classmates, and it was the beginning of his disenchantment with the world to know they all received the same degree. His wealthy fellow students would never be caught where he was now, standing in the unemployment office getting ready to beg for a few more weeks of subsistence.

"We're taking you off the government teat, so to speak," Mrs. Buendia abruptly announced.

"What?"

"No more for you."

"Please, ma'am. Can I have some more?"

"Cute. Dickens, right? *Oliver Twist.*" For the first time Mrs. Buendia smiled. "You know, I teach a course in ESL over at City College. . . ."

Mrs. Buendia gave Raphe ninety more days of unemployment, a "gift" because of some new law passed by Congress. After that, however, he was on his own. He could apply for welfare and food stamps, but Buendia warned him that he'd only get those if he was penniless. He'd have to sell his home, drain all his savings, and even siphon the meager dollars in his 401K account. After all that financial ruin, he could then apply, and maybe—only maybe—get further assistance. Raphe thought of the woman with three kids in front of him in line at Safeway, and how she so slowly and agonizingly tore each food stamp stub from her booklet to pay her bill. How can someone like that so easily get government help, but he would have to be humiliated first?

The only good news was an actual job tip from Buendia, and remarkably it was in his field. A biotech start-up in SoMa needed help with its web site. When he called, an eager staffer asked him to come in the next day. Raphe couldn't believe his good fortune—the company was only a few blocks away from 225 Folsom. He could do the interview on his lunch break. Harrington, surprisingly, didn't mind covering for Raphe two days in a row. "I am on the lick out, these dias," he explained.

DIABEAT-IT worked on a cure for diabetes. Raphe thought the name contrived and silly for such a serious illness, but had to admit he was impressed from the moment he walked through the door. So much of SoMa's tech world sat in converted old wrecks of buildings, but not this place. It was less than two years old and gleamed of stainless steel, glass, and blinding white floors. Lila, from human resources, explained that the designer's goal was to create a sparkling "clean room" motif. It worked. The style exposed even the minutest speck of dirt, requiring janitorial crews to be inexorably vigilant.

"If you don't mind," Lila cleared her throat, "we'd like to have you do a little test of sorts." She ushered Raphe over to a workstation. "Your resume shows you have exceptional credentials for this work, but we like applicants to do a little skills check." Lila showed Raphe the company's web site. It wasn't too impressive, since it was really just a promotional tool. No business was transacted through the site. As far as Raphe could tell, it was updated with an occasional press release related to the FDA approval process for the company's drug. Only six announcements had been made in the past year.

Despite the simple content, the site was barely functional. It was oddly slow and several internal links were dead. "Can you fix it?" Lila asked.

Raphe accessed the programming. Whoever wrote it was a hack. The HTML work was sloppy. Even someone who dropped out of C++ class back in Brown could have done a better job. "Sure. The code just needs some rewriting."

"Excellent. How long will it take?"

To make it perfect, Raphe figured he would have to scrap at least half of the code. Still, the site was remarkably small, an easy job for someone with his background. It seemed incredible to him that "Web Site Manager" was to be a full-time position. They must have something bigger in mind down the line.

"To fix it right, I'd say it would take about four hours of intense programming."

"Wow," Lila smiled. "Then you'd better get to it."

"Huh?"

"Four hours. You'll be out of here by five. That's when I have to leave for the day, so that's perfect."

"I don't understand."

"What's to understand? You need to fix the site. That's the job application."

Raphe smoldered. He'd heard of situations like this. Companies looking to save a few bucks would post "job openings" for web site work, but what they really wanted was free labor. *It ought to be against the law,* he thought, irked that the state unemployment office had sent him on this scam.

"No."

"What do you mean, no? Don't you want the job?"

"What job would that be?"

"Uh, to work on our web site."

"This web site?" Raphe felt the old anger start to rise in him, the same bitter feeling he had back in the dot-com days when his labor supported the cash flow of so many others. "This is the whole thing?"

"Yes. It's all we need." Lila was flustered. A guilty look washed over her face.

"So when I fix it, *then* what would I do?" Raphe got up, and strapped his backpack over his shoulder. "If you want consulting work done to fix your site, you need to pay for it. Fuck! Look at this place. You've got more money than God! And you go around trying to cheat guys like me!"

Lila stiffened. She raised her hands, as if ready to fend off an attack.

Raphe turned and stormed into the hallway, heading back toward the heavenly, white glow of the lobby. As he was about to reach the door, a jolt of red broke into his peripheral vision. Red hair. That beautiful red hair. Raphe found himself instantly calmed. The woman smiled warmly at him.

"Hey," she said. "Don't you work with Mr. Harrington?"

17

"You're gonna wear those?" Julie looked at Raphe's sneakers, an old pair of Vans.

"Yeah. They're comfortable." Raphe looked down for his own inspection, tipping his foot to the side. He remembered the day he bought them two years ago. He'd never dream of spending a hundred dollars on sneakers now.

"Maybe. But your feet are going to be killing you in a couple hours." Julie walked over and nuzzled Raphe's neck. "I have quite a hike planned for us."

"You still haven't told me where we're going," said Raphe, the end of his sentence softly evaporating. He loved when she kissed his neck. So gentle, barely a wisp, yet the touch of her lips there—right *there*—sent a charge through his entire body. The one spot made him melt. Only two of his lovers had ever found it. First Baptiste and now Julie.

"Ahhhh," Raphe whispered. "Let's just stay here and crawl back into bed."

"But we just got out of bed," Julie kissed again. "It's already one in the afternoon. There aren't too many hours of sunlight left."

"Nature can wait," Raphe moaned.

"The Rockports," Julie said.

"What?"

"Put on the hiking shoes," Julie breathed into his ear as she released him and walked into the kitchen. Raphe's eyes followed her, soaking up the vision of that red hair with the same thrill he felt the first time he saw her out the window of 225 Folsom.

Had it been only two weeks since they first spoke? He remembered how stunned he was to bump into her that day in the heavenly, white lobby of DIABEAT-IT.

For months during his mail sorting duties, Raphe had rehearsed in his head all the clever things he would say when he finally had the chance to speak with her. He would be so witty, yet manly—the combination would sweep her off her feet and into his arms. But when the moment finally came, Raphe—the writer—found himself unable to form words.

"You OK?" Julie said after a few moments went by, and all Raphe seemed to do was make choking sounds.

"Uh, yes," Raphe cleared his throat. "You just caught me a little off guard. I didn't expect to see anyone here that I knew."

"I work here. I'm Julie," she said, extending her hand.

"I know," Raphe fumbled to take her grasp. "Harrington told me your name. I'm Raphe."

"Raphe? That's an interesting name. If I remember right, that's an anatomical term."

"Really? I never knew that."

A puzzled look came over Julie's face, as if she just recalled something strange. She shook her head and let out a little laugh. "No, that can't be it."

"Oh."

"You headed out?"

"Yeah. I was just talking to the people up in your HR department . . . about some work."

"Really? You're a scientist, too?"

"No, computers. Dot-com. But you probably knew it was something like that since I work behind the desk at 225 Folsom."

"I was just on my way to have some herbal tea," Julie smiled. "Wanna join me?"

Would I ever! Raphe wanted to scream, but instead managed to control himself and put out a restrained, but enthusiastic, "Sure."

They ventured off to a tiny café that specialized in teas from around the world. Julie picked for them something made from the South African Rooibos leaf. It smelled pungent to Raphe, but the taste was remarkably sweet and soothing. Julie smiled as she explained it was a brew praised for its mystical ability to create bonds between people. As they chatted about their lives, Raphe couldn't remember ever being so charmed by a woman. Julie was as smart as she was beautiful. Right after MIT, she came to San Francisco to work for DIABEAT-IT. Her grandmother's death from "the sugar" drew her to the research. As she spoke, Raphe began to see Julie for what she was with her brains, personality, and packaging—a rising star in biotech. Raphe nervously pulled on his soul patch. The more he heard, the more anxious he became. His heart sank. He feared Julie was the type of successful woman who would never have anything to do with a guy like him.

He'd seen it so many times since moving to The City. The beautiful women in their twenties inevitably had their pick of men. Guys came to San Francisco thinking that as a place with so many gay men, it would be the perfect spot to be single and straight. Women must be desperate to find *normal* guys.

How quickly they'd learn they were wrong. San Francisco was also one of the most expensive cities in the world, so the women who decided to live there tended to be ambitious in order to survive. They had powerful careers, lucrative jobs, and were on the fast track to success in the worlds of finance, computers, or biotech. They called the shots, and some even developed a checklist to determine which men to date.

For a guy to qualify, he needed the accoutrements of wealth. An expensive car. A great job. A home in a trendy neighborhood—owned, not rented. A charming personality and fit body were lower on the list, but important. Few men Raphe's age could make the grade, which explained why the sidewalk news racks of *Yank Magazine* were always empty by Friday night. San Francisco women, meanwhile, either dated much older men or simply buried themselves in their careers.

But as Julie continued to speak, Raphe began to think she might be different. The tone of her voice was sweet and embracing, not pushy. She'd immediately paid for the tea when it arrived. "Please, I would love it if you would let me do this for you," she insisted. Raphe had never met another woman in The City who ever picked up a tab.

Perhaps her checklist didn't require a costly admission, Raphe thought. Just chemistry. Maybe it was because she grew up in Nebraska, where Raphe concluded the values were more wholesome.

"So you said this tea is some sort of love potion," Raphe said as he took a big sip. Not that it mattered. He was infatuated the first time he saw her out the window of the shop.

"Oh, I wouldn't go that far," Julie laughed. "Although it's known for mellowing people out. Maybe that helps break down resistance."

"You believe that?"

"Sure."

"It doesn't sound very scientific," Raphe teased. "I mean, you're in biotech."

"There's more to me than just science. And there's more in this universe than what you can see in a microscope."

"Like?" Raphe couldn't take his eyes off her. It was if he were hypnotized.

"Like us, for example." Julie smiled wide. Her teeth were as stunning as her hair.

"Us?"

"Do you think it's just random that after all this time of being a few feet from each other every morning, suddenly we find ourselves face-to-face, brought together finally by a completely unrelated chain of events that landed you in the lobby of my office at the split-second I decided to go out for tea? And I've been craving this *exact* tea all day. Coincidence? Well, I didn't make all this happen."

"Neither did I."

"Then who did? Look, the way people connect, it's . . . mystical. It's not about scoping out each other's bank accounts and resumes. It happens when two people connect with each other—and only each other. A type of fate."

Fate? And she believes in mystical teas. For an MIT grad, it didn't make sense. Julie straddled two worlds, the sacred and the profane. Yet she wasn't torn by the conflict. She seemed to embrace it all with such ease. In a way, she reminded Raphe of his own journey. Someone who also sat on a fence.

As they sipped the tea, Julie admitted to watching Raphe as much as he'd been eyeing her. She confessed to taking glimpses of him as she left for work each morning, cursing the days when the glare from the sun prevented a clear view inside the shop. Sometimes she would just stand and stare for several moments, until she saw Raphe start to turn in her direction. Then she'd pivot and be off, with no one but herself knowing how long she'd been admiring.

"It was like a game of cat and mouse. I wanted you to catch me looking! For some reason, I've known for more than a year that we'd end up meeting. But something inside told me it would happen in some unlikely way. I even went as far as to put a needle in a haystack and place a listing on the *Missed Connections* page of craigslist."

Craigslist! How many times had he skipped right by the *Missed Connections* section, thinking that no one would ever want him enough to put a posting there. All that time there was a message waiting for him from the beautiful, red-haired woman upstairs. Raphe cursed himself for wasting so much time exploring places like BARTM4M. Hidden in the billions of pages of the internet, his answer was there all along. He'd been looking in the wrong place.

"Pretty passive-aggressive, right?" Julie confessed.

"No." Raphe found it hard to speak again, overwhelmed by the thoughts filling his head. He'd never met anyone so open with her feelings. She wanted him, as much as he always wanted her. Yet he'd been off on a journey into another world. The internet was a devilish prophet. Instead of leading him to Julie, it had brought him to Baptiste. "I guess I just don't understand. Why didn't you just say hello? I wanted you to say hello . . . so much."

"*You* could have said hello."

"I wanted to run out onto the street every morning."

"I wanted you to." Julie's right eye glossed over. She turned her head down to the table and stared into her cup of tea. "Boy, we're quite a pair. Like something out of some bad romance novel."

"I want us to be," Raphe said.

"A bad romance novel?"

"No. A pair."

Julie giggled softly, regaining her composure. "Well, that's life in The City for you. We're all living on top of each other, crammed into the tiny tip of this little peninsula. Yet we're too afraid to be intimate."

"No. Not at all. It's OK to be careful." Raphe moved his hand across the table to gently put it upon hers. "I've learned that it's OK for things to move slowly. Some things are worth waiting for."

"Raphe?"

"Julie?" He liked saying her name out loud. He wanted to scream it so the whole world heard.

"I don't want to wait any longer."

They fled the tea shop and nearly sprinted back to 225 Folsom. Raphe ducked below the window so Harrington wouldn't see him head upstairs to Julie's apartment. As soon as the door closed, Julie's mouth was on his. Her hands grabbed the back of Raphe's head. At first, his arms went limp by his sides. He'd wanted her for so long, just her lips against his created an overpowering cascade of sensations.

He caught his breath and moved his arms around her, his thumb finding the spot beneath her shoulder blade. He pulled her closer and felt her breasts press into him. Her tongue explored his mouth, and he lunged his into hers in return. He inhaled her scent, her hair smelling freshly washed with herbal shampoo. After so many months of wanting, he savored every taste, touch, and smell. He wasn't sure if minutes had passed, or hours.

Abruptly, Julie's mouth pulled away, and she pushed back. She stared intensely at Raphe's chest and began frantically unbuttoning his shirt. When she got to the last button, she kept going and undid his jeans.

"Are you sure?" Raphe asked, startled by how aggressive Julie had become.

"This isn't the tea talking," she said, breathing heavily. Her forehead shined with sweat. With one swoop she lifted off her top and tossed it onto the floor.

She wore no bra. *Her breasts don't need one,* Raphe thought. They were like large upsidedown teacups with no sag, and nipples that burst in shocking red compared to her fair skin. He reached forward to touch, but she opened his shirt and lunged at him, wriggling onto his hairy chest.

While clutching, she took tiny steps backward until she'd

pulled them both into her bedroom. As they moved, Raphe's open jeans slipped down. By the time they reached the bed, the pants were at his ankles.

Julie looked up into Raphe's eyes, then down to the front of his boxers. He was so aroused, he'd popped through the fly. She took him in her hand as she kicked off her shoes and slipped out of her slacks and panties. She got onto the bed on all fours, never letting her grasp leave Raphe, and moved her face toward his belly. Then she kissed gently where her hand had been.

More than the touch, it was the anticipation that nearly put Raphe over the edge. He could climax right now if he wasn't careful.

How different it was with Julie. Was this how love felt in the flesh?

Did he even kiss that girl Lolly? Sex with Lolly was rough, with him pounding her like he'd seen the guy do to the prostitute at the Power Exchange. He let Lolly do dirty things he'd never done with a girl, like sticking her finger inside him and making him taste his own semen when they were done. Sex with Lolly was the most intense he'd had with a woman, but it wasn't real. It was an act—role-playing for an afternoon.

Julie nuzzled and licked.

How different than Baptiste. Julie was so tentative, while Baptiste would have devoured him by now, knowing all the places to caress with his tongue to bring Raphe close before pulling back at just the right—

Stop! Raphe pushed Baptiste from his mind. Julie's lack of expertise wasn't a flaw. It was perfection. What had the so-called skills of men brought him? *This* is what he craved now. Someone who did *not* know how every inch of his body worked. It seemed only fair. He didn't know every inch of Julie's body yet. They would make those discoveries together.

He didn't need a whore like Lolly. He didn't need the firm hand of Baptiste. He needed to be just a guy with a girl.

He bent over and pressed his lips against Julie's. He wrangled out of his shoes, kicked away his jeans, and freed himself from his boxers. He got next to Julie on the bed and explored every inch of her body with his hands and mouth. Her smell was exotic compared to anyone else he'd been with. Was it the red hair? Did that create a different scent and taste? When she was drenched from his mouth, her body arching as if begging, he finally entered her. He kept going until she convulsed and dug her nails into his shoulder. Then he let himself release. He stayed inside her until they nodded off to sleep.

The next morning Raphe went home to get his laptop and clothes. He hadn't slept in his own condo since. Two weeks had passed that seemed like two minutes.

Raphe emerged from his daydream of that first day, noticing he'd become aroused at the memory. He thought of begging Julie to come back into the bedroom. She had other plans. A hike? It seemed important to her. He'd be a good sport. He kicked off the Vans and put on the Rockports. Julie tossed him a daypack, and they made their way down to the curb. "You wanna take my car?" Raphe asked.

"Car?" Julie smirked. "We don't need a car."

"Where are we going? Taking the ferry to Angel Island?"

"Nope. We're not even leaving The City."

"What?"

"I promised you a hike," Julie said as she kissed his neck again. "I never said we were going anywhere."

The adventure turned out to be an urban hike through the neighborhoods and hills of San Francisco. They made their way across SoMa and into the Mission, with Julie gleefully noting the colorful barrio murals as if she'd made archeological discoveries. Walking through the gay Castro neighborhood, Raphe at first felt uneasy—worried he might bump into someone he knew. Instead, he noticed how more men than ever seemed to check him out. He was with a woman now—back to being straight—and that made him somehow even more desirable. Raphe avoided eye contact with the men who took second looks, but marveled to himself at the extra attention.

They climbed up steep Diamond Heights making it to the top of Twin Peaks just in time to see the sun starting to set over the ocean. They stared westward, nuzzling each other as strong winds whipped at the jackets Julie had packed just for this moment. I could be naked, Raphe thought, and still be warm in her arms. They snacked from a bag of sticky-sweet, organic Barhi dates.

By the time they climbed down and walked back along Market Street to City Hall, it was night. Lights beamed off the gold highlights on the building's towering dome, adding yet another magical touch to the most romantic day Raphe had ever experienced.

"Thank you," he said.

"For what?"

"For this day. For you. I've lived here for years, and I've never had a day like this. Now I know why couples in love from all over the world come here. I never understood until now."

"Well, it's not over."

"What do you mean?"

"We're camping out tonight."

"Camping? Like in the park?"

"I think we can do better than that," Julie explained. "Besides, I think it will be fun to study the native nocturnal species."

Julie led them across the vast Civic Center plaza, then turned up Larkin Street to an oasis in the middle of the run-down Tenderloin neighborhood called The Phoenix. At first glance it reminded Raphe of an old-fashioned drive-in motel, built in the style of something found by the side of the highway in the sixties. Just two floors, with large, draped windows facing a courtyard with a kidney-shaped pool.

Adjacent to the courtyard was a hot, new nightclub, the Bambuddha Lounge. Decorated in a fusion of Buddhist religious artwork and dramatic hard-edged white and wood furnishings, it was the latest place for men and women to play. The beautiful people, and others.

Raphe collapsed onto the bed. The kitschy motel exterior was a facade. Inside, the rooms were as hip as the club. Just about everything was bright white—the bedding, the walls, the desk, the chair, the towels, the bathroom tile, the pencil and pad next to the phone, the phone. The room had that same heavenly feeling of the lobby of DIABEAT-IT, where Julie and Raphe first said hello.

"It's lovely," Raphe grinned. "The best camping I've ever done."

Julie crawled onto the bed next to him. "I wanted to do something special. For you. You know, I'm crazy about you."

"Why?"

"What do you mean?" she asked.

"Well, you're everything any man could ever want. Beautiful, brilliant, caring. I still don't understand. Why me?"

"Fate."

"Yeah?'

"That and the fact that you're so sweet, smart, and sexy." Julie crawled up behind Raphe on the bed, spooning her body against his.

"Fate. You really believe that stuff?"

"I do." Julie kissed Raphe's neck.

They changed into dress clothes—another secret Julie had carefully packed into their bags. Downstairs at the club they sipped Sidecars and soaked up the sexy atmosphere. Julie said she was surprised to discover Raphe even knew what a Sidecar was. She thought he'd be a Jack and Coke type of guy.

Raphe looked over the crowd. An unattractive squad of women in one corner loudly discussed various men who they had "sent packing."

"He was so jealous of me," one said.

"He couldn't keep his hands off me," gloated another.

Not one of the women looked as if it were possible she'd had a date in the past decade, yet they supported each others' tales as if genuine. Bars like these, Raphe thought, are churches of delusion, where alcohol heals the wounds of inadequacy. At least for the night.

He watched as eager, handsome men in their twenties prowled the crowd, chatting up the pretty, younger women. The men oversold themselves and used gestures that were too broad. Raphe caught the whiff of gas in the air. Straight bars always smelled like farts. Must be the nerves of everyone in the room, their stomach acids munching away at their insides. So many people wanting to hook up, but the rules of the game made it such an anxious, impossible task.

Gay bars didn't smell like farts. At those, it was only a matter of when, not if.

Raphe suppressed that thought and held Julie's hand. The misery of the straight singles scene was behind him. So were hook-ups with women like Lolly, and the frenetic world of Baptiste. He had his girl now. The red-haired woman from upstairs at 225 Folsom was his.

At 3:00 A.M. they escaped their room to skinny-dip in the hotel pool. Tiles in the bottom of the pool were designed into countless shapes of the number 9. Or were they 6's? The water was cool, but Raphe still became hard. Once inside Julie, he found warmth. Then heat. She put her arms around his neck. As she got closer, the clasp became more intense, almost to the point of cutting off Raphe's air. Then spasms, and collapse.

They'd climaxed at the same time. Nothing could seem more natural—a perfect fit.

Raphe noticed that some of the other guests peeked out their windows. They'd been watching.

He didn't care. After all he'd been through, he was glad for all to see who he really was.

FALL

18

Their walk took them past the new store on Mission, the one that specialized in sales of wind chimes and pepper spray.

"You don't look very good, man." Baptiste had seen Raphe a few times in the past two months, only connecting once physically. They talked on the phone almost every day, but it was clear Baptiste was losing his convert. But to what? Surely, not . . .

"I really need a vacation," Raphe sighed.

"Again? Jesus. Didn't you have one just the other day? How many times are you gonna do that?" Baptiste worried Raphe had developed an obsession with these so-called *vacations*. An addiction. It just couldn't be healthy.

"No, uh, I mean I need to get out of The City," Raphe backtracked. He'd been editing his thoughts with Baptiste ever since he met Julie, the day she seemed to magically appear like an angel in that blinding, white biotech lobby. He wanted to share his joy, but knew there was no way Baptiste could understand. Raphe wasn't sure he had a handle on it. Once again, too much had happened too soon.

"Oh, *that* type of vacation," Baptiste laughed. "I thought you were talking about, you know, the *other* type of vacation. The kind you get down in Pacifica."

Raphe had received one of *those* vacations just a few hours ago. He was still in the afterglow. The rush. That remarkable feeling of absolution. It was *exactly* that type of vacation he craved.

"I'm just burned out. Maybe I'll head up to Calistoga for a week."

"Well, you do look a little drained these days."

Raphe used the same cover story with Julie—a retreat from The City to work on his novel. It was a lie he felt guilty about, but he knew it was best to protect her from the truth. Julie was the reason he got involved in all this in the first place. Innocently, of course, but she had pushed him, and now he was hooked. He knew if he told her the truth, it would lead to some big, dramatic scene. What if she walked out on him? He couldn't risk that. He loved her.

No, it had to be handled secretly. He'd heard about places up in Calistoga where he could get it out of his system once and for all. He would do it as many times as it took for him to be sick of it.

Raphe remembered how his mother Ellen once told him that as a teenager she developed a nauseous aversion to cheese soufflé. In home economics class, back in the fifties, all the girls had to learn to make a proper French cheese soufflé. When done, the smell that filled the room of twenty little ovens was luscious and overwhelming—like nothing the working class New England girls had ever experienced in their corn beef and cabbage lives. Ellen dove into hers as if she'd not eaten in a week. One spoonful to taste soon turned into ten, and in a matter of minutes she had consumed the entire dish. It was too much of a good thing, and her small frame soon rejected the rich concoction in an orange explosion onto the beige, linoleum floor. She would never have cheese soufflé again. Decades later, the thought still made her gag.

Raphe needed his own type of cheese soufflé epiphany.

The trip to Calistoga took several days to plan. He reserved a room in a cheap motel for the week. He could come and go anonymously. He didn't want anyone following his daily appointments and object to what he was doing. He was pretty sure alternative medicine wasn't like pharmacies, where computers tracked if someone tried to fill the same prescription at more than one store. As long as he didn't go to the same place twice, no one would ever know.

He booked himself into a different clinic each day, using a variety of aliases. If it didn't work, he vowed to return home and fall into Julie's arms and finally admit his weakness. Maybe she could rescue him.

She owed him that much. She started it.

Even though she worked in a field that required the daily manipulation of nature's plan, Julie was anything but artificial. Every strand of her stunning, red hair was natural, making her a genuine ruby in a world of imitations. She was also obsessed with holistic healthcare. She didn't see any conflict with fudging DNA during the day and drinking wheat grass shakes at night. Her embrace of two such different worlds was one of the reasons Raphe adored her. On Saturday mornings they would venture into the herb stores in Chinatown where Raphe found himself amazed at Julie's knowledge of all the different mysterious substances that peppered the shelves in hundreds of glass jars. Many of the shopkeepers knew her, and beamed whenever "Red Lady" entered their stores.

"Ever have a high colonic?" Julie casually asked one day.

"Is that some kind of drink?" Raphe imagined it to be something containing ginger root.

"No, no, no. It's a health procedure. Colonic irrigation. It's very good for you."

"What is it?"

"It's a type of cleaning—for your insides."

It all sounded quite reasonable, until Julie got to the details. Raphe squirmed as he imagined what it would be like to have a garden hose stuck up his butt to have his colon power-washed. "What if it burst?"

"Don't be ridiculous. It's not like that at all," Julie admonished.

"I think I'm gonna pass."

"I wish you wouldn't say that."

"Why? What's the big deal?"

"Well, I didn't say anything because I didn't want to hurt your feelings."

"Hurt my feelings? What are you talking about?"

"Look, we've been sleeping together every night since we met." Julie looked directly into Raphe's eyes.

"Yeah?" He gulped.

"And I love it. Except for one thing."

"What?"

"In the middle of the night you tend to . . ." She paused.

"What?"

"You, uh . . . release."

"Release?"

"Gas."

"Really? Shit. I'm sorry. I had no idea." Raphe thought back to the gassy men he'd made fun of at the Bambuddha Lounge. Was he also nervous inside? If so, why? What was his body telling him?

"Hey, it's not like it's something you're doing on purpose," she said, gently touching his arm to console. "In a way, it shows how completely relaxed you are in bed with me. I know that. But it can be a little, uh, overwhelming."

"And you think this high colon thing will help?"

"A high *colonic*," she said with the emphasis of a teacher explaining a new vocabulary word to a slow student. "The fact is that gas is mostly produced by little irritants we have in our system. Sometimes the food we eat causes it. Other times it's done by parasites. We all have them in us. Sometimes they get a little out of control, and we need to put them in their place. A high colonic will wash them out."

Of all reasons to be dumped by a woman, Raphe never imagined it would be for nocturnal gas. The idea of having something sprayed up his ass repulsed him. His mind flashed to the moment when he was brutally violated. *Mark Hazodo. I hate that guy.* But the alternatives—losing Julie and forever being branded a *night farter*—were worse. Why had Baptiste never mentioned it?

"Will it hurt?"

Getting an appointment at the clinic in Pacifica took a week. Two handsome young Hollywood actors on "The Tonight Show" the previous week had dished about how they used high colonics as a way to stay in shape. Since then the clinic had been booked solid.

When the day arrived, Raphe was nervous. Waiting for the appointment made his anxiety worse than if he'd been able to get it done the day Julie mentioned it. It didn't help that Julie had adopted the routine of sprinkling her pillow with a few drops of some aromatherapy oil each night before they turned in "just as a precaution." That nightly whiff of orangey, sweet marjoram became a potent reminder of his flatulent failure.

The clinician was an overweight, middle-aged woman named Sarah. Before starting she asked questions about Raphe's diet, scolding him every time he mentioned any type of meat. He noticed an embroidered, framed sign on her office wall that read, "Don't eat anything that has parents." Raphe wondered why, if the woman maintained such a healthy diet herself, she was so fat.

It took a few minutes for Raphe to adjust to the woman's explanation of the upcoming procedure. In a strangely contrived lingo apparently aimed at avoiding profanities, Sarah never used any of the words Raphe would have associated with going to the bathroom. He wasn't crude enough to believe she'd have a potty mouth and use words like "shit" or "crap." But he at least expected to hear clinical descriptions such as "bowel movement" or "excrement."

Sarah used none of those words. Instead, she substituted cute little expressions. The entire procedure was called a "vacation." The moment of expulsion itself was simply known as an "exit." The substance that would be emitted was nicknamed the "baggage." If he felt pain at anytime while being "loaded," he should just tell her to "abort," and she would do an "emergency exit."

Raphe wondered if he were really getting a high colonic or taking a trip on a jet.

He had to remove all his clothes and put on a hospital gown, but not in the usual way. She instructed him to put his legs through the armholes, and simply hold the skirt section up against his chest. There was no point in trying to tie the drawstring in the back, since being "peek-a-boo" was essential. Yes, she would see his "opening," but that was just part of the "vacation experience." It was nothing to be ashamed of.

He stumbled down the hall from the dressing room, clutching the johnny to his chest. It reminded him of the way his teenage sister guarded her modesty with a towel as she emerged from the shower and darted to her room. He remembered how he'd taunted her mercilessly for having such large breasts when she was just fourteen and he was ten. If she could see him now, she'd have the last laugh.

"This is the CleanStream 3900," Sarah explained as she pointed to a large, white machine built into the wall. Tentacles of hoses, pressure gauges, and control panels emerged from the imposing device. Sarah said it was filled with sterilized water. All the hoses were also sterilized and would be disposed of immediately following the session. Nothing was ever reused with patients. "We want everyone to have a healthy vacation!"

Sarah instructed Raphe to lie on a doctor's exam table on his back. It wasn't what he expected. He'd imagined himself squatting over a toilet.

"Not at all!" Sarah gleefully chided. "The CleanStream 3900 takes care of everything!"

New age music filled the room, and Raphe shut his eyes. After he was relaxed, Sarah told him to turn on his side. She gently parted his bare cheeks as her finger massaged a large glob of lubricant on his "little opening."

"Give me your hand," she said. He reached behind, and she placed in his grasp the end of the hose, which had also been liberally slicked. Sarah guided his hand so the head of the inch-thick tube nudged up to its destination. "You need to push it in yourself," Sarah soothed. "Take your time. It won't hurt if you are in control. Relax."

Relax. That's what Baptiste said the first time he entered. After hours of teasing foreplay that included massaging with fingers, oil, and tongue, Raphe remembered begging in his head for it to finally happen. When it did, he was ready and willing. The colonic was different. The plastic hose was larger than Raphe imagined—he had studied enema bottles at the grocery in anticipation, and this was at least five times that girth. It was stiff, without any of the give of Baptiste's flesh. Yet the gel somehow allowed the hose to slip inside, quite easily to Raphe's surprise. In a strange way, it actually felt pleasant. He wasn't aroused as he had been with men, but he couldn't deny the enjoyment of the sensation.

Once in place, Sarah secured the hose by taping it to Raphe's cheeks. He turned onto his back so his weight would further hold it in place. Then Sarah started what she called the "fulfillment stage." Warm water slowly ventured inside. At first Raphe wasn't sure anything was happening, since the machine had so precisely calibrated the water to exactly match his body temperature. It wasn't until pressure began to mount that Raphe realized his insides were being flooded. Raphe imagined the rivers of the CleanStream 3900 exploring his bowels like a rain-bloated lake spilling over into pristine fields. It was nature doing its duty.

Raphe felt a little stoned, as if he'd taken a hit from some particularly mellow pot. That was to be expected, Sarah had warned ahead of time. The toxins released during the procedure often have a relaxing effect on patients, putting them into a zone of contentment. In this daydreaming state, Raphe imagined the scared little parasites in his colon. The snakes that had invaded those pristine fields, now dying in the floodwaters, unable to escape the wrath of the cleansing . . .

Ouch.

"You feeling a little pain, sweetie?" Sarah asked as Raphe snapped back to reality.

"I think I really have to go to the bathroom now." Raphe panicked, worried the pressure he now felt in his abdomen would cause him to soil the table.

"Just sit back and relax and enjoy the ride," Sarah soothed. She turned off the pressure, and with the push of a button the flux of sterile water stopped at the source. The machine then switched a valve that reversed the flow down into a separate tube that began to take the sclerotic waste away. The pain ceased immediately, followed by a feeling of complete release. It wasn't just the departure of the implanted liquid, but with it Raphe's tremendous backlog of stress and frustration. He felt his emotional baggage—men, women, money—join the other waste down the clear tube and back into the machine for disposal.

Sarah watched carefully, noting with concern anytime she saw what she deemed to be a meat by-product making its exit. "People are killing themselves with red meat. Just look at that! It does nothing but clog your pipes!"

When the exit was complete, the process started all over again. The warm waters gushed in, the garbage flowed out. The cycle continued five more times, and with each cleansing Raphe felt the sensations multiply. At each peak he felt more stoned, and at the end of each release more relaxed and at peace.

As he dressed to leave, Sarah offered him follow-up sessions at a discount. Five for the price of four. Despite his limited funds, Raphe eagerly wrote a check.

Raphe hadn't planned to tell anyone about the colonics, but when Baptiste mentioned one day on the phone that he wanted to lose a couple pounds, Raphe found himself eagerly sharing the experience. The reaction to his enthusiasm wasn't what he expected. Instead, Baptiste thought it was the funniest thing he'd ever heard, and soon repeated the story to all their friends, adding his own scatological humor into the retelling.

"Vacation?" Baptiste burst out. "You mean she calls taking a crap a vacation? Geesh! So if I only have to take a little dump, do I just call that a weekend in Tahoe? After a big meal, do I say I'm gonna have a trip to Europe soon?"

The anecdote became a hit, and soon the joke infected Raphe's entire gay circle. Steve asked if at the office he should now excuse himself using the euphemism "I'm running down to Carmel" if he had to pee, and "I'm off to Montana" if it were more than that. Jeremy said he almost "vacationed" his pants when he first heard the tale.

Raphe tried to take all the razzing in stride. After all, Julie loved him even more for doing it and claimed to notice an immediate improvement.

"Are you sure this is healthy?" he asked one day, beginning to become nervous that he was enjoying the vacations too much. It just couldn't be natural.

"It is *such* an improvement," Julie said. "No more waking up in the middle of the night gasping for air. It's wonderful."

"Yeah, but is it normal? I mean, I don't know any other guys who get this done."

"Maybe they should," Julie said. Then her expression changed, as if she was suddenly aware that something wasn't right. "You look upset."

"I'm OK, it's just that . . ."

"Hey, don't worry about this. Just because others guys aren't having it doesn't mean anything weird about you. If there's one thing I've learned in biotech, it's that we're all different. A drug that heals one person isn't going to work for everyone else. We've all got our kinks. This works for you, and that's nothing to be ashamed about."

It wasn't shame. It wasn't aversion. Quite the opposite. Raphe couldn't admit the truth to Julie. After only a few sessions, he'd become addicted. With all his troubles seeming to flow away each time, treatments soon became once a week.

"How about twice a week?" Raphe asked Sarah.

"Sweetie, vacations should not be taken too often," she explained. "Although I have to admit, I've never met anyone who caught on so quickly. It's like this machine was built for you. You have a gift."

He was man mated with machine. Wasn't that what those fools in dot-com promised to do? Humanity intimately joined with technology. It was nothing like *this*.

"Please?" Raphe begged. "Twice a week?"

"No," Sarah smiled. "That's just too much of a good thing."

With Sarah's refusal, Raphe found another clinic in Berkeley to add into the mix. Wednesday nights he went to Sarah in Pacifica. Saturday mornings he headed to Berkeley. He lied to Julie and told her he'd started with a personal trainer at a gym across town.

When that still wasn't enough, he located a man in Pacific Heights on the internet who claimed to have a small clinic in the basement of his home. Desperate for a fix one night, Raphe went over. He walked in to find the man standing naked in a windowless, black-painted room holding an enema bag in one hand and his erection in the other. As he fled, Raphe realized he had a problem. Once again he'd fallen prey to an obsession, just like he did with Dr. Kaplan. He had to snap out of it. If for no other reason, he was going broke trying to pay for all the sessions.

In Calistoga he found enough different spas for colonics seven days in a row. After just two days he felt spent, his body exhausted by not having time to recover between sessions. *This is going to work. I will get this obsession out of my system by gorging on it.*

Strangely, the exhaustion did not bring rest. He tossed and turned in the spartan motel bed, unable to succumb to sleep. He missed not having Julie beside him, but it was more than that—his mind would not let him doze. It was akin to the excitement of a child waiting for Christmas Day. What would tomorrow's session be like? Would it be the best of all? He obsessed over the little differences of the various clinics and spas he'd visited. He noted the subtle variations of language the assorted clinicians would use when administering the procedure. A woman at one of the Calistoga venues once let the word "shit" slip, which made him giggle. And he noticed how the machine used was a CleanStream 4100. Not the CleanStream 3900! Did the higher number mean it was better? Was it going deeper than any of the others?

When Sunday arrived, Raphe was weary, but he considered himself finally cured. He nearly limped to his car, his body so weak from the daily purging of all nutrients. He'd lost fifteen pounds, according to the motel scale. Surely Julie will notice. He plotted to blame it on some sort of macrobiotic diet a spa forced him to consume.

At least that would be his cover story—no need to worry her with the truth. The week of *vacations* had worked exactly as planned. As he had the last one administered that morning, he concluded that he'd had enough. He saw his gaunt frame in the mirror as he dressed to go home. This was rock bottom. No more.

As he started the car, Raphe felt a slight jab in his stomach. What was that? Did the vibration of the car make something feel unsettled? No, it wasn't the car. He knew that. It was one of those horrible little parasites.

One was still alive. They didn't get them all.

19

"I lied to the Precor today," Baptiste said. "How pathetic is that?"

"Is that someone at the law firm?" Raphe asked.

"The Precor is not a *who*. It's a *what*. The name of the stair-master at the gym. I told it I weighed 175. I'm really 181. Pathetic."

Baptiste often talked about his weight. Raphe knew better than to say anything to challenge him or even enter the conversation. After a moment or two of venting, the subject would quickly change to safer territory. When it came to questions about someone's weight, especially Baptiste's, there was never a correct answer.

As if it really mattered to Raphe. In all the months since they'd met, Raphe had never seen Baptiste as anything less than a hunk. *Hunk.* As a writer, he wondered why he'd never been able to come up with a better word. Baptiste had a handsome, youthful face, but his body was fully a man's. Years of working out to fight off the progression of his thirties had created over-sized arms and legs, and firm, ample, and round pectorals.

Building muscle didn't interest Raphe as much. When he went to the gym, he always did cardio routines—the crosstrainer his latest favorite—and a few of the weight machines. He liked the idea of big muscles, but only on others. Without much effort, he was able to stay athletic and trim. The gym was mostly an escape.

Raphe liked being back in Baptiste's life, at least part of the time. After Julie tried to change him with the debilitating colonics, it was Baptiste who came to the rescue. Unable to confess his weakness to the woman of his dreams, Raphe sought what he thought would be a stronger embrace. Sins were easier shared with other sinners.

Raphe told Baptiste everything.

His money fears. In just weeks he would be forced to survive on only what Harrington paid him. The equity loan was still contingent on cleaning up the mess of ID theft. That could take months.

Then he admitted his addiction to colonics. Baptiste said he'd noticed the weight loss and feared the worse. He was relieved to finally learn the truth, and that it was not AIDS.

Hardest of all, Raphe confessed his romance with Julie.

"It's OK," Baptiste consoled. "I knew something was up. But it's not too late to get you back on the right track. You can still be saved."

Raphe was amazed how conciliatory Baptiste seemed. He'd missed that *anything goes* life. It was what made Baptiste's world so attractive. He doubted Julie would feel the same, no matter how wonderful she was.

Baptiste offered to do what he could to get Raphe's credit fixed—he knew someone in law enforcement who might be able to help. Then he put Raphe on a strict diet of water and saltines for two days, to arrest the disturbance in his bowels. Amazed that such a simple idea effected a cure, Raphe again began to see Baptiste as some sort of miracle worker. Life once more was easier. He distanced himself from Julie, claiming he needed to spend more nights at his own place "to work on the book." She seemed excited to hear he was getting on with his novel and stopped into the shop each morning to deliver a passionate kiss "for inspiration."

Instead, Raphe spent those nights with Baptiste. He brought his laptop and tried his best to write. But the blank screen would stay that way, with barely a dribble of words dispensed in the course of the day. He erased even those, dismissing them as useless, pointless, or stupid. It wasn't just a case of writer's block. He couldn't blame Baptiste as a distraction, since he rarely got home from the law firm before eight. It was worse than all that, Raphe concluded. It was the worst possible scenario for a writer.

He simply had nothing to say.

When his brain felt sufficiently fried by his failures, Raphe headed for the huge 24 Hour Fitness complex on Potrero. It was only a few minutes away, but felt miles from his troubles. When in the zone of a workout, with music on his headset blasting in his ears, he could clear his mind of the struggle. Gay or straight. Julie or Baptiste. He wanted to be in both worlds, but didn't feel like he completely belonged to either.

Raphe found the gyms in San Francisco full of little stories. Like the muscled Mexican man with the teardrop tattoo just below his right eye. Raphe imagined it the result of a gang initiation, where the man probably had to kill someone to prove his worth. Of course, Raphe didn't know if this was true. It was one of dozens of fantastic backgrounds he invented for the characters he studied as he leisurely went nowhere on the Life Fitness Trainer 9500.

Other stories he didn't need to make up. His observations filled in the gaps. Even though 24 Hour Fitness was the so-called *straight* gym in SoMa, he took note of how the men checked each other out, mostly in subtle ways. When it appeared a man was watching a television hung from the ceiling, he was actually peering at the mirrored walls to absorb the reflected image of another man jogging on a treadmill at the other end of the room. Some men wore dark sunglasses in the workout room so they could more discretely stare at the rows of perfect glutes that strained a few feet away.

Only in the showers did the game become more overt. Smoked glass walls partitioned each stall, allowing for both discretion and a slightly obscured peek at the next man. Standing toward the open front of the chamber gave an unobstructed view into all the berths on the opposite side of the small room. Conversely, huddling in the back under the spout offered privacy. This ability to hide or reveal oneself in an instant created endless opportunities for mischief. A gay must have designed this place, Raphe figured.

Most of the time nothing would happen. Men would just bathe in front of each other, stealing quick glimpses of beefy physiques when there was no possibility of being snared taking a peek. Even if caught, no one cried foul. Guys seemed to like to show it off. Unless they were Mormons. The Mormons, Raphe observed, showered in their underwear.

Occasionally the gay guys would cruise each other into play. If there were enough, the room would erupt into a quick circle jerk, only to end with stifled gasps as white jolts splashed across the filthy tile floor.

Then there was something Raphe saw several times that he called the *stealth attack*. Two blond, young muscled guys were masters of the technique. He nicknamed the two men Dick and Dick, though he had no idea what their real names were. He wondered if they were some bored couple, looking for a new thrill for their relationship. At the very least, they were a team. If Raphe saw them in the gym, he made sure to pace his workout so he ended up in the showers at the same time.

The only thing he could compare it to was yawning, that involuntary reaction people have when they see someone gape, then they too suddenly have the urge. He knew yawns were not contagious. Yet they produced this reflex reaction, a mystery of human biology.

The same was true with hard-ons, Raphe observed. If a man saw another with an erection, he automatically became hard. It didn't matter if he was gay or straight.

Dick and Dick cornered their victim, always another good-looking man. They would not know the guy's orientation, but at this gym he was likely to be straight. One of the Dicks would position himself directly across, at the front of his chamber in the unobstructed view. The other Dick would get into the stall next to the target, and stand so close to the smoked glass that even the details of his pubic hair became clear.

Then they would start. They wouldn't look at the subject—they would stare at each other. At first, they caressed themselves, working their hands down to between their legs. They would use gobs of liquid soap, until they had washed themselves into full arousal. Then they would stroke, focusing their eyes on each other's hands.

Even if the prey had avoided seeing anything up until this point, the unmistakable arm motions of masturbation would grab his attention, even if only caught in periphery. Curiosity would force him to sneak a glance. To the front, and to the side, he couldn't help but see the perfect bodies of two handsome men clearly approaching climax. In that instant, and it only took a moment, the man's own passion would rise. He might not even notice it at first. Then he'd look down, embarrassed for his lack of self-control.

It wasn't sexual desire speaking, as much as the call of na-ture, like the reflexive yawn. If the target turned out to be gay, Raphe noticed, it quickly became a free-for-all. Soon all three men would be watching each other and smiling, enjoying themselves to completion.

If it was a straight man, the event would end abruptly. Within seconds of becoming erect, and without even the slightest touch or effort, he would spasm. Seized by the taboo of the scene, a torrent would flow.

A shocked look of shame would envelop the man's face. That's what Dick and Dick wanted to see—the payoff they desired. They'd let go of themselves, look at each other, and laugh. The straight man would try to scrub off the remnants of his humiliation as quickly as possible and bolt into the locker room to suit up and leave. Soon he'd be out in the lobby to meet his wife or girlfriend, his hair still dripping wet.

For Raphe, this was possibly the hottest sex he'd seen since moving to San Francisco. It was erotic, somewhat dangerous, and weirdly involuntary. He wanted to turn the episode into a short story, but figured it would just be viewed as a fiction no one would want to read. The world simply didn't believe in sexual grays the way he knew they existed.

Most people wouldn't *want* to know. Perhaps they feared that exploring these thoughts would shake their black and white view. He couldn't blame them for embracing an easier peace of mind. To know otherwise had consequences. If he'd never opened that letter to Dr. Kaplan, never been tempted to take that first step into other worlds, would he be more content?

He tried to purge the struggle from his mind. No one would want to read about that.

Instead, he spent time in front of his laptop painfully straining to extract stories from worlds he didn't really care about. The so-called *normal* world, the safe places he was supposed to capture if he was to be successful in the pursuit of a career in literary fiction. But he just couldn't relate to that plotless, first person universe. He'd read recently how the new fiction editor of the *New Yorker* sought only work that "eschewed narrative, characters and meaning." Instead, she wanted experiments with words plunked on top of each other in unusual ways. Raphe felt exasperated. Isn't that what the jumble puzzle in the newspaper is for?

The way he saw it, Raphe just didn't have the baggage needed to be a great writer. He didn't have any pained relationship with his family to explore. They got along fine. No hugging or "I love you" stuff, but the typical normal and formal New England deal. Raphe hated the current trend where just about everything had to be derivative of a classic work, so that too could be bundled as a companion book to further line publishers' pockets. No cancer. No drug problem. No sexual abuse as a child. Without these topics burning in his soul, he felt destined to be a literary loser. His life just didn't provide enough material.

"You wanna do a carjacking?" Baptiste asked one night.

"Huh?"

"You seem down. You know, maybe it will help."

"A carjacking? Are you fucking nuts?"

Baptiste was always coming up with crazy ideas he thought would help Raphe's writing. He was sweet that way, even though as a corporate attorney he knew very little about fiction.

"It's dangerous," Raphe further protested.

"No it's not. I did it when I was in college. It was so fucking easy, and so . . . well . . . hot."

"Jesus, Baptiste. I can't believe you're suggesting something like this. You're a lawyer. If we get caught and arrested, you'll lose everything. For someone like you, this would be a huge scandal—front page of the newspaper."

"That's not gonna happen. I know how to do this. Besides, it will give you something to write about." Baptiste traipsed his fingers through Raphe's short hair, just as he always did when he wanted to be affectionate. "I can see it all now. You will get all nervous just before. Lots of anxiety. Maybe little drops of perspiration down your back." He let his fingers trickle down Raphe's spine to illustrate the point. Gently he pulled his hand away.

Then, without warning, he violently smacked Raphe's behind. "Then we do it!"

"Hey! That hurt."

"Yeah, but it was also a *thrill*. Something you didn't expect. Exciting, even. That's what I'm talking about! You sit at your computer and struggle to write about shit you know nothing about. You've admitted it to me yourself. Let's go out and do something you *can* write about."

"We could get caught."

"We're not gonna get caught. I know exactly what to do. Like I said, I did it back in college. In those days I was broke, lonely, and drifting. I did a carjacking with a buddy. It was so exciting. Yeah, it was dangerous. Especially in those days. But I felt so alive after I did it. Somehow it lifted me out of my funk. And let's face it—you're in a funk."

A funk. Maybe that was it. Maybe he wasn't a complete failure. Maybe all he needed was to be inspired. He was never going to hate his mother, or go back in time to be a teenage runaway or foster kid. Perhaps his little adventures in SoMa could be the inspiration for his novel.

"You're saying that as Mr. Corporate Attorney, you owe it all to a night of carjacking in college?"

"If you put it that way? Sure."

They took Raphe's car. The older, dark blue Toyota seemed like it would attract less attention than Baptiste's red Boxster.

"How about if we plant ourselves down on Ringold Street?" Baptiste suggested.

"That won't work. Too many lights."

"Well, we need a dark street."

"I know, I know," Raphe snapped. "I heard you the first five times you said it."

Baptiste smiled. "Already getting edgy, huh?"

"So this is what edgy feels like? If that's all I get to experience for the sake of my writing . . ."

"Shhhh!" Baptiste pointed down the block. "There. That street up on the left."

"Natoma?"

"Yeah. That's the one. It's dark and it leads right to Tenth and the highway if we want to get away fast."

The street was empty of parked cars. Raphe noticed signs for 4AM STREET CLEANING the next morning, forcing residents to park elsewhere for the night or face a ticket. The lights on the outside of a storage building at one end of the block were out, making for a dim, desolate section of street. Raphe pulled over.

"Pull up more," Baptiste whispered. "Tenth is just a few feet up. We need to be close enough to see all the traffic going by."

Tenth Street was one of the busiest in SoMa, at all times of day and night. It provided the exit from downtown and the neighborhoods to the major freeways to both Oakland and Silicon Valley.

"Perfect. You see that. You and I can sit here without anyone taking notice. But we are so close to hundreds of people passing by that we can see their faces. All of them unsuspecting of what we have planned."

"I'm nervous," Raphe turned off the engine. "But, in a weird way . . . excited."

"Cool."

"I mean, I think I can do this."

"I knew you could."

Raphe let out a deep breath, composed himself, and looked into Baptiste's eyes. "I'm ready. Let's do it."

With near ritualistic motion, Baptiste led the way. He undid his belt and pants, then pushed them down to the dirty floor. Raphe followed, and found himself jolted by the cold sensation of the old car's faux leather against his flesh. They pushed back and tilted their seats so Raphe's moving arm could have free rein away from the awkward presence of the steering wheel.

They stared into the passing cars, sometimes looking directly into the eyes of the men and women who drove past. Each contact lasted only a fraction of a second, but multiplied by dozens of times it felt like an entire audience watching. A few cars crawled by on Natoma, the curious glancing to see what the two men were doing. One older man idled and stared for nearly a minute before another car approached and pushed him along.

The erotic additive of danger replaced any of Raphe's fears of being caught. The men tried to hold back as long as they could, but the thrill soon overwhelmed them, sending their excitement onto the floor mats in unison.

As they drove off in silence, Raphe opened the windows to release the funky air trapped inside.

20

Lauren and Jessica rounded the corner at Mission and 6th and nearly collided with a man urinating against the side of a building. He was dirty, dressed in a ripped tweed winter coat. The splatter landed just inches from Lauren's open-toed Kate Spades.

"What the fuck!" she yelped.

Jessica glared at her friend with a raised eyebrow.

"Don't give me that look." Lauren was exasperated. "It's broad daylight, and the guy's taking a piss on the sidewalk. He almost splashed me!"

The man turned and offered the women a toothless grin. He pushed himself back into his pants and zipped up.

"You are the *last person* allowed to complain," said Jessica.

"How can you say that? You know what happened to me in that My Place bar!"

Jessica pointed her forefinger at Lauren's mouth. "Don't! That's not what this is about, and you know it. We wouldn't be in this shithole neighborhood if you hadn't . . . ugh!"

Lauren knew not to say another word. Maybe this time she'd pushed her friend too far. All she'd been trying to do was get them to meet some hot city guys, but each adventure seemed to end in disaster. It was as if this entire town of Frisco were shouting "Go Away!" at them. Thank God she'd at least made it with that cute guy Raphe from the room4rent ads. If not for that, this would have been her longest dry spell on record. Even so, she was insatiably horny lately. It was like an itch that never got scratched.

Lauren turned and scanned the corners of the intersection. Jessica was right. This was a shithole. Pawn shops, homeless skanks with shopping carts, and dozens of junkies walking around like zombies. Her dad warned her about coming down to this area. He said it was the worst part of SoMa, maybe the most dangerous block in all of San Francisco. It was only eleven in the morning and already half the street weirdos looked wasted out of their minds.

Across the south side of Mission she spotted their destination. The Rose Hotel.

"There it is!" she said.

The entrance wasn't like any hotel she'd seen before. Instead of a bellboy, the women were greeted by a glass-and-steel-fortified door. When Lauren pulled on the handle, the door didn't open.

"What type of fucking hotel is this?"

"Lolly, geesh, don't you know anything? This isn't a Hilton. It's a homeless hotel. An SRO."

"SRO? What the hell is that?"

Jessica rolled her eyes. "It means single room occupancy. It's like a dorm."

"Well, *excuse me* for not having all the insider scoop on the ins and outs of skid row," Lauren mocked. "How do you know so much?"

"Newspapers. Ever heard of them? I read them. You should try it sometime."

Jessica pressed a button on the intercom. An unintelligible squawk came from the speaker, then a buzzer sounded to open the door. Jessica hurried inside.

Fuck, she's really pissed, Lauren thought. It wasn't like Jessica

to be so abrupt. She'd barely spoken a word the entire drive into
The City.

The small lobby of the Rose was actually a welcome retreat
from the filthy neighborhood. It was simple but spotlessly clean.
It had the plain tile and institutional smell of a college dorm.
Not fancy, but safe.

"The sign says it's this way." Jessica walked through a doorway at the back of the lobby, and Lauren followed. They entered
a small room with a few scattered plastic chairs. Taped to the
wall was a piece of notebook paper with words in black magic
marker scrawl: "Waiting Area." No one else was there. Jessica sat
so her back faced Lauren.

A large, purple metal door opened at the far end of the
room. A smiling African-American woman holding a thick
manila folder walked out. "Ah, you two must be Lauren and Jessica."

The two women nodded.

"Terrific," the woman beamed. "You're our last cases for
today. Come on inside."

She's nice, Lauren thought. All things considered.

When they walked into the room, they faced a panel of four
people seated behind a long table. Two men and two women.

"Please, sit down," said a young man who sat in the middle.
He had a wave of short dark-blond hair, blue eyes, and a boyish
face. He wore a tight pullover blue sweater that revealed an athletic frame. Lauren gave Jessica a quick look that said, *Not bad!*
Jessica returned a stare with the unmistakable retort, *Don't you
dare!*

"Welcome to South of Market Community Court," the
young man said with a rehearsed cadence. "We think this is a
better alternative than Superior Court. If we settle this matter
here today, there won't be any guilt on your record. In fact, the
arrest won't even stay on your record—as long as you don't commit a similar offense in the next twelve months. To the left and

right of me are volunteers from the neighborhood. They will be hearing your case."

Lauren's father was livid when he heard about the charge she faced. "Only in San Francisco!" he ranted. In all his years as a corporate lawyer, he'd never heard of such a ridiculous thing. As much as he railed against the city's stupidity, she could tell he wasn't completely on her side. He was always judging her. When the letter came that said she could resolve things in this weird, little kangaroo court, her dad was quick to chime in. "You'd better grab that deal and make this mess go away. It's like a damn get-out-of-jail-free card!"

"Do you have any questions so far?" the young man asked. Lauren and Jessica shook their heads. "Good. One of the volunteers is going to read the police report. After that you'll have the chance to respond and give your side of the story."

The man nodded to the black woman at the end of the row, the same one who had welcomed them.

"At 23:30 hours on the night of the 15th, officers Menendez and Blake were on routine patrol in the area around 1015 Folsom Street. . . ."

1015 Folsom. The hottest club in the city. Lauren's mind wandered back to that night. She and Jes came in for an event called "Atria." A famous DJ had flown in from New York with the latest house music mixes. Great Cosmos. Cool guys. It was supposed to be an edgy crowd. Not kinky like that bondage place, but gritty. When they got there, it seemed like everyone was high on something. No one was buying them drinks, like the guys would in Concord. In fact, she didn't see *anyone* with a cocktail. Instead, they all guzzled huge bottles of water. Why was everyone so thirsty?

"Responding to a complaint from neighbors," the woman continued to read from the police report, "officers Menendez and Blake exited their patrol vehicle and perambulated on foot down Harriet Street alley in the southward direction . . ."

The girls in the club were all skinny bitches. And with the gallons of water they drank, the line for the ladies' room was fifty deep. Lauren remembered wandering the club, hoping to find a restroom where the line wasn't so long. It was hopeless.

"When advancing to the mid-block region, officers Menendez and Blake spotted two females, later identified as . . ."

After two hours, her bladder felt like it might burst. She grabbed Jessica and bolted out an exit into a dark alley. Where was she? She didn't know this street. If there was a gas station or something around, she didn't see any. In pain and desperation, she got between two cars parked in the alley . . .

"Between a blue 1996 Ford Bronco and a convertible gold 1982 Mercedes 380SL roadster, officers Menendez and Blake witnessed the two females engaged in what appeared to be . . ."

Lauren remembered pushing down her panties, lifting her skirt, and squatting. She held onto the two cars for balance and let go. As the tinkles hit the pavement, the agony finally began to subside. Then . . . fuck! Cops!

"Officers Menendez and Blake cited the two females. One for public urination. The other for conspiracy to commit public urination. The two were released on their own recognizance with the promise to appear." The panelist closed the police report.

"Is that what happened?" the young man in the center asked.

Lauren thought of arguing. What was she supposed to do? It wasn't healthy to hold it for so long. The club is really to blame for not having enough bathrooms. Maybe she should sue the water company that supplies the club, since that's what started the problem in the first place. *Calm down,* she told herself. Her father said Community Court was the best deal around, and she should just shut up and take her medicine. No matter what the court decided, the verdict was better than sitting before a real judge and having a criminal record. OK, she could play along. She opened her mouth, ready to confess.

"Yes!" Jessica interrupted, a little too loudly. "That's *exactly* what happened."

"Do you agree?" the young man looked at Lauren.

"Uh, sure," she said.

The panelists mumbled to each other a moment.

One of the volunteers, a middle-aged woman with short, red hair, smiled at Jessica, then Lauren. "Look, ladies, I live near that club. I've got kids. We're constantly calling the police about people using that alley as a toilet. How would you like it if someone did that in your front yard?"

Lauren wanted to reach across and slap the bitch. My front yard? A dirty, dark alley in SoMa is not the same as a front yard! *Take your medicine*, she heard her father's voice say. *It's a damn get-out-of-jail-free card!*

"No, ma'am. Of course not. I'm sorry." Lauren nearly gagged on each word.

"Well, then," the young man smiled wide. "The guidelines are pretty simple in cases like this. Two days of community service. You'll both come back into The City, probably on Saturdays, and do volunteer work in the neighborhood. It will give you a chance to make up for the damage you did to the community."

Two days! Lauren was enraged. She had to give up two days of her life for taking a pee in the street! What about the guy who almost pissed on her this morning? People like that get away with everything. No, not her. If you're from the burbs, this town treats you like shit. She held in her outrage. She had to. Her father would be furious if she screwed up the deal.

When they got back into the waiting room, Jessica turned to Lauren. "I hope you're happy."

"What?"

"You're out of control! I keep watching your back, and what do I get for it? Two days of community service!"

"I'm sorry, Jes. I had no idea . . ."

"Grow up! When it comes to getting a city guy, all your common sense evaporates! Let's stop these stupid trips into SoMa. There's nothing here for you but trouble."

"It's not that bad, is it?" a voice said from behind them. It was the young man who headed the panel.

"Oh, hey," Lauren grinned. Now that he was standing up, she could see he was as well-built from the waist down as he was under the sweater. "My friend is just upset. It's not like us, to, uh, you know . . ."

"Get caught with your pants down?" the man laughed. He held out his hand. "I'm Noah."

"You can call me Lolly." Lauren smirked. "You know . . . like the pop."

Jessica rolled her eyes.

"I'd hate for you to leave here with such a bad impression of SoMa. Many of us think it's the best part of The City."

"Why?" Jessica asked, her voice revealing her skepticism.

"Well, think of it this way." Noah said, his arms grabbing the air with enthusiasm. "San Francisco is the most open city in the world. You can come here and be whatever you want to be. SoMa is The City's playground. Here you can do whatever you want to do."

"Except pee in the streets," Jessica deadpanned.

"Touché," Noah chuckled.

"I know what you mean," Lauren said. "We've seen some stuff."

"Oh?" Noah leaned in closer to Lauren. "Like what?"

"We went to the Cocktail Club at a bar called My Place," Lauren offered nonchalantly.

"My Place? You've been there?" Noah seemed shocked.

"Yeah," Lauren studied her fingernails. "No biggie."

"Are you kidding me?" Jessica looked aghast.

"And we went to Bondage-a-Go-Go," Lauren said proudly.

"No way." Noah shook his head. "You did not go to Bondage-a-Go-Go. There's no way someone as sweet as you would wind up in a place like that."

"Maybe I'm not as sweet as I look. I know all the dirty little secrets of SoMa."

"That's it!" Jessica burst. "I'm leaving! Lolly, you're on your own. I'm taking BART home."

Jessica marched down the hall to the hotel lobby.

"What's with her?" Noah asked.

"Ah, don't mind her," Lauren dismissed with a wave. "So what's your job here on the court? You the judge?"

"Officially, my title is arbiter. It's like a judge. I'm supposed to make sure things go smoothly."

"Well, your honor . . ." Lauren traipsed her finger down Noah's chest. Through the sweater, she could feel his firm pectorals. "I'm not sure I've learned my lesson. I think more justice needs to·be handed out."

"You've really been to Bondage-a-Go-Go?"

"Even been to the secret room upstairs."

"Fuck!"

Lauren smiled wide. "Well, that's a start."

Noah made some calls on his cellphone as they walked down noisy Mission Street. After a few blocks they came to the enormous Argent Hotel. In a handoff that seemed incredibly fast to Lauren, Noah returned from the reception desk with a key. "A little nicer than the Rose Hotel, eh?" he said.

The room was filled with light from the floor-to-ceiling windows that overlooked artsy Yerba Buena Gardens below. They grabbed at each other's clothes until they were naked. There was little pretense of romance. This was about animalistic heat and fucking. Lauren got down on her knees and took

Noah into her mouth. He moaned. She got up and took his hand to lead him to the bed.

"No!" Noah sounded panicked. "Not the bed. Uh, the floor. Yes, the floor. I want to get rug burns from you, you Bondage-a-Go-Go whore!"

Lauren liked the verbal abuse. A take-charge man. It was about time.

Noah got on his back and told her to mount him. "Not on your knees, bitch. I want you squatting. Like you did between those two cars to take a piss. Get on me and ride!"

Lauren did as she was told. She shut her eyes and clenched her muscles as she inched up and down, holding herself steady with her hand on the window glass. It felt good. Then there was a distracting noise. What was that? Was the TV on? It sounded like clapping. Very faint. Applause maybe.

She opened her eyes and turned toward the window. A dozen men in uniforms stood in the gardens looking up. One had a video camera. Others were passing around a couple pairs of binoculars. The men laughed, pointed, hooted, and clapped.

"What the hell?" She got off Noah and scrambled toward the back of the room, picking her blouse off the floor to hold against her chest. "Those guys! They can see us!"

"Duh," said Noah.

"What do you mean?" Lauren felt anger rising.

"I thought you said you knew all the dirty, little secrets of SoMa. This is the Argent Hotel."

"So?"

"Uh, floor-to-ceiling windows? Get it? With the curtains open, everyone can see everything that goes on in these rooms. Perfect for exhibitionists. It's famous."

Exhibitionists! She'd been paraded out for all to see without her permission.

"Who are those guys?" she demanded.

"Just some of my friends. They work here."

"Fuck you!"

"Whoa, bitch. Who's the one who kept bragging about how she knew all about—"

"Asshole!" Lauren got up and went to the bathroom.

"Where are you going?"

"I'm going to wipe you off of me!"

"Not here, you're not."

"What do you mean, *not here*?"

"Hey, we're just borrowing this room for a few minutes. Can't get the bed dirty, or use the towels. That's not part of the deal."

"Part of the deal?" What type of guy was this? Even Putt gave her a tissue. "I thought you rented this room. For fuck's sake—you're a judge!"

"Man, you're a stupid bitch. I'm not a real judge. That's just volunteer work."

"Then who the fuck are you?" Lauren screamed.

"Chill, will ya? Don't you get it?" Noah looked at Lauren with disdain. "I'm the bellboy."

Lauren walked over to the window, her blouse still held to cover her chest. When she reached Noah, she took her free hand and slapped him across the face as hard as she could. Pain shot into her hand. She shook her wrist, trying to make it subside. It hurt like hell. But it was a good hurt. From now on, she wasn't going down without a fight.

21

"Do you want me to be naked?" Griffin asked as he set up his table of lotions and other apparatus. "It's up to you."

"Uh, naked?" Raphe was confused. "*You?*"

"Sure. I'll take off my clothes while I do it to you."

"Well, uh, won't I be lying face down the whole time?"

"Yes, mostly." Griffin said. He turned up the dial on a strange electrical contraption that contained tubes filled with a glistening amethyst-colored substance. Raphe wondered if it was some sort of aromatherapy system. The room had that kind of smell.

"If I'm on my stomach staring into a pillow, then there really isn't much of a point, is there? I mean, I won't actually see you, right?"

"Sure, it's just that some guys . . ." Griffin paused. He seemed surprised, or amused. It was hard for Raphe to tell. "Yes, I suppose you're right."

Not that Raphe wouldn't have wanted to see Griffin naked. Even in his clothes, Raphe could tell Griffin had a tight, muscular build. A Bowflex workout system sat in the far corner of the room, not a spec of dust on it. Griffin was cheerful with an ever-present smile. Probably a great kisser, too. With his shining dark hair, Griffin was the type Raphe would have eagerly tricked with in other circumstances. In the gay world of SoMa, he'd learned that sex was as easy as a handshake, almost a common courtesy. The "naked" offer didn't come as a shock to Raphe, though maybe his own refusal did. Was this a sign that he'd fallen in love?

If so, was it with Baptiste? Or Julie?

This was not the moment to think about that. He came here to rid himself of that struggle, at least for the next hour. He needed the release. He'd awakened at three that morning in a panic attack, his mind caught in a loop of agonizing conflicts. He couldn't choose between the two. With either one, there was too much to give up. Baptiste said he didn't mind if Raphe continued to see Julie, if that's what brought him happiness. But Raphe saw through those assuring words as a ploy, a clever lawyer's technique for twisting the Wisdom of Solomon. It was easy to predict that Julie would never be so gracious and would kill their relationship, rather than see it shared—and shared with another man, no less! Baptiste was as smart as he was suave, proposing a bargain he knew no woman would ever accept.

He couldn't bear the thought of losing Julie, that red hair walking out of his life forever. His desire for her hadn't waned, even though he'd reconnected with Baptiste. By seeing them both—by needing them both—Raphe knew he dabbled with catastrophe. The logical side of his mind tortured him for the conflict, but overwhelming emotions trumped reason.

From those nightmares of lost love, Raphe's restless mind that morning then turned to money. Unemployment would run out in ten days. At the rate he was spending he'd be penniless in three months, even with the wages he brought in from Harrington. To fund all the colonics he'd stopped paying his car insurance premiums, and prayed each time he drove that he'd avoid being caught. This led to feeling jittery behind the wheel, actually making him more prone to an accident.

Stop it! Raphe shouted inside his head. He was doing it again, reliving the nightmares. For the next hour he had to relax. Besides, Baptiste was paying for the session. He insisted on it.

No, Griffin could keep his goddamned clothes on. This was strictly business—a service to be provided. It wasn't about Griffin's sexual gratification or glorification of his worthy physique. He could keep his pants on. Besides, there would be plenty of nudity this afternoon. Unfortunately, Raphe dreaded, it would be his own.

Despite all he'd experienced, Raphe still hated that initial moment of being naked in front of a stranger, especially in the gay world. Baptiste assured him he didn't have anything to be ashamed of, that his body was one to be coveted. Still, he saw how men in The City worked so hard on their appearances. They toiled at the gyms to craft each curve to perfection. They cultivated wardrobes with astonishing detail. Even the dressed-down, working class sloppy look was one that was highly manufactured. A costume. Whenever Raphe spotted a man with messy *bed head* hair, he knew it wasn't because the guy had just crawled out from under the sheets—that coiffure took at least twenty minutes of intense work to achieve. None of these efforts appealed to Raphe, so when it came to his own semblance, he thought himself an outcast. The guy who will never quite fit in. If he was really gay, God had forgotten to give him the queer eye fashion gene.

Even when clothes weren't involved—or maybe especially so—Raphe felt intimidated by the competitive nature of the gay looks game. One exceptionally sunny day, Baptiste suggested they go to San Gregorio, the cruisy nude beach south of San Francisco. Besides being loaded with perfect bodies, the stretch was notorious for dozens of little structures made from driftwood that men crawled into for sex. It took little more than a furtive glance to initiate a sweaty session in one of these so-called "condos." Those who didn't want to join were welcome to watch.

Raphe begged off, blaming a fear of skin cancer from too much sun, even though the descriptions Baptiste gave of the spontaneous, sandy orgies tempted him. If there were a checklist involved to qualify as a San Francisco gay, Raphe felt he would surely fail. House music. No. Meticulously groomed. No. Designer clothes. No. Perfect physique. No, not compared to the gym beauties.

If Baptiste hadn't insisted on today's session, Raphe would have never come. Did he really need to do this to fit in? Why did the people who said they loved him push him to pursue such drastic measures? He thought back to Julie's high colonics. It was like they both wanted to mold him into something he wasn't, to better suit *their* needs and desires. The pushing made him uneasy in the worlds of both Baptiste and Julie.

Still, he promised Baptiste he would at least try this, and he had to admit Griffin seemed an excellent choice for the job. When Griffin answered the phone, he was so pleasant, even in the face of a barrage of pointed questions from Raphe. Yes, he'd done it many times before. Yes, he was a professional. Yes, it would be very discreet. Pain? Well, that really depends on the individual. . . .

After exchanging greetings and being shown to the table, Raphe stripped completely, frenetically tossing his clothes into a pile on the floor. He knew if he went slowly, he would chicken out and keep his underwear on. That would have only delayed the inevitable, giving the afternoon the tensity of a strip tease. Get it over with. Waiting could create some sort of anticipation that might make him aroused, like when he was a teenager at the nude beach and was forced to lie facedown to hide his lack of self-control. How humiliating.

Raphe got onto the table, stretching out prone with his face turned sideways on a large bed pillow. Its freshly laundered smell comforted him. He shut his eyes.

He felt Griffin's hand gently brush his back. "It *has* been a long time, hasn't it?"

"Actually, I've never done it before," Raphe said. The mood and smell of the room, the embrace of the soft table and Griffin's soothing voice made Raphe relaxed enough to think he could doze off, even though he feared agony from what was just ahead.

"So I'm your first?" Griffin seemed genuinely concerned, the tone in his voice reminding Raphe of his grandmother. "Don't you worry. I'm going to take good care of you."

Raphe heard a click and a slight buzzing vibrating through the air. The sound got closer, passing by his ear and down to the base of his spine. It felt good as it touched his flesh.

"The secret to doing this right," Griffin said, "is making sure it's just the right length." Raphe felt pressure, but no pain. Enjoy this prelude. Torment would be just ahead. What was wrong with him? He knew so many gay men who enjoyed having this done—they got off on it. In some ways, he wanted to be one of those men, to fit in so completely that something like this would become routine, even desired. Gay. Straight. Neither world was completely inviting.

Baptiste promised this would help open him up and make Raphe more comfortable around other gay men. Once finished, they could go to places like Dolores Park together and freely mingle, with Raphe then feeling like he belonged to the club. The park was nicknamed Dolores Beach by the locals, even though there wasn't a lake or drop of water in sight. Instead there was a sea of towels and blankets, colorful platters serving up a buffet of The City's most stunning men, all sunning themselves shirtless. After today, Baptiste promised, Raphe could join their ranks and feel completely at home.

Raphe craved belonging like that. To be accepted. He bit

down into the pillow, preparing himself for the intrusion of pain he was sure would strike at any moment.

"Yes, that's the trick," Griffin said, his voice now slightly singsong, the way people tend to talk when they fall into creative concentration. "You need to make sure all the hair is exactly three quarters of an inch before you do anything." The vibration from the electric trimmer felt soothing.

After clipping, Raphe's back was wiped and patted with a soft towel. Then Griffin grabbed one of the glistening bottles from the heating tray and applied the wax.

"It contains honey," Griffin explained. "It's a special blend I'm trying out." It was warm, but not too hot against Raphe's skin. Griffin pressed down a piece of cloth firmly over the ooze. Raphe reached under and grabbed the legs of the massage table, bracing himself for tearing and suffering.

Pffft.

That was it. He knew it had happened because he felt a slight jolt, but where was the pain? Had it really been done at all? Surely it wasn't possible to have it done without the constant need to hold back tears. He'd heard the pain could be excruciating, especially the first time. Raphe thought back to the colonics that went so easily as well. Was he some type of freak whose body was built to endure discomfort?

"The second trick," Griffin continued in his lilt, "is to make sure to follow the direction of the hair and pull it from its roots. Otherwise, all you're doing is breaking it at the base. That really hurts, and it doesn't last for long."

When the last area was waxed, Griffin sprinkled powder and rubbed to soothe. "Now I need you to lie on your back."

With the heavy weight of impending embarrassment, Raphe made the turn. But if Griffin had any misgivings about Raphe's body, he didn't share them. No giggles. No telltale cough. Raphe felt at ease. It wasn't that he was more proud of his physique, or he'd achieved some progress in gay body perfection. Griffin's

caring manner had made him comfortable. Now it seemed somehow okay to lie completely exposed.

Griffin took out the clipper again, and started on the chest.
Baptiste had explained that "manscaping" involved complete
gay grooming body hair care. That meant trimming down the
chest to create a uniformed, sculptured look. It was all about
staying current and fighting the sprouting elements that betrayed one's true age.

"Guys try to do this themselves, but here's where they always make a mistake. They take off too much. Then they end up
looking weird—like adolescent boys." Griffin clipped the pubic
hair. Raphe smiled, pleased he had the self-control to get
through all this. A handsome man had just spent half an hour
touching him all over, and not once did he feel aroused. Was it
maturity? Surely he'd grown up since those days on the nude
beach when he was a teenager. Maybe he was finally learning to
accept the eccentricities of the gay world and was no longer rattled by new experiences in it. Of course, there was no need to
make any of this sexual, since it was little more than a mundane
haircut.

The buzzing moved up against Raphe's shaft. To get close
enough, Griffin took it into his hands and pulled directly up, allowing the clipper to traipse down to the base. Raphe felt a
slight panic. Willpower was one thing, but Griffin was holding it
in his hand and tugging. That combined with the vibrations of
the trimmer—how much could a man endure? He began
thinking of other things. Baseball. No, that's a cliché. How about
a shopping list? He started making mental notes of the things he
needed to pick up at the store later, but by the time he reached
two percent milk it was too late. He found himself fully erect
and pointed directly at the overhead light.

"Um?"

"Oh, it's OK," Griffin said, continuing his styling with the
trimmer. He apparently wasn't bothered at all. Instead, he ap-

peared relieved, as if his work had just been made easier now
that fallen timber had been cleared from the path. "You shouldn't
be embarrassed. With the buzzing there's no way to stop it. Frankly,
you lasted longer than most."

Even after Griffin let go, and the vibrations ended, Raphe's
arousal would not end. It acted as if it were somehow proud that
it finally got to reveal itself in all its glory, putting on an award-
winning performance, and it wasn't going to let the moment
end anytime soon. *Cut it out*, Raphe begged. Even when Griffin
presented a hand mirror so Raphe could see every inch of the
finished job, the standing ovation continued.

How strange it looked. With the hair all trimmed so neatly,
the clock of age had been turned back. Maybe too far. It looked
childish. Without all the hair, his body seemed that of a boy, except for the erection. With that so prevalent, the image made no
visual sense. He grasped it to try to hide it. Is this really what he
desired? Is this what he had to do to finally belong?

"Thank you for making me feel so comfortable," Raphe
said as he got dressed and paid. "You really provide a unique service."

"I'm happy to help. I know there's a real need for something
like this. It's not like you can ask for it at Supercuts. Feel free to
tell your friends."

Raphe nodded. "I do have one question, though."

"Yes?"

"Well, it's about the nude part. When I first arrived, you
asked me if I wanted *you* to do this naked. I'm just curious,"
Raphe hesitated. "I mean, how often do people say yes—that
they want you to be nude, too? Is it rare?"

"Oh, honey," Griffin said sadly. "You are the first person to
ever say no."

22

In his new circle of gay friends, Raphe learned that few were known by only their first names. Instead, a colorful adjective was added as a precursor to better determine exactly who was being discussed. Since there were at least three Bobs, one was referred to as Tall Bob. Another was known as Fat, Bald Bob. The third was called Loud Shirt Bob, because he once wore a particularly noisy polyester burst of a top to a party. Baptiste explained that people weren't being cruel. They were just descriptive, since so many uninspired parents in the sixties and seventies had depended on monosyllabic common names for their sons. Without adding titles, how would you know who anyone was talking about?

Fair enough, Raphe thought, until he realized the trend went well beyond just distinguishing between men with ordinary first names. *Everyone* seemed to have a descriptor added, even if his moniker was unique. Raphe asked to know what his was, but Baptiste refused to say.

This week's edition of Game Night was small compared to others. Just the two couples. Black Jeremy and White Steve playing Trivial Pursuit with Raphe and Baptiste. *Bad Boy Baptiste.* Raphe wondered how he earned that nickname.

"Madonna," Jeremy said flatly.

"I haven't even asked the question yet," said Steve with comically exaggerated exasperation.

"Arts and Entertainment?"

"Yeah."

"Then the answer is Madonna," Jeremy smirked knowingly. "This is the eighties version of the game. At least half the answers to the entertainment ones are Madonna."

"That's ridiculous."

"OK. Go ahead. What's the question?"

Steve turned up the card to his face, carefully cradling it to hide the answers from everyone else at the table. He cleared his voice, and paused for dramatic effect. "Which Detroit-born singer is known as the *Material Girl*? Dammit!"

"Yeah! A pink wedge!" Jeremy crowned his playing piece, then threw his arms up in the air as if he'd just scored a touchdown. Raphe and Baptiste laughed in unison. Moments like these were what made Game Night so fun. It was one of the trendy things to do, providing an escape from the routine of the bars. If they had been straight, they might play these games with their own children. Since they didn't have that type of family, they created their own, embraced the nostalgia of their youth, and turned back the clock to be kids themselves.

"Did you hear what happened to Cheap Dave?" Steve chimed in, purposefully making Jeremy wait for the next clue. Dave had the unpleasant habit of always scrutinizing every group restaurant tab so he would only pay for exactly what he had consumed, right down to the penny, rather than simply split the bill evenly. It was a habit that earned him the title "cheap," although no one ever called him that to his face. "He got arrested at the airport."

"Don't tell me," Baptiste said. "During the shoe check at security they noticed those Pradas he wears are fakes."

"And pretty bad ones at that," Jeremy joined in. "It's even spelled wrong!"

"No, nothing like that." Steve's expression suddenly became serious. "He got picked up for cruising the bathroom."

"The bathroom?" Raphe was constantly amazed by the endless tales of where and when men cruised each other. When he was straight—he was still a little straight, wasn't he?—he'd been oblivious to this other world of cat and mouse sex games. Now he noticed it happening nearly everywhere he went. A furtive glance, a wayward hand against his behind in the cramped MUNI metro, the scene at the gym. He assumed all of these things existed before he ever made his way to men. Why hadn't he seen them before?

"You know how it is," Steve continued, then looked at Raphe. "Oh, I keep forgetting. You're new." He explained that the bathrooms at San Francisco International were notorious for hook-ups—they seemed to be designed specifically for men to check each other out. The walls and ceilings were made of shiny, black tiles, each with enough gloss to act as reflective, dark mirrors. A man sitting in a stall simply had to look straight up to see directly into the cubicles on either side. If a neighbor also peered up, they would make eye contact, and an erotic exchange could begin. Leaning back they would gratify themselves in full view of one another, the visual stimulus prompting quick climax. Word of mouth had made the scene such a craze that it gained a mention on the web site cruisingforsex.com. The publicity made the bathrooms at SFO a destination for gay men from all over the world, to the point where even the feeble airport police began to take notice.

"So there's Cheap Dave, whacking away in unison with some young guy, and suddenly there's a loud bang on the stall door. It's one of those big, black police batons," Steve continued. "Those same black tiles that allow you to look over to the next guy also give the cops a view into what you're doing from ten feet away. Cheap Dave got nabbed."

"That's awful," said Raphe, remembering his own trauma of being caught in the act with a friend when he was a teenager.

"It's worse than that. Turns out the other guy was only fifteen. So now Dave faces charges as a sex offender. He was arrested, taken downtown to the jail, and forced to hire a very expensive lawyer. He missed his flight to Turkey!"

"If he had just kept it zipped up," Baptiste scolded, "he was just hours away from having all the teenage boys he could possibly have wanted."

Jeremy got the next play wrong, a science category question about photosynthesis. When it came to Raphe's turn, he picked up the dice and clenched them in his fist. "I want to play a different game."

"What? I am so close to winning!" Jeremy squealed.

"No, that's not what I meant. We can keep playing this. I'm just curious. You know," he looked over to Steve, "because I am so *new*. I have some questions."

"Oh! So you want to play *I've Never*," Steve jumped in, a little bit too enthusiastically. "That's a great game. Each guy takes turns saying something he's never done, but suspects the others at the table have. If he's right, and they admit it, then he gets a point. Let me go first . . . uh . . . I've never blown anyone at North Baker Beach."

"Shut up!" yelped Jeremy. "I told you that in confidence— and that was long before we ever met. . . ."

Raphe laughed. He enjoyed the little bits of staged drama between the two men. Would he and Baptiste get to that level of playfulness in their relationship? Or would he have that with Julie? "Guys, that's not want I meant. I want to know about real games. Games that guys play with each other. You know, in order to score. I'm writing a book, and I think this would be great material. You already told me about the airport and Cheap Dave. I want to hear some more unusual ways that guys find other guys."

The three other men looked to each other. "You're serious?" Steve asked.

"Yeah, I want to know some of the ways you picked up guys, or were picked up. The really strange stuff."

"OK, I'll go first," said Jeremy, not waiting to give anyone else a chance to speak. "I was walking down Howard Street one day, and a guy rode up in a Jeep. One of those open-topped ones. Just swerved right over to the sidewalk, pulled a fifty dollar bill out of his pocket and not so subtly waved it next to his knee so I could see."

"Not the fifty dollar story again," moaned Steve.

"Shut up! You'll get your turn." Jeremy continued, "So I looked over, with my eyebrows raised in a little *Is that for me?* expression. It was surreal. I'm around thirty at this point, and well past what I would have thought was the age to be a prostitute. And the guy was hot! He was a little older, with bits of gray at his temples, but he was handsome in a rugged way. White guy, of course. I suppose there should have been a little voice inside me that screamed *serial killer* or something. It was weird. I wasn't scared. Instead, I felt this instantaneous urge of excitement. Without saying a word, I climbed up in the Jeep. This was near 11th, so he took a couple turns until we ended at the dead end of Dore Ally off Folsom Street. In broad daylight mind you, but for some reason I just didn't care. I took his fifty, dropped my pants, and let him suck me off right there. I never came so fast."

"Last time you told this story it was a twenty," Baptiste jabbed. He took a big gulp from his third martini. It was Friday night, his usual time to toss back a few to unwind.

"Fuck you."

"I heard it was a five," Steve jumped in.

"Fuck you!" Jeremy reacted in mock offense "OK, smart guy. You tell Raphe a story. Your turn."

"OK, I've got one." Steve put both hands down flat on the

table, assuming the position of a serious storyteller, purposefully making eye contact with each of the men as he spoke. "I was headed out late one night for a trick—back in my single days, of course—and went down Stillman, one of those alley streets. About halfway up the block a man and woman are having a fight. She's yelling at him about what a loser he is, how she hates him, and all this shit. As I get closer, I can see she has something in her arms. A bundle or something. I can't get a good look at the guy, because he's out in the middle of the street, and cars on the sidewalk are blocking my view. But from the waist up, he is a really good-looking guy. Hispanic. No shirt. Beautiful, lean, hairless brown body, with longish, dark hair. He's yelling back to her, in Spanish. I can't understand what he's saying, but it's clear he's really drunk.

"I'm thinking maybe I should turn back and find another way to go, but something about the fight draws me closer. Maybe because the guy seemed kind of hot. As I got near, the girl becomes just bullshit crazy mad. She's now yelling at the top of her lungs, also in Spanish, but you don't need a translator to know she's fed up with this guy. Then she takes the bundle and throws it down the block . . . in my direction! I duck as it just misses my head and lands on the pavement behind me. The girl then runs into a nearby doorway, still swearing her head off.

"When I turn around, I see behind me that the bundle was really a pile of clothes. Shirt, shoes, socks . . . and jeans . . . and underwear. That's when the guy comes over from the street onto the sidewalk ahead of me. Turns out they are *his* clothes. He's naked!

"So you have to picture the scene. There I am face to face with this beautiful Latino stud. He's naked, and the only thing between him and his clothes . . . is me. His girlfriend has ditched him, or kicked him out. To top it all off, apparently they musta been in the middle of something when all this drama happened, or maybe the fight got him excited, because the guy is *hard*. He's pointed straight at me with a big uncut, so firm the skin has been pushed back almost all the way.

"I can't help myself. I just stare right at it. He notices me looking, and in a moment of shame that somehow got through all that alcohol, he puts his hand down to try to cover himself. But he can't. No hand is big enough to hide that thing. He fumbles for a moment, and ends up clutching his shaft for cover, but lets out a little moan at the recognition of his own touch.

"I make eye contact with him and smile. He grins back. Honestly, I don't know what he was thinking, but I went for it. I walked right over and took him in my hand. Next thing I know I'm sunk down and going at it."

"Shit," Raphe exhaled. He'd visualized every moment of Steve's story. He even knew that block on Stillman. "A straight Latino hunk. That's incredible."

"No kidding! It was like a fantasy. One minute I'm headed off for a run-of-the-mill late night blo and go, and next thing you know I am dining on Mexican *al fresco*! But then the guy says the most messed-up thing."

"What?" Raphe said breathlessly.

"As I have the guy in my mouth—in my mouth!—he says, 'You aren't one of those *gays*, are you?' I couldn't believe it. Even for a drunk guy that was possibly the stupidest thing I've ever heard. So I spit him out, got up from the ground, and walked away. He just stood there stunned, still pointing out at full tilt, his clothes in a pile, and me disappearing into the distance. The guy didn't know which way to turn."

"You finished?" Jeremy snapped. "In the two years we've been together, I musta heard the Latino story at least twenty times. You gonna throw those dice, Raphe?"

Raphe tossed the cubes to the board, where they landed with a muffled thud from the moist envelope of sweat that now covered them. "Madonna," he said.

"What?" griped Steve.

"Arts and Entertainment. The answer is Madonna."

"Oh, please. Not that silliness again. I haven't even picked up the card."

"Go ahead."

Steve reached for the clue, once again keeping the text shielded from the other players. He cleared his throat. "'In 1985, what pop music singer married actor Sean Penn?' Dammit!"

Raphe smiled. "Your turn, Baptiste."

"No, it's not. You got the question right, so you get to roll again."

"Not this," Raphe explained. "It's your turn to tell a story."

"A cruising tale? OK. I've got one. It sounds like everyone thinks these stories about picking up straight guys are hot, so I'll tell one of those. Actually, it's not really a specific story. Instead, I'll share with you a technique."

Baptiste took another big gulp from his martini, on the rocks with a twist, no olive. "When I want to bag a straight guy, I go right for the soft spot."

"His nuts?" Jeremy giggled.

"I get to his nuts—eventually. And the rest of him," Baptiste smirked. "But how I corrupt him has nothing to do with sex, at least not at first. I start by lubricating him with . . . flattery. A nice, friendly, nonthreatening dinner. I make sure there's plenty of strong red wine, since that tends to chip away any inhibitions. I like to take them to Bacar, since that's right around the corner from my house. I convince the guy he's too drunk to get home, and suggest he crash at my place. Once we get there, I pull out a bottle of nice scotch. Something smooth that goes down easy and eliminates any anxieties. Once we get comfortable, that's when I pull out the special weapon—the one thing guaranteed to make a straight guy fall to his knees."

"Your big cock?" Steve joked.

"I'm talking, of course, about the guy's relationship *with his father*," Baptiste continued. Raphe noticed the other men nodded their heads in agreement. "Get him to talk about that. Straight guys are so emotional about how they relate to their dads. How they never get hugged and all that shit. Most of them start crying, or at least get tears in their eyes. You hold them. That's when you know you've got them. Before you know it, you're fucking them, and then you own that ass. He'll do whatever you want."

Raphe felt something on his cheek. Something foreign. It was different than the sensation of someone touching his skin. Whatever it was rolled down his face, hugging the curve of his nose, until it landed on his lips. Instinctively his tongue darted forward to taste. Salty. The taste of a tear. Betrayal, Raphe discovered, did not have a bitter flavor. It was akin to the sea, the same taste that flowed from men.

"You asshole," Raphe finally spoke, his knees unsteady as he stood up to leave. He wanted to flee as soon as Baptiste started telling his tale, but he was too paralyzed to move. At first he felt embarrassment that his love was revealing their story to others in such a callous, cruel way. Then he realized it was not *his* story, but in fact the recipe for countless conquests by Baptiste of which Raphe was only the latest. Raphe's shame turned to anger, then hate. *Bad Boy Baptiste.* What had he done to deserve this?

Julie's face flashed in his mind. She would never turn on him like this.

He left the door ajar as he walked out, but no one followed.

"What's that about?" asked Jeremy.

"Fuck," said Baptiste, dropping his head to the table in disgust. "I forgot. That's how I got him into bed the first time."

"You need to be more careful," chastised Steve. "They don't call him Retard Raphe for nothing."

23

With unemployment running out the next week, Raphe looked desperately for ways to pinch pennies. In addition to dropping his car insurance, he canceled his satellite TV service and no longer picked up a latte on his way to work. He decided to fall behind in his condo dues after reading in his homeowner's agreement that he'd need to owe at least a year's worth of payments before any action could be taken. A year. Surely, he'd be back on his feet by then. He'd neglected to chip away at the little extras he'd paid for with his phone service, but turned out to be grateful for this omission. Calls from Baptiste came in almost hourly all weekend, and caller ID allowed Raphe to simply turn and look at the phone with scorn.

"Hey, handsome." It was Julie, stopping by 225 Folsom on her way to work. "Where you been?"

"Hey," Raphe replied somberly from behind the counter.

"Ah, Monday morning Raphe. I remember that mood. Writing not going well?"

"It's OK."

"Get much done over the weekend?"

"Some," he lied.

"My trip down to Carmel for the off-site went well . . . thanks for asking."

"Sorry." Raphe stared down to the counter. From the corner of his eye he saw Mr. Harrington watching and listening from the other side of the room. He should mind his own business.

"What's the matter? I was kinda hoping I'd hear from you last night when I got home. You know, it has been five days since I saw you. I thought maybe you missed me a little."

"I did. Really. Sorry, I'm just in a shitty mood this morning. Feeling a lot of pressure right now."

"Not the stomach thing again? You said you were over that. Maybe you need to get another colonic."

"No! I mean, no, it's not that. I just had a revelation over the weekend."

"A revelation. Hmmm, that sounds serious. Wanna tell me about it?"

Raphe paused. He couldn't share with Julie any of the drama with Baptiste. Here she was, the most incredible woman he'd ever met, and for some strange reason *she* wanted *him*. *Snap out of it and stop being such a morose jerk*, he scolded himself. *You'll lose her, too.*

"I missed you."

"Really?" Julie's voice sounded hopeful.

"Yeah. That's it. That's what all this is about—my revelation." He was making it up as he spoke, but a truth began to emerge in his mind. After being forsaken by Baptiste, Julie was the only light remaining in his life. He needed her. He loved her. "I feel better now, just seeing you."

It was true. The red hair, the perfect smile, the pull of her— it was the wake-up call Raphe needed to emerge from the cloud of Baptiste's betrayal. Raphe cupped his hands out over the counter and held them there until Julie dropped hers into his.

The next few minutes were a blur, even while they were happening. Raphe tried later to recall all the details, but everything happened so quickly it was like watching a videotape on fast-forward, with ripples distorting the picture.

"Hold it right there!" a loud, deep firm voice commanded. "Let go of the girl!"

"What?" Raphe turned toward the front door. A man dressed all in black stood with a pistol drawn, the barrel pointed squarely at Raphe's head. A half dozen others in the same uniforms scurried in behind the man, also armed. Harrington, who was mulling about near the mailboxes, immediately dropped to the floor, his arms stretched out.

"Don't shit me! Don't shit me!" Harrington cried.

Julie cautiously pulled away from Raphe's grasp and stepped back. They both put their arms up in the air. Raphe noticed the insignia on the men's uniforms. FBI. It was the raid Harrington always feared.

"Get down on the floor you MUTHAFUCKER!" the commander of the operation yelled at Raphe, continuing to point his gun. Shaking, Raphe stepped out from behind the counter and slowly got to his knees. Gently he placed his palms on the filthy tile, stretched prone, and closed his eyes in terror.

"You all right, miss?" Raphe heard the officer ask Julie.

"Yes," she stammered. "I-I'm fine. What's this all about?"

"You work here? Reconnaissance said there were only two involved in the shop, the older Hispanic and the younger Caucasian."

"No, I live upstairs," Julie meekly explained. "What's happening?"

"Bad things, ma'am. Bad things."

"What type of bad things?"

As Julie and the officer spoke, the other gunmen scattered throughout the office, trying to determine if there was anyone else present or hiding. When they finally realized it was just one room—"This dump doesn't even have a bathroom!" one officer said amazed—the all clear was given.

"Stand up!" one of the officers said as Raphe felt a kick in his side. As he groveled to his feet, he saw the horror in Julie's face. All he could do was shake his head, hoping she would understand this had nothing to do with him. An officer violently grabbed Raphe's wrists and jerked them behind his back into handcuffs.

"What bad things?" Julie asked again, her words now soaked in fear.

"Scams. Cons. Identity thefts. A lot of lives have been ruined because of this place," the commander said as he gestured to the officers across the room to lift Harrington off the floor, also in cuffs. Raphe noticed how Harrington no longer had the jovial face he carried with him to work each morning, that expression now replaced with something angry and sinister. The commander wiped sweat from his brow up into his thick salt-and-pepper hair, using the moisture as makeshift grooming to keep the wavy locks off his face. Raphe noticed the man's moustache also had specks of gray and was meticulously trimmed.

"I don't understand. It's just post office boxes." Julie was exasperated. "You must have it wrong. You make this sound like organized crime."

"That's exactly what it is, ma'am," the lead officer explained. "Not just this shop, but others like it across The City. Raids like this are happening at all of them as we speak. We're closing 'em down. Half the scams you see on the internet are run out of this chain."

"So what does that have to do with Raphe?" Julie looked into Raphe's eyes. He could see her desperation.

"If he works here, he's part of it."

"That can't be true. He's just a clerk." Julie walked over to Raphe. "Tell the officer you had nothing to do with this," she pleaded. "Raphe. Tell them. Raphe!"

"Did you say Raphe?" the officer asked.

"Yes."

"That's me," Raphe finally spoke, his voice crackling.

"Well, miss, maybe you're right." The officer put his gun back in its holster and walked over to Raphe. From his back pocket, he pulled out the warrant, unfolded it, flipped several pages, and held it up to Raphe's face. "Is this you?"

There on page four was Raphe's name. The paragraph described a complaint filed by Troy Stuber at California National Bank, detailing Raphe's identity theft out of the Haight Street branch of Harrington's empire.

"Yeah, that's me!" Raphe practically yelled his relief. "That's the complaint filed by my bank. Someone used my name to run up a scam, and the bank said it would launch an investigation. Yes, that's me!"

"You isshole!" Harrington burst out. "You betray me!"

"No, Mr. Harrington. Honest. I mean, I knew there was someone with a mailbox at your shop in the Haight that ripped me off. But I never blamed you. It was the bank—"

"You bistard!" Harrington struggled to free his hands from the cuffs to lunge at Raphe, but two officers held him back. "I'll keel you!"

"Mr. Harrington, no. Really. It wasn't me."

"I'll keel you!"

"Okay, now. Everyone just shut up!" The commander gave the entire room an ugly glare. "It turns out that Mr. Raphe here has friends in high places." The agent motioned for another officer to remove Raphe's handcuffs.

"I do?"

"Yes, a *special* friend of the agency. Mr. Baptiste Martinez. He contacted me over the weekend and told me you needed help. Something about a bank loan being in jeopardy for a long time because of this scam. I've known Baptiste for years. He's a great guy."

"Who's this Baptiste?" Julie asked.

"Just a friend of mine."

"A good friend, I guess," said Julie. She looked relieved, but puzzled.

"I'll say," the commander continued, now smiling with a knowing grin at Raphe. "He told me you're his new boyfriend. Congratulations. Baptiste is quite a catch."

WINTER

24

"Lolly, I don't want to put this on my forehead," Jessica said as she stared at the round, blue sticker. "It's gonna leave a mark."

"Oh Jes, gimme a break. You've got enough makeup on to repel a terrorist attack. That little bit of glue ain't gonna hurt."

"But I don't get it. Why do I have to stick a blue dot on my forehead? I'm not Indian, you know. Besides, they have pink dots, too. We shoulda picked the pink dots. You know, pink is for girls. Blue is for boys."

Lauren sighed. How many times would she have to explain this?

It was her first time, too, at a Pink Slip Party, one of the last vestiges of life from the smoldering ruins of SoMa's dot-com world. The nightclub on Harrison opened on a slow weeknight for high-tech workers and potential employers to gather. People looking for jobs wore pink dots on their foreheads. Those doing the hiring marked themselves with blue. The idea was to break the ice quickly in a casual atmosphere, lubricated by alcohol, so both sides could walk away with new leads.

"Jes, how many times have we come all the way in from Concord to the clubs in SoMa to meet guys?"

"Seems like a million."

"Right. And how many times have we found an awesome guy?"

"Uh, never?"

"That's right."

"So why are we here?"

"Because this time, I'm finally gonna call the shots. I'm gonna find a hot-looking guy, and I'm gonna make him do what *I* want," Lauren said as she pulled down her tight, green sweater, inspecting to make sure it looked snug in the right places. "I've made a decision, Jes. I don't need a boyfriend. What I really need is a 'fuck buddy.'"

"Lolly!" Jessica didn't even try to hide her disgust. She wondered when Lauren would grow up and realize sex wasn't the only way to attract a man, at least not the type you could keep.

"The fact is I'm gonna be twenty-seven soon. I've got *needs*."

"If all you want to do is have sex, you can do that back in Concord. What about that guy Jay over at H&R Block? He's kinda cute."

"An accountant? Geesh! I don't want to be a pincushion for some prick to give a few pokes until he loses it." Lauren believed she could size up a man's sexual abilities with just one glance. She'd sit outside Starbucks at the mall and make predictions about each man who passed. *Cums too quickly. Doesn't even know what a clitoris is. Bad kisser.* And on rare occasions, *Oh yeah.*

Even if she saw one she thought was worthy, she knew bagging him would be all too easy. City guys—they were the challenge. Although except for the room4rent fucking, she had to admit it wasn't going very well.

"I'm sick of being a receptacle! I want a man who's sexy and creative. Even a little bad. Someone who will become dedicated to *me*. I have a better chance finding all that with guys in The City. Let's face it, they're smarter and more sophisticated. What's that word? Oh, yeah. They're urban."

"You mean, urbane."

Lauren marched them over to the corner of the room where the two women had full view of the event. Hundreds of pink dots all swarming around a handful of blues.

"Lolly, I still don't get it," Jessica said. "If we put these blue dots on, people are going to think we're from some company doing hiring."

"Exactly."

"But we're not!"

"Take a look out there, Jes. As soon as we press these dots on our heads, we'll be the center of attention. At most SoMa bars, we're just another couple of blondes from the burbs. But when these dots go on, it will be boys, boys, boys!"

"And then what?"

"Then I get to pick the best one, and invite him for an *in-depth* interview."

"Yeah, some out-of-work loser."

"Oh, I'll put him to work, Jes. Besides, I told you, I'm looking to be worshipped—every nasty part of me. At least for a night or two. What's that old saying? I gotta get 'em in the church first, *then* make 'em listen to the sermon."

"You're going to hell, Lolly."

"At least I'm honest."

"What company are you gonna pretend you're from? You'd better have a good story, or else they're gonna know you're a faker."

"I dunno. What's a good one? Oh, I know. I'll say I'm working with that one in all the commercials. You know, the one with the cute sock puppet dog that does all those jokes."

"Pets.com?"

"Yeah! That's the one. It's perfect."

"Bankrupt."

"What?"

"Pets.com went out of business," Jessica smirked. "A *long* time ago."

"Shit. OK, how about Webvan? That's kinda kewl."

"Busted."

"Fuck. What's that one your kid brother got his college textbooks from?"

"Bigwords.com?"

"Yeah."

"Gone . . . years ago."

"Jes, you're not helping! Isn't there *any* company still open?"

"If you're gonna be a liar and pretend to be hiring for a big dot-com company, then maybe you shoulda read a newspaper in the last three years. The reason there are so many pink dots is because everyone's out of work!"

"Oh, fuck that. I'll just make one up."

Lauren grabbed the blue dots, pressed one onto her forehead, and the other onto Jessica's. They got only a few feet into the crowd when a stout, masculine-looking woman stopped them.

"What company are you from?" the woman barked.

"Uh, it's called," Lauren paused. "Lauren.com!"

"You mean, like Ralph Lauren?" the woman asked as she took a fresh résumé out of a manila envelope.

"No, it's different than that."

"Well, it doesn't matter what you're selling. I'm in IT. I can fix anything." She thrust her résumé into Lauren's hand, then turned and searched for the next nearest blue dot.

"What the fuck is IT?" Lauren whispered to Jessica.

Variations on the same awkward scene repeated over the course of the next hour. Instead of men, Lauren clutched a stack of résumés in her arms. Each person seemed increasingly more dysfunctional as the evening wore on, with some so nonverbal they could only muster the courage to hand over a résumé and silently slip away.

"Hi. You hiring?"

The voice came from behind Lauren. Sexy and masculine, it sounded somewhat familiar. Lauren looked to Jessica, who could see who it was. When her friend's face lit up in a smile, followed by an eager subtle series of head nods, Lauren turned around.

It was Raphe—the handsome guy with the short hair and soul patch from the room4rent day. Lauren caught her breath, suppressed the rise of embarrassment that tried to envelop her, and put on her best game face.

"You?" Raphe said. "Lolly, right?"

"Nice of you to remember."

"Well, uh, I hadn't heard from you since that day. I was kinda hoping that . . ."

"Let's not talk about that right now," Lauren said, using her eyes to gesture toward Jessica.

"Well, it's so good to see you again," Raphe said as he reached out and gently took her hand in his. It wasn't a hand-shake, so much as a touch of affirmation. "And you're a blue dot."

Raphe couldn't believe his luck. Maybe things were chang-ing for him, the breeze of karma finally blowing in the good di-rection for once. Since the raid on 225 Folsom he'd hit a new low. Even standing in the Pink Slip Party, the horror of that day came rushing back like a slap in the face. Whenever he was in a crowd lately, he relived the pain.

Julie had dumped him on the spot, not even bothering to take him out of earshot of the FBI squad and Harrington.

"You're queer?" she had yelled.

"Julie. It's not what you think. . . ."

"You have a *boyfriend*!"

"I never said that," Raphe said. The FBI commander backed off slowly, seeming to realize his remark had fouled the room more than any tear gas canister.

"Fuck! It sounds like everyone else knows about it!" Julie bit into the knuckle of her forefinger. "When were you gonna tell me? Is this why you haven't been around for weeks? Or maybe that was your real revelation this weekend—that you like to . . . suck cock!"

"Julie. Don't," Raphe begged. He was past any hope of salvaging his pride, having his life implode like this in front of an audience of other men—the commander, the FBI agents, and Harrington. They all stared. He tried to block them out by tunneling his vision on Julie. He saw the pain she felt. The confusion. How could he explain to her what he really didn't understand himself?

"I'm not gay."

"Then what are you?" Julie spoke bitterly.

"I'm Raphe. Just Raphe. I can't describe it any other way."

"And this Baptiste?"

"He's real."

"Gay?"

"Yes."

"And you're not? Is this supposed to be some sort of cruel joke? *I'm not gay, but my boyfriend is . . .*"

"Julie . . ."

"You cheated on me! You have no idea how many men ask me out. But I picked *you*. I thought you picked me," she wept.

"I did—"

"I should have known from the first time you told me your name. Raphe! Do you even know what that name means? That should have been my first clue!"

Raphe didn't understand what she was talking about. His name? Raphe was his mother's maiden name. That's all. "Julie—"

"No, no, no. Don't say *my* name. It sounds dirty coming out of your mouth. A mouth that's been . . . god-knows-where."

"I still love you," Raphe implored.

"Love? How can you say that? Love means you want to be

with me. And only with me! The way I wanted to be with you—*only* you." Julie's face changed. From being on the verge of hysteria her expression had calmed into a look far more wounding. Bitterness. "You can't even decide between men and women."

"It's not about making a decision. It's not as simple as choosing sides."

"Not simple? Look, I live in San Francisco, too. Our great fucking open society where everyone who comes here gets a clean slate to be whatever he wants. Especially when it comes to sex. We get all the options here. No judgments! I get it. So don't make me out to be some sort of bigot. I will not allow you to do that. This isn't about going this way or that way. It's about you being with me. Only me. You weren't. You lied. You betrayed me."

Julie sighed. The resignation in her voice hit Raphe in the gut. His mind flashed back to the hurt he felt when the tables were turned—when he discovered he'd been the victim of Baptiste's deceit. He'd inflicted on Julie the same horrible pain. Was there any worse feeling than betrayal? Now Raphe was the villain. It didn't feel any better to be on the other side.

"But I still love you," he begged.

Raphe wanted Julie to say she still loved him, too. That she could accept the fact that he was stuck somewhere in the middle of things, trying to sort it all out. It wasn't about picking sides, distinguishing between right and wrong, white or black. His life was about shades of gray, a multitude of different grays, like the gritty buildings that populated SoMa.

No such embrace came from Julie. She opened her mouth to speak. Instead of words, she put her hand over it to try to stifle a combination of gasp and wail that didn't sound quite human to Raphe—a despair so deep he'd never heard anything like it before. Julie looked around the room, searching the faces of the police officers as if for help or solace. They looked down at their shoes, nervously avoiding her eyes. Then in a sudden panic, Julie bolted from the store. Raphe was paralyzed, unable to do anything other than watch as her bright, red light dimmed from his life, heading down the street until her ruby glow could no longer be seen.

That night the phone rang and the caller ID again revealed it was Baptiste. This time Raphe picked up the phone. Baptiste had heard from the commander all the details of the raid and the scene with Julie. He apologized for setting the disaster in motion, explaining that he was just trying to do something to make amends and help Raphe after being "such an asshole" at Game Night. Lonely and wounded, Raphe went to Baptiste that night, and once again felt the strength he needed. No more dramas, Baptiste assured, pledging to make everything between them right again.

Baptiste did as promised, Raphe marveled. More than friendship or sex, they began to develop a type of intimacy Raphe never thought possible with a man. In the month since their reunion, they'd rarely slept apart. No more swinging with others or exploring The City's kinky underground. Now it was just the two of them. Reading the Sunday paper in bed, watching TV, browsing bookstores—all done together as a couple. Raphe found it astonishing how mundane it all seemed. After all, he was with a man. That's not *normal*.

Baptiste appeared to be in a state of bliss—he never stopped smiling. The only thing he said he worried about was Raphe's job, or lack thereof. He vowed to get Raphe back on his feet. "A man is not fully a man unless he's working," Baptiste said, claiming it was something he constantly heard growing up in the Mission. It was Baptiste who found the posting for the Pink Slip Party on the internet and suggested Raphe go and network. Without the money coming in from Harrington, and unemployment gone now, Raphe desperately needed a real job.

A job. It was the only thing holding him back.

Raphe emerged back into the present to the noise of the Pink Slip Party, staring into Lolly's eyes.

"You hiring?" Raphe forced a smile.

"I'm certainly in the market for someone," Lauren smirked.

Raphe enthusiastically handed over his résumé. They had fun that day, didn't they? He tried to remember if he'd done anything that might have offended Lolly, the woman who now held his fate in her hands.

"Brown, class of 1999, huh?" Lauren bit onto the eraser end of a pencil for dramatic effect. "You haven't been in the job market for many years." She remembered how fun he was the day of the room rental hook up, with his athletic build and that tuft of hair under his chin. She liked the way it brushed her cheek when he kissed her earlobe. Now, forced to do her bidding, she could feel those little hairs caress wherever she demanded. And not just another one-time thing. This would be their second time. Forget the idea of a fuck buddy. Fate had given her the opening she really wanted—to finally make a city guy her own.

"Well, no. But I've worked on dozens of sites—I was at a major web developer before it went under. I have a ton of experience. I can do anything: programming, design, project management. You name it—anything."

"Anything? It sounds like you're bragging," Lauren toyed.

"No, I mean it. I've never failed to bring a project in. I do whatever it takes. Long hours, all-nighters."

"You know, Raphe, I think you have potential. You are perfect for a position I have in mind."

"Well, thank you, Miss, uh . . ."

"You can call me Lauren."

Raphe was puzzled. Didn't she introduce herself last time as *Lolly*? Maybe that was some sort of nickname. "And you work for Lauren.com?"

"I own it, actually."

Raphe thought back again to that afternoon. He was pretty sure she told him then that she was some big time recruiter from the financial district. Of course, maybe she just wanted to keep the truth confidential. After all, it was now clear she was quite successful. It made sense to him that she'd need to be careful about what she shared with people she didn't know very well. "That's awesome. And what exactly does your company do? I can't wait to sign on and take a look at the site."

"Well, let's talk about all that. It's just, well," Lauren looked around the room, "so crowded in here. I wonder if there's any place quieter where we can be alone."

"I live just a block from here, remember?" Raphe grimaced when he realized he shouldn't have said that in front of the other woman. She must be some work colleague of Lauren's, he figured. "I mean, you can see right here on my résumé." He pointed. "That's my address. I live very close. Unless you think that's not appropriate. After all, you don't know me very well."

"Oh, I know you just fine, Raphe," Lauren giggled as she dangled his résumé in her fingers. "See, I've got your whole life right here."

"Can I talk to you?" Jessica interrupted.

"Raphe, this is my personal assistant Jessica . . ."

"*Privately*," Jessica said through clenched teeth, refusing to respond when Raphe offered his hand to shake. The two women turned and huddled a few feet away.

"Cute, huh?" Lauren bragged.

"Are you shitting me? Lolly, you don't even know this guy. We're not talking about some nightclub or bar where you can yell for help if you get in trouble—you're going to his apartment."

"So?"

"So? So as your best friend, I have to finally say . . . *no*. Do *not* do this. It's so self-destructive. It has to stop. I just can't stand here anymore and do nothing!"

Lauren looked at her friend. In that instant the girl she'd known since childhood—they even double dated together—was transformed into her judging father. That same superior tone of disgust and condemnation.

"I'm not asking you to stand there and do nothing," Lauren said. She took the stack of résumés she'd accumulated throughout the evening and plopped the bulk into Jessica's arms. "Hold these."

Raphe gently grasped Lauren's hand and tugged her through the crowd of pink dots and out a side door that led to a small alley. Up the block, just past the fisting club with the tattered sign "America: Open for Business," they reached Raphe's building.

It was just as Lauren remembered, with the breathtaking views, more spectacular now that it was night. The thousands of lights from The City sparkled like diamonds.

"Oh, yeah. The place," Raphe said, recalling the pretense of their first meeting with some embarrassment. "I never did get that other bedroom rented out. I guess there's a glut of rentals now on the market. Who would've ever thought that could happen in San Francisco? When I first moved here, The City was booming. You couldn't find an apartment no matter how much money you had." Raphe paused. "I'm sorry. You came here to interview me for a job, and now I'm babbling. Talk about making the wrong impression."

"You're not making the wrong impression," Lauren flirted. "In fact, you're doing quite the opposite."

"Hey, let's look up your site," Raphe walked into his bedroom and fired up his computer.

In a panic, Lauren wedged herself between Raphe and the screen. She pushed the keyboard shelf under and slowly wiggled herself onto the edge of the desk, placing the opening of her skirt within Raphe's reach.

"Oh, let's not look at the site right now," she said, in the sexiest, bossy voice she could muster. "It doesn't matter what Lauren. com is today. What I want to know is what Lauren.com can be . . . in your capable hands."

She bent down and took Raphe's grasp into her own. The rest took little more encouragement.

It was different than their first time. Lauren now took control, and Raphe obliged. He wanted so much to please—a job at Lauren.com could be the answer to so many problems. Lauren's demanding spirit reminded Raphe, in a way, of sex with men. Like when he was with—

Baptiste! What was he doing? They'd just made their peace and agreed to give it a try as a couple.

"I want us to commit," Baptiste had said. "That's all I've ever wanted. Just you and me. No more messing around with other guys. And, for god's sake, no more women. Agreed?"

"Yes."

The moment repeated in Raphe's mind. Already he was cheating.

It's a job, he told himself. As long as he kept himself emotionally detached and just followed Lauren's orders, he convinced himself he could justify the experience as a type of work application. Wouldn't Baptiste want Raphe to contribute to their partnership as an equal? That's what *partner* implied. He was fucking Lauren *for Baptiste*. For the health of *their relationship*.

Raphe ran his fingers and lips over Lauren's body, acting as if each inch of flesh represented a new sensation for him. His pleasure became completely secondary to hers. He buried his face inside her for what seemed like nearly an hour, flicking his tongue on her cues to bring her to climax. He eagerly followed her instructions on exactly where to press on the inside, as if no one had ever told him of this place before. He only entered her when she demanded, then followed her every instruction precisely for speed and force. The sex was all about *her* needs. Raphe held back and released after several hours, and only when commanded by Lauren to do so.

In the morning, they greeted the day with laughter, noticing they each still wore the telltale dots on their foreheads.

"So did I get the job?" Raphe asked with a grin.

"Well, you did pull an all-nighter, as promised."

"I told you I do whatever it takes," he said. "But seriously, did I get the job?"

"Well, about that job . . ."

"What?"

"There's a little problem with Lauren.com."

"What? You want me to go down on you again? Did I do it wrong?"

"Oh, Raphe, no. You were great. I've never been with a guy who was so into pleasing *me*. You pushed all the right buttons, followed all my commandments."

"Then what is it? What's the problem with Lauren.com? I'm sure I can fix it, no matter what it is."

"The problem with Lauren.com . . ." She paused and pulled the sheet up over her mouth. "Promise you're not going to hate me?"

"What is it?" Raphe had stopped smiling.

"Well, there is no such thing as Lauren.com. I made it up. I just wanted to meet some cute guys, and I thought . . ."

"No such thing!" He jumped out of the bed, pulled the sheet off Lauren, and wrapped it around his naked waist. "No such thing! I don't understand. Then what the hell was all this about? You just used me . . . for sex?"

"Hey!" Lauren covered herself with a pillow. "Guys use girls for sex all the time. Besides, you only had sex with me because you thought it was going to get you a job. Remember? So who's using who here?"

"I can't believe this," Raphe mumbled. "I can't believe this!"

"Jesus Christ! It's not that bad! At least you got laid! Isn't that all guys want?"

"What this guy wants, you stupid bitch, is to be able to pay his fucking bills! I am going to lose this place if I don't come up with a way to pay for it. Now I can't even do that. And even worse . . ."

Raphe sat on the edge of the bed, his body collapsed into tears. He sobbed so uncontrollably Lauren sat down beside him and tentatively stroked his back. She'd never seen a man cry before.

"I'm so sorry, honey. I had no idea things were so bad. I never meant to hurt you. I just wanted to have some fun. I guess I was only thinking of myself. You're right. I'm a bitch. I only cared about getting a cute guy. It was all about me, and you got hurt. I'm sorry about that. I really am."

Raphe kept crying.

"But it's going to be OK. You'll find a job. And if you can't afford to keep the condo, you'll just find another place to live. It's only an address. You gotta have faith."

"It's worse than that," Raphe moaned.

"Worse? I don't understand." Lauren became indignant. This guy acted like having sex with her was some awful crime. Who was he to judge her? That tone in his voice. Just like her father's admonitions. "How can having sex with me be so bad?"

Raphe wept harder. He fell onto his back on the bed, then yelped through the tears. "I cheated on my boyfriend!"

"What?"

"Baptiste! The man I love!"

"What the fuck are you saying? You telling me that you're one of *them*? A gay?" The anger flew up through Lauren. Betrayed *his boyfriend*! What the fuck? A goddamn queer! The gays had stolen another one from her, someone she'd loved not once, but twice! He was on the path to be hers! It wasn't right.

Lauren seethed. This weeping faggot, through his girlish tears, had the audacity to sit in judgment of *her*? As if she had done something wrong. If a man used smooth talking to get a woman in bed, he'd be seen as clever. Like her brother. The jock who screwed half the girls in high school, so popular her father bestowed him with the beloved nickname "Stud." How different it was for her. The slap at eleven when she got the earrings. "Slut!" At thirteen a nosy neighbor called her parents after spotting Lauren kissing a boy at the movies. Just a little kiss to thank him for inviting her. When she got home that night, her father beat her so severely she had to wear long sleeves for two weeks to hide the bruises. "Whore!"

Now this man. This Raphe. Gay—not really a man at all. He actually thinks he can call the shots? Reject her and make her feel ashamed for who she is? No. Her way was the right way. *He* was the infidel. He and his kind threatened everything.

The rage quickened under her skin, making her blood feel as if it simmered, blistering into a sharp pain, like the stab of a knife, behind her right temple. It made her wince, thinking only that she needed to make it stop. End it, she told herself. This was the line crossed too often. Someone needed to defend her faith against shit like this, to teach a lesson to those who refused her.

She saw what she needed on the desk, remembering it from the first time she visited. With preternatural agility and speed, she leaped from the bed, grabbed the weapon, and struck.

Raphe was too startled by the sudden attack to defend himself and didn't realize what happened at first. Somehow she had pinned him to the bed before fleeing from the room.

Then there was the pain. Agony like nothing he would ever be able to describe. It came from his left hand, a throb that pulsed up his entire arm. He tried, but couldn't move it. He turned his head to look. Blood on the sheets, seeping out at a volume so frightening it made him convulse. His hand was pinned to the mattress, stabbed through the middle by the schwag letter opener, still gaudy with its fake tribal design and tacky message.

"Uganda get it."

I sure did, Raphe thought. *I sure did.*

25

"That would be great if we were just another lame dot-com," Mark Hazodo said, clearly bored.

It was the fifth time in a week he'd sat through a weak presentation by marketing consultants for NeverEnd. His company. He founded it. But the VC guys insisted he listen to all the pitches. It was the third round of venture capital funding, and to secure the fourth Mark had to finalize his plan for where the company would go after the IPO. VC money was so hard to come by these days, especially for anything tech.

Flash. Splash. MP3. *Do these idiots really think I don't know what this stuff is? Like they have to explain it to me?* Mark grew up on the web. Now guys twice his age, with a fraction of his knowledge, thought they could advise him. They were still in the twentieth century, along with their wardrobes.

"Gentlemen." Mark tried to speak calmly, but with each word his voice infused with growing passion and anger. "The name of my company is NeverEnd. It's a game that allows players to construct their own universe of characters and plots. It is as limitless as the number of ideas these ten million users can contrive. They sneak into this fantasy world of their own making. They do not want rap music pumped out of their computer speakers as they sit in their ten-by-twelve beige cubicles. They don't need links to homegrown porn stories of Picard-slash-Riker. And they do not want frames popping onto their screens with bulletins about Jennifer Aniston!"

Mark stormed out of the conference room, his cheeks slightly flush, annoyed with himself for *showing face* to others. How much more of this could he take? Don't these VC guys get it? When you're a company on the cutting edge, there's no one up ahead to show you the way.

"Another bad one?" Jeannine asked as Mark turned the corner toward his office.

"I don't know what bugged me more. The fact that the information was so dated, or the fifty-year-old guy who made the pitch wearing a Fox Racing sweatshirt."

"He was getting jiggy with it, huh?"

"Word to your muh-tha." Mark mocked a gangsta gesture.

"I'm glad you still have your sense of humor," Jeannine smiled. "I understand this is a big month for you."

"I guess."

"You guess? Twenty-five years old. That's a milestone in a man's life."

"Yeah. Now begins the slide. . . ."

"You'll be forced to cut back on *E* and *K*," Jeannine laughed.

"What will I do without them?"

"Don't forget the inevitable bouts of *ED* just a few years ahead."

"Like Bob Dole?"

"Pretty soon that hair gel is going to start looking foolish."

Mark grinned and put his arm around Jeannine in exaggerated affection. "Thanks. Thanks so much for making me feel better."

Jeannine was the only one in the company who wasn't afraid of Mark, and he loved her for that. Putting her in charge of HR was his best hire, even if she was a bit nosy about his personal life and kept track of things like birthdays. She was the only one to make him somewhat humble and grounded. Maybe it was the fact that she looked like a dowdy, middle-aged housewife, even though she was barely thirty. The company's Mom, he nicknamed her.

That week a *Wired* magazine cover story dubbed Mark the boy genius of video games, recognized for reaping astonishing success when the rest of SoMa's tech world lay in the ashes of the scorched dot-com earth. He'd turned his lifelong love of head games, intrigue, and collecting experiences into a way of life for millions of gamers. Mark was on fire.

"Don't forget about tonight," Jeannine reminded.

"Do I have to?"

"It will be really fucked up if you aren't there." She tugged his arm to bring him in close. "I know you think all this is bullshit, but you run this place. You need to give people who work for you the chance to do some quality ass-kissing. It's important to them."

"Why?"

"Honey, if you don't let people brownnose, they'll start to think you don't love them."

Love them? These people didn't really know him. They thought they did, and that they had some sort of relationship with him, but the face—the compartment—Mark contrived for them to see was mostly fiction. They were just employees. Paid friends.

"Think of it as another game, Mark," Jeannine said. "See how many people you can trick into thinking you really like them."

"A game." Mark grinned. "I'll be there."

Mark never came to this part of Mission Street. At least not to stop. He'd driven by plenty of times while headed in or out of

SoMa, usually on a trick. He'd never actually pulled over to park and walk around. Twenty-first and Mission was a mixture of dollar stores, drug addicts, and people who didn't speak English.

Up the street he spotted an out of place building with a beautiful facade and valet parking. In the Mission? This must be it. The address matched the one Jeannine had scribbled on a Post-it for him.

"You here for the Mark Hazodo party?" the valet asked.

"Better than that, buddy. I *am* Mark Hazodo!" He tossed the young man the keys to his black Range Rover and walked in under the marquee.

Foreign Cinema was a combination outdoor movie theater with fine dining. Old, foreign films projected onto a huge, painted white brick wall overlooking the motif of a sidewalk café. Mark heard the food was incredible, but a friend warned the clientele was mostly obnoxious Eurotrash and Pacific Heights brats. He wasn't sure which group was worse. They were both self-centered with inherited wealth whose only pathetic ambitions were to earn bad reputations.

None of that tonight, Mark reasoned. He made his way down a long, cement corridor to enter. At the end of the hall, he saw one of the company's underlings spot him then slip behind a set of red, swinging doors.

"Excuse me, sir." A hostess standing behind a wooden podium stopped Mark as he approached. "Tonight is a private party. The restaurant is closed for regular business. This event is by invitation only."

Mark smiled. "Ah, so your job is to stall me while they get their act together, eh?"

"You've seen right through me," the hostess flirted.

"How much time did they tell you to kill before letting me in?"

"Only a few seconds," she said as she peeked over her shoulder through a little, round window in the door. "You can go in now."

Mark paused for a moment as he placed his hands on the swinging, double doors. Then with one dramatic swoosh he pushed them both open.

"For he's a jolly good fellow! For he's a jolly good fellow! For he's a jolly good fellow . . ."

As the crowd of more than two hundred continued their corny serenade, someone placed a bubbling glass of J in Mark's hand, and the endless series of pats on the back began. He was ushered to the chair of honor at the end of a long table especially assembled and covered in a gleaming, white linen tablecloth for the occasion. The VC guys had gone all out.

One by one the guests paid their deference.

What did he plan to do this weekend to celebrate? Mark had his fake responses carefully memorized.

Meeting Gina in Carmel.

Yeah, she really wanted to be here tonight, but got stuck in LA for work.

No, not sure where we'll be staying.

Yup, I heard the Inn at Spanish Bay is great, but it's up to her.

Gina made all the arrangements.

It's going to be a surprise.

Never met her? We'll have to set that up someday. . . .

What a bunch of dumb fucks, Mark thought. They'll believe any fiction I spin, as long as I look sincere. Even a fake girl-friend. He remembered his real plans for his birthday weekend and smiled.

26

The surgeons told Raphe he was lucky. Somehow the blade went right through without destroying any tendons or fragile bones. They gave him all the free samples of Vicodin they had on hand when Raphe admitted he didn't have health insurance. The doctors said the healing would be painful, since the hands were the main pathways to feeling, but there would be no permanent damage.

Maybe not physically, Raphe thought.

Breathless, Baptiste burst into the ER cubicle. His face was full of worry. Staccato panicked yelps flew out in between gasps for air. "I got here as soon as I could! Are you OK? Oh, my God! Look at you! Are you OK? When I got your call, I freaked! Are you OK?"

Raphe tried to come up with a story to explain what happened. Some writer. His fabricated tale started at the Pink Slip Party and ended in an assault by homeless crack addicts in an alley on the walk home.

Baptiste spotted the bloodied "Uganda get it" letter opener, the one he'd seen countless times on the desk next to Raphe's bed.

"And these attackers had just been to your bedroom, stole

this . . . and then coincidentally used it to stab you?" The tone of Baptiste's voice quickly changed from concern to prosecution.

When Raphe was attacked, he called 911. The EMT crew mistook the weapon for something actually from Africa and brought it to the hospital for testing, fearing the possibility of some foreign contamination. Now it was bagged and waiting as evidence for the police.

That awful feeling of being caught overwhelmed Raphe, just as it had when he was a teenager. Then again with Julie during the raid at 225 Folsom. He was guilty, no doubt, and figured his only hope was a full confession. "OK. I wasn't attacked on the street."

"No shit."

"What really happened is . . ."

"I don't care what *really* happened."

"What?"

"You don't have to be a fucking attorney to add up the facts in this case. You had someone in your bedroom! A fucking trick gone bad, and now I'm here to help you clean up your mess. Again! Like when you let that Asian guy Mark cum in your ass!"

"It's not like that." The image of Mark Hazodo's face flashed in Raphe's mind. In the ER waiting room he'd seen a copy of *Wired* featuring Mark on the cover. *Mark Hazodo. I hate that guy.*

"You weren't screwing some guy last night?" There was anger in Baptiste's voice.

"No." Raphe looked at his bandaged hand. *Tell the truth,* he told himself. No matter how bad the truth is, it's better than spinning a lie that would surely trap him later. "I was with . . . a girl."

Raphe shut his eyes, prepared for a verbal assault. Instead, the room was silent. Several beats went by. Nothing. He heard a patient in a nearby room coughing loudly. Still nothing from Baptiste. Not even the sound of breathing. Raphe sheepishly opened his eyes, his face begging for forgiveness.

"You know, Raphe, you're a piece of shit," Baptiste said, his voice scratchy. He thought back to the first moment he spotted Raphe on the platform of the BART station. Such a handsome man. A clean slate of sorts, the type Baptiste believed he could mold. He'd hoped Raphe was a keeper. New—not yet damaged like so many San Francisco men. Despite how he acted, Baptiste had long ago tired of hedonism. Deep down, he wanted the real thing. Love. Uncomplicated, devoted love.

"I was at that job party, and she said she had work for me. The next thing you know—"

"The next thing you know," Baptiste stopped himself. In court he'd grilled many witnesses on the stand, trying to separate the truth from their deceit. Was that what he really wanted to come home to each night? "The next thing you know," defeat soaked his words, "you've lost a boyfriend."

Raphe returned home from the hospital, not quite sleeping or living, and curled up onto his bed. He stewed in the haze of painkillers for two days, unable to assuage the torment of what he'd done to Baptiste. He betrayed the only one left who loved him. Now guilt. It hurt more than his hand. The bloody spot where he was stabbed remained on the sheets, a constant reminder of his failure. He was too far into the abyss to think of anything as practical as laundry or cleaning or eating. He obsessed about calling Baptiste to grovel for forgiveness, but when he tried to write that dialogue in his mind, he realized it all sounded so pathetic.

Wednesday night he drew up enough strength to move the few feet over from his bed to his keyboard. Without satellite, his television was worthless, The City's hilly terrain made over-the-air reception nearly impossible. Now his computer was all that connected him to the outside world. Maybe he'd find some bit of salvation there to roll away the stone and free him from his cave of misery.

Raphe!

Do you even know what that name means?

That should have been my first clue!

Julie's final screams of anguish rolled through his mind. He'd hurt her horribly, too. Also in a way that could never be forgiven. What did she mean about his name? A clue? A clue to what?

He went to websters.com and typed in "Raphe."

ra·phe also **rha·phe** ($r\bar{a}'$ $f\bar{e}$)

n. pl. **ra·phae** ($-f\bar{e}'$)

1. *Anatomy.* A seamlike line or ridge between two similar parts of a body organ, as in the scrotum.

There were other definitions, but he was sure Julie once said his name had an anatomical meaning. This must have been what she meant. A seam? On the scrotum? He didn't know such a thing existed. He peeled down his boxers, noting how fetid they'd become after three days of wear. The manscaping session had trimmed away so much hair that very little had grown back, making his body continue to appear almost adolescent, allowing for an unobstructed view to areas below he'd never studied before. He cupped his testicles and held them under the light of his desk lamp. There it was. A seam.

Why had he never noticed it before? Fascinated, he took his forefinger and gently traced the seam down from the base of his shaft to beneath the twin sacks. It didn't end there. He felt it continue, all the way to his anus. Like it connected the two areas.

He went to the bathroom to get the hand mirror that came

with the clipper kit he used to trim his soul patch. Putting it on
the floor, he squatted over the reflection to see what he had
been touching. A perfect line that ended in two vastly different
worlds. At one end was his manhood, the source of procreation
and pleasure with women. At the other was the part of him men
desired most, where they offered the type of ecstasy a woman
could never provide.

The raphe. It was a line between these two places. It was in
the middle, enjoying its proximity to both destinations, the
dominant and the submissive. In between. It didn't pick sides.

Raphe put his face in his hands and cried. He never believed in destiny, but here it was shining up from the silvered
glass beneath him. The word fate that Julie so often used to describe their love. From birth, his *fate* was to be somewhere in the
middle. The universe had conspired to even name him this way,
lest he be too stupid to figure it out on his own.

He once thought desire existed in ones and zeros, like the
computer code language of his former tech life, a forced choice
of this way or that. When he loved both Julie and Baptiste, he
damned the idea of forced choice. He tried to take both paths.
Now he saw there was a space that existed between those ones
and zeros. The raphe. Himself. Raphe.

The pull of obsession, one that had grabbed him so many
times before, hit again. Back at his computer, he went to
google.com. He entered the word "raphe" and the search engine brought him to medical web sites with exhaustively detailed descriptions and definitions, even photographs. He surfed
for hours, trying to learn all he could. He read how all human
beings are at one early stage of life *female*, and only those with
the additional Y chromosome morph into men. The raphe,
some scientists believed, was what remained of what was once a
nascent vagina, abandoned in mid-creation to be replaced by a
penis. Labia, stunted and retarded. A mixed message about gender. Just like himself.

As he clicked through the endless screens of information and theories, a new idea began to form. A revelation. He might be *named* Raphe, a fantastic coincidence at the very least, but surely he was not the only one like this. There had to be others. Those unable to commit to either end of the seam. Others who didn't fit in perfectly into the worlds of straight or gay. Those, like him, who were the seam itself. There had to be a whole tribe of others also living in the gray. He needed to find them. Maybe they could show him how to be happy, and how to love.

Again, he prayed for the computer to deliver an answer. His fingers raced over the keys, tapping into web sites that had guided him in the past.

A posting on craigslist grabbed his eye.

MEN OR WOMEN. WHY CHOOSE? (sf)

Once he clicked on the heading, he found just one word: *Blacksheet*. It was underlined and colored blue, making it a link to another web site. He clicked again.

Blacksheet turned out to be a code for The City's bisexual underworld. He couldn't find any explanation on the site for where the term originated. Instead, he saw photographs of people engaged in orgies, their faces all carefully blurred to conceal their true identities. Men and women. Women and women. Men and men.

Blacksheet called to him through the electronic otherworld of the web. Maybe the answer never was just Julie. Or just Baptiste. He couldn't be the only Raphe. Blacksheet seemed like the best chance for finding someone like himself. For the first time in days he felt a surge of energy and excitement pulse through his body. Blacksheet had a party that night.

He sent an e-mail describing himself. Within minutes a return message appeared in his mailbox, with instructions on where to meet. It was also in SoMa, at a place called the Purple House on Folsom near 12th.

Raphe undressed to shower. He'd left the bandages on his wounded hand for too long, causing the gauze and scab to fuse. He soaked it in a sink of warm water, until the clot dissolved enough to remove the wrap. Despite his careful efforts, the moment of detaching still stung. Raphe took two more Vicodin before jumping in under the soothing jets of warm water. At least the hand wasn't bleeding anymore.

"What the hell happened to your hand?" the bouncer sneered. He looked perfect for the job with nasty eyes, two days' growth of stubble, and arms so pumped up they sent a menacing message of impending violence to anyone who might cross him.

"Just a little accident. It's fine, really," Raphe explained, somewhat sheepishly. "Just needs to be kept bandaged."

"You're gonna need to wear a glove over it." The bouncer pulled from a box on a nearby shelf an off-white rubber doctor's glove, the type that would be used during an exam. He dangled it in front of Raphe's face.

"That?"

"No glove. No love."

Raphe took the glove from the bouncer. "Now," ordered the brute, watching as Raphe struggled to get it over his wounded left hand. The pain was still there, like a constant ache. The ER doctors had also given him latex gloves to put over the wound, but he'd resisted—it just looked so strange, like that of a comic book character. Or worse, since there was only one glove, like a white Michael Jackson. Well, more white, he mused. As he walked down the hall of the purple house, Raphe laughed aloud at his own little joke.

"What's so funny?"

Raphe turned to see an attractive man with umber hair in a

side room pulling off his T-shirt. The man was lean, maybe too skinny. Raphe could see the guy's rib bones, and his pecs were so slight they compared to those of a teenager. Only the face showed age, too much of it to match the boyish body.

"Oh, nothing," said Raphe. "Well, maybe a little Vicodin talking, actually."

"Vicodin," the man smiled. "An excellent buzz, man. Still, you really don't want to laugh at an orgy. Naked people tend to take it the wrong way."

The man introduced himself as Andrew. He showed Raphe where to strip down and grab a towel. As he disrobed, Raphe felt none of the shame he'd experienced in the past, that nervousness now expelled by the drugs. He noticed Andrew staring as he dropped his briefs.

"Vicodin is awesome, man. But it can be a cock killer," Andrew smirked. "And that's a nice cock."

"What?"

"It's a great drug, but messes with your hydraulics. Hard to get it up."

"I don't have that problem," Raphe said as he wrapped a towel snug around his waist.

"Still, why chance it?"

"What do you mean?"

"I've got something to help keep you going, even in the face of Vicky."

"Vicky? Who's she?"

"Vicky?" Andrew grinned. "Vicky is short for Vicodin. A nickname."

"Oh."

"But she's got a great sister. And when they meet, those girls sure know how to party together."

"A sister?"

"Yeah," Andrew held his hand out. In his grasp was a tiny bottle of a crystallized powder. "Vicky, say hello to Tina."

27

Raphe's soul patch had gradually disappeared. He hadn't shaved since the night of the Pink Slip Party. In five days his beard grew in so much that his little tuft lost all definition, slowly melding into the forest of other hair.

"Is there any left?"

"Only one hit, man. Any more Vicky?"

"Gone."

Crashing. They'd been up since the Purple House. The crystal energized Raphe just as Andrew promised, but not just his sex drive. He'd been wide awake for days. Raphe tried to recall all the details of what had happened. He could only cull bits and pieces from the sleepless rattle in his head. He knew for sure that after the orgy they went to Andrew's apartment, an upscale condo on Hawthorne. Raphe remembered walking in and being impressed by the artwork on the walls and the trendy Limn furnishings—signs of very expensive taste.

"You own this?" Raphe asked.

"Naw. A couple of women I know let me live here. They pay for it."

"Shit. I'd love to have friends like that."

Andrew gave Raphe a sweeping look from head to toe, his first chance to get a detailed glance since they left the Blacksheet party. It was so dark in there. He knew Raphe was young and handsome—one of those metrosexual types—but Andrew had no idea how much until that moment. Yes, the women of the lesbian sorority would love to have a young stud like this as one of their Boy Toys. That hand needs to heal first. No, Andrew realized. What was he thinking? If he ever even mentioned the sorority he'd be banished for life. Let it go, he told himself. Just fuck this guy, have some fun, and leave it at that.

Andrew broke into his stash of meth and they'd been awake ever since. Three days. Raphe discovered that crystal made him able to explore sex in ways he never realized were possible. It pushed senses to an extreme level of alertness, so every sensation was distorted and magnified, especially when concentrating on a single feeling. If he thought about the pain in his palm, it would quickly turn into throbbing agony. That torment completely disappeared when he focused on another part of his body for pleasure. In the past, sex meant working toward the climax, an expulsion of joy. On crystal, there appeared to be no destination, only a journey, one more intense than any single orgasm.

An area of flesh could be caressed for an eternity without boredom, creating an endless supply of ecstasy and fascination. They sucked each other's nipples with all the gratification of newborns attached to their mothers. When they finally detached from each other, Raphe realized that four hours had passed in this one position. His nipple was bloated into a raw, swollen, reddish welt.

The crystal had also made the Blacksheet party an inchoate fright for Raphe. When he first came to The City years earlier, a colleague at the web-design firm joked that "San Francisco is a city of great food and great sin. And one of these days I'm gonna eat at one of those restaurants." But when a banquet of sex lay before him, Raphe found it too overwhelming. Enslaved by the effects of the drug, Raphe wanted to explore just one thing. In an orgy that wasn't possible. He was the youngest person in the place and quickly found himself passed around like a joint.

He remembered how the living room of the Purple House was empty, the floor covered in rubbery mats that reminded Raphe of the padding used for wrestling tournaments back at his high school. When he first entered the room with Andrew, people stared at Raphe's left hand with its latex glove. An overweight woman who looked to be in her forties eagerly asked Raphe if he was a "fisting top." When he said no, the woman sulked off, but others who overheard the conversation came over. A woman kissed his neck, while a man went to the opposite side to lick Raphe's earlobe while loosening his towel. The hit of crystal Andrew gave him then kicked in full, weakening Raphe's sense of time and control. He was pulled to the floor and turned onto his back. Both women and men rode him. No matter how many mounted, their styles and skills an intense variety of sensations, Raphe could not climax. Even when he concentrated to try to go over the top, it would not happen. Something had stunted him. Vicky? Tina?

Andrew pulled Raphe up from the floor.

"This crowd is ugly," he said. "I have a better idea for enjoying this crystal. You game?"

During the taxi ride to Andrew's apartment, he explained how the Purple House was part of a sex cult, operating out of similarly painted homes throughout the world. Then he mumbled some nonsense about two old lesbians he let rape him as their Boy Toy. Raphe couldn't keep up with the conversation. It was a blur. Tina had all his attention now.

That was three days ago.

"Ever do a contact high?" Andrew drew a long drag from a joint.

"You gonna blow that smoke into my mouth? We did shotguns back in high school," Raphe said. "Kiddie stuff."

"Not this shit. I'm talking about Tina."

"A contact high with crystal? There's no such thing."

"For a fucking newbie you sure think you know a lot." Andrew took another drag. The pot was putting him in a good place, now that Vicky was spent. He always liked to have something to take the edge off when he did lots of crystal. It was healthier. "There's a way to do it. And it would work for you, man, since you don't usually party with Tina."

"And you?"

"I'm hard-core, bud. I'd have to take the primary hit, and then let you take the ride with me from there."

"Ride?"

"Ever hear of a 'booty bump'?" Andrew asked as he took another drag.

"Sounds like a dance."

"Well, it definitely gets you grooving. It's the most powerful way to party with crystal, without using needles." Andrew looked at the joint and paused for a moment. "Smoking is one way to get high, but it's not the most intense. It's slow, and mellow—awesome right now for this weed. With Tina, you want her all the way inside the house—not just stuck in the front hallway."

"And the booty bump?"

"Well, you take some crystal, and you let it dissolve in water. Then you take a syringe . . ."

"Hey, I thought you said no needles." Even through the blur of all the sex and drugs, needles scared the shit out of Raphe. How could people do such awful things to their bodies for the sake of pleasure?

"Wait, man. Let me finish." Andrew took another toke. "You melt some crystal in water and then suck it up into the syringe—a syringe *without* the needle. Just the plunger. Then you drop trou, and squirt it up your hole."

"You're joking."

"It works, man. The tissue down there is real thin and porous. It's as intense as opening up a vein. And a lot safer. And no blood."

Raphe tried to imagine the scene. A sudden fear hit that he would soon lose his high. Then what? Back to reality. *His* reality. "Let's do it."

"There's a problem, man. That's what I was trying to tell you," Andrew rambled, "and why I asked if you'd ever done a contact high."

"What do you mean?"

"Well, I only have enough Tina left to get *me* going—even with a booty bump."

"Oh," said Raphe, disappointed. "You go ahead. I'll just watch."

"That's not what I meant. Since you're like, uh, almost a virgin, I know a way for us to share. I need the whole dose to make the trip. But I can get you off by recycling."

"Recycling?" Raphe asked.

Andrew set it up. He went to the kitchen and grabbed a large bottle of Calistoga from the refrigerator and stood there until he had consumed all the cold contents. He drank too quickly, provoking a momentary ache in his temple. From a small box in his bedroom he grabbed the remains of a syringe. Once the meth was dissolved into a glass with a skim of water, Andrew sucked the mixture up into the plunger.

He removed all his clothes and stretched out prone onto his bed. He instructed Raphe to take the syringe, gently pry open his hole with his fingers, stick the plunger in as far as it could go, and squirt the liquid up inside.

"I'm gonna lie here and hold it in, so it gets soaked up," Andrew explained. "When it kicks in, then it's your turn."

Within moments, Andrew felt the familiar rush crawl up his body, from the back of his neck and over his forehead to his face. From there the sensation trickled down his chest, landing below his waist to create an uncontrollable urge. He wasn't sure how much time had gone by—meth tended to do that—but all the liquid had flowed through his system and reached its critical mass. His bladder ached from all the water he guzzled. He got up from the bed and pulled Raphe with him to the floor. He peeled down Raphe's boxers and ordered him onto his knees, head down in supplication. Andrew spit on his hand to lubricate and stroked himself hard. When he knew he was ready, he entered—giving Raphe no warning. Once inside, Andrew took a deep breath to relax. He felt the erection begin to subside. Not too much, or he'd fall out. He couldn't go soft, just slightly less than hard. Enough to create the opening for flow—the trick every man with a morning hard-on and full bladder knew. He pushed until the stream of urine released. Relief. The crystal made the sensation feel joyous, like an extended, mild orgasm. He continued to push, knowing it was more liquid than any man could hold in his bowels. Still, Raphe did not cry out or object.

"Don't move, man. I'm gonna pull out now." That should do it, Andrew sighed. He thought of the club boys who would trade piss on Tina. They'd each do a hit and then dance for hours, filling themselves with bottled water all night long. When they'd feel their high start to wane, they'd head to a men's room stall where they'd drink each other's piss to make the buzz last a little longer. The routine would repeat until the sun came up the next day. *Amateurs*, Andrew thought. You can recycle crystal to keep a high going that way, but it was nothing compared to pissing up someone's ass. Why go through the stomach when there's a more direct route?

He marveled over his protégé's ability to hold on. It had already been several minutes, and there was no sign of weakening. On meth, this guy Raphe was a natural, able to take anything without complaints or fear. Some guys could turn into such pussies on Tina, but not this kid. It was like a shield for him. Andrew couldn't introduce him to the Boy Toys women, since that would violate his agreement. But if this kid was up for making some money, his immunity to this type of pain would make him perfect for . . .

"Hold it in there, man!" Andrew yelled as something dripped down to the floor. "Clench! You want the bump, don't you?"

Raphe felt a sensation. It was the crystal, all right. A new burst, riding on the coattails of his waning current high, now pushing him up to yet another level. Remarkable. Yes, this is where he needed to be. A thought flashed in his mind. Was this safe? He recalled the panic of being taken by Mark Hazodo without a condom. Had the crystal destroyed his inhibitions? No, this was different. Andrew wouldn't hurt him. They had Tina in common. Besides, this was just liquid—like those enemas, the *vacations*. He had a real knack for those. Now this.

"Oh, man—Tina is definitely in the house!" Raphe laughed. "And she got in through the back door!"

Raphe closed his eyes. In the rush, all his anxieties disappeared. Julie. Baptiste. That bitch who stabbed him. Money. Job. Mortgage payments. He felt as if he could hold in this liquid forever, as long as this freedom lasted. He never wanted to leave this place. He was finally home, and he knew he'd do anything to stay right here.

28

Lauren looked at the thick, green letters sprayed on the brick wall. The writing was so huge she had to step back to see what four-letter word was spelled.

"Stupid kids," she said to Jessica. "It's supposed to start with a C, not a K."

Jessica sneered back. "You should know."

"Hey!" Lauren snapped.

"Just get back to work." Jessica dipped her brush in the solvent and went back to scrubbing the wall.

"Don't be calling me names." Lauren crossed her arms. "It's your fault we're cleaning graffiti."

"*My* fault?" Jessica dropped the brush into the bucket. "Look at me! I'm wearing a dirty, orange vest with the letters DPW on the back. It stinks like someone else's BO. Like I'm a . . . garbage man!"

"Oh, chill out."

"And how the hell is this my fault? You were the one who got us sentenced to community service!"

"Jes—"

"No, tell me. Please share with me your incredible wisdom on this." Jessica raised her arms. "Here we are back in SoMa, cleaning a skank alley filled with godknowswhat, working an entire Saturday, all because you got caught with your pants down. And this is my fault?"

"Well, when they asked us what we could do, you were the one who said you liked drawing and artwork."

"I thought they'd have us volunteer at a day-care with kids!" Jessica's cheeks turned scarlet. "I meant coloring with crayons, not removing obscene graffiti. I wouldn't have worn sandals if I knew I'd be doing this shit."

Lauren thought about arguing back. After all, she wore sandals, too—it wasn't like Jessica suffered alone. And Lauren's orange vest stank even worse, like ten packs of cigarettes. But when she looked at Jessica's red face, she could see her best friend was at the end of her rope.

"I'm sorry," Lauren said.

Jessica silently picked up her brush and started scouring again. Her hands were raw.

"Face it, honey. The only *manual* labor we know is done by a guy named *Manuel*," Lauren joked.

Jessica cracked a smile.

Lauren giggled.

Jessica let the brush plunk back in the bucket and cackled. Lauren laughed so hard she snorted, which hit her as even funnier. In the silliness, she lost her balance and stepped a few paces back without looking.

"Shit!"

"Lolly, what is it?" asked Jessica, still snickering.

"Shit! Shit! Shit!" Lauren yelped and kicked her foot.

"What?"

"I stepped in a big pile of dog shit!" Lauren shook her leg, trying to get the mess off. It was no use. Crap squished between her toes, oozing into the straps of her sandal.

Jessica's eyes widened. "That's not dog shit."

"Whaddaya mean?"

"Well, dogs don't wipe themselves with toilet paper."

Lauren gagged. Next to the mess sat a wad of used tissue. What type of person goes to the bathroom in an alley? It's disgusting!

She felt a pang in her stomach. She'd done the same thing. Only she was arrested for it. Two days of community service for peeing in the street! That's why she was here in this gross SoMa alley, the same place she'd used as a toilet, condemned to clean. It wasn't fair. Taking a little tinkle wasn't nearly as bad as *this*. Someone took a shit on the sidewalk, and she stepped in it! It was like all of SoMa conspired against her. Because she's from the burbs? She bet the cops never arrested whoever took this dump.

She scraped her foot on the curb. It still wasn't coming off! She was going to have to walk around for the rest of the day smelling like poop! It was probably homeless poop! Who knew what was in it? Maybe she'd die from touching it! She had to get it off. Terror began to overwhelm her. She couldn't catch her breath. She touched her forehead. It was wet. She was sweating like a pig. She never perspired—not even in spin class.

She grabbed Jessica's bucket of cleanser.

"No!" Jessica shouted.

Lauren poured the liquid over her foot. It was brackish and smelled strongly of ammonia, but the shit seeped away. She could see her toes again. Her skin stung a little, but better to be scalded by chemicals than covered in crap.

She tossed the empty plastic bucket up against the brick wall and watched as it clunked to the ground and rolled a few feet down the sidewalk. What was happening to her? It seemed like the whole world was shitting on her. Her eyes watered. Fumes from the solvent? It was more than that. Her head throbbed. She felt woozy. She sat down on the curb, put her face in her hands, and wept.

"Lolly?" Jessica panicked.

Lauren wailed.

"You're crying? You *never* cry."

Jes was right. Lauren never cried. So why now? It wasn't because she stepped in crap. She'd been messed up ever since *that day*. She hadn't had a good night's rest since. When she got into bed, all she could think of was snuggling in the sheets with that guy. He'd betrayed her, and she struck back. Then the blood. God, what had she done? She'd get more than community service now. Maybe prison!

"Lolly! Calm down. This isn't like you. I mean, it's just some shit. It's not the end of the world. We'll go find a place where you can wash up. It will be OK—"

"It's not that," Lauren sobbed.

"Then what is it?"

Lauren had to tell her. Not just because they were best friends. Jessica was smart. She'd know what to do.

"I'm in big trouble," Lauren struggled to speak.

"What?"

"That guy from the Pink Slip Party."

"You're not making any sense," Jessica said as she sat down on the curb. She put her hand on Lauren's back and gently rubbed. "You mean the guy you went home with?"

"Yeah. Raphe."

"What happened?"

"Well, I thought we had a good time. We did it all night long. Then the next morning . . ." Lauren put her face back in her hands. The tears flowed again. She saw the look of shock on Raphe's face. None of this would have happened, if he wasn't a . . .

"It's gonna be OK. Just tell me."

"The next morning we get up, and he tells me he's got *a boyfriend*. He's a gay! Something in me snapped. I picked up a knife and stabbed him."

"Lolly—"

"Then I ran away. I don't know what came over me. All I

wanted was a cool city guy. Every day I've been waiting for the police to come and take me to jail. I can't sleep, I can't think straight. . . ." She tried to wipe the tears away with her sleeve, but they kept coming.

"Was he breathing when you left?"

"Sure. His hand was bleeding pretty bad, though."

"His hand?"

"Well, that's where I stabbed him!" Lauren blubbered, "Haven't you been listening to me?"

"OK, OK, OK," Jessica soothed. "I'm sure he's fine. You just stabbed him in the hand. I bet he didn't even call the police."

"I dunno . . ."

"You don't even know if he was seriously hurt. Maybe the knife didn't go in very far."

"I'm pretty sure . . ."

"Maybe you just nicked him."

"But . . ."

"I bet it wasn't anything worse than a paper cut."

"I . . ." Lauren tried to remember exactly what she saw that day. It all happened so fast, and she'd never looked back. Jessica was right. She didn't know anything for sure. Maybe Raphe wasn't really hurt. If he was, wouldn't the police have arrested her by now? Of course, she never gave Raphe her full name, or told him where she really lived. Hell, even if Raphe did go to the police, she'd never be caught. . . .

"That said," Jessica continued, "I'm worried about you. Honey, you've been over the edge for a while now. I've never seen you so boy crazy, and coming to SoMa has been nothing but trouble. Why can't we just stick to the guys back home?"

Lauren thought about the guys in Concord. Rob. Mike. Paul. Doug. They were all nuts about her. But they were all so *vanilla*. If she went with one of them, wouldn't that make her just as flavorless? She was meant for more than that.

"They're boring, Jes."

"Maybe. I'm just not so sure we're made for this much excitement."

"There's no turning back now," Lauren said. She stood up from the curb and extended her hand to Jessica. "Let's go."

They walked out of the alley, leaving their cleaning supplies behind. Lauren figured she'd make up some story about why they never finished. She'd say they got mugged.

She stopped and turned to look at the brick wall. They hadn't made a dent in removing the graffiti. The word "KUNT" was still there in all its enormous, green glory.

What a word. Spelled with a K it seemed like it could have a different meaning. Suddenly it wasn't so offensive. It had a toughness to it. Empowering even. Maybe that's how she'd think of herself from now on. That's what you needed to survive in SoMa. Be one tough kunt, ready for the battle.

Lauren smiled. *Don't mess with this one.*

29

Mark Hazodo felt something under his shoe. It was metal and scraped on the dusty, cement floor. He turned up his foot to find an old soda cap stuck to the sole of his sneaker.

Figures, he thought. After all, this was once a soda bottling plant. Actually, it was a soda bottling plant until two months ago when he bought out the old, Italian owners. For three generations they bottled their own local brand there in SoMa at the corner of Fourth and Brannan. All those years of dedication, hard work, and struggling to keep the family business alive. What was it all for? Mark made their lifelong toil disappear in an instant, with less cash than he ever expected. The dot-com bust meant buildings were selling cheap these days.

It was prime SoMa real estate. Mark could throw a rock from the roof and hit South Park, once home to so many internet start-ups it earned the nicknames Silicon Alley and Goatee Gulch. Three years earlier there wasn't enough available space for all the new media companies begging for the desired SoMa zip codes. If a company wasn't an "03" or an "07," somehow it didn't get the attention of VC money. One corrupt city supervisor actually proposed extending the zip codes deep into the Mission, as a way to help some friends who owned property there. No one talked like that anymore. Now most of the buildings sat vacant and "dot-com" was only ever mentioned with disgust.

The old bottling equipment was finally gone, so Mark could now fully absorb the marvel of his own brilliance. More than 40,000 square feet of raw industrial space with ceilings so high it looked like an aircraft hanger. Twenty-foot paned windows started at what conceivably could be a third story level. With no tall buildings nearby, the sunlight beamed in to create a magical effect.

He'd take his purchase and rent it back to NeverEnd for a rate that would set records in the current market. Since he signed the paperwork and the property was held by a Delaware corporation he created online with pseudonyms, no one would suspect anything. The money hiding game.

He walked toward the center of the huge room. It was all there. Just as he ordered. He'd hired the staff at the theater prop store near Market and Van Ness to create a scene. It was for a play, he told them. He gave them meticulous instructions on what needed to be on "the set" for the performance. The prop guys' attention to detail was nothing short of exquisite. Maybe they thought he was making a porn movie, and they'd get a mention in the credits.

In the center of the room sat a king size bed, modern but made from beautifully stained wood. Covering the old cement floor, a huge Persian carpet stretched from under the bed to create the dimensions of a large home. Around the edge of the carpet were eclectic furnishings and portable lights. The black leather massage table was a nice touch.

He put his Tumi case on the bed and took out his Vaio laptop. He walked over to a faux Louis XIV desk and chair. Power on. Phone line in. He put his ad up on craigslist under the heading "Birthday Boy."

He inserted a photo of himself, the same face shot used with the recent feature story *Wired* published on him. It was a sexy photo. The *Wired* staff insisted he not shave for a few days, creating a smattering of stubble that created a rugged edge. Mark had stared at the photo many times and once even masturbated to it. *With this picture, I'd even fuck me.*

Normally he wouldn't be so brazen, for fear of having his secret life exposed. But the picture was already so public he knew he could just claim it was stolen and misused by someone else. The video game business was so backstabbing and competitive. It would be a logical explanation. Besides, he couldn't imagine the VC guys or his work colleagues trolling gay sex listings. His parents didn't even own a computer.

The text of his online posting got right to the point: "Celebrating 25 years. Handsome. Masculine. Japanese-American. 5'10, 160lbs, muscular and firm. Hung 8X6. $$$. Will take on all comers in a marathon session to fulfill all fantasies, both yours and mine." For fast response, he included his Instant Messenger account.

The number of IM replies created more open windows than the computer could handle. He'd never before seen the warning YOU HAVE TOO MANY SCREENS OPEN AT THIS TIME.

First he had to pick a spotter, someone to watch his back. A guy who called himself Ward said he'd done it before. At thirty, Ward seemed to have all the right qualifications: a regular at Gold's, The Sling, and The Hole in the Wall. He lived nearby on Potrero Hill. With a dark biker-style goatee and shaved head, his picture made him look menacing enough to be obeyed. He could pack up some toys and be over in thirty minutes.

Perfect.

"Man! I can't believe this place! It is killer!" Ward said as he walked in with a large olive green army surplus duffel strapped over his shoulder. "How did you ever find it, bro? I can see some wild parties happening in this space!"

"Just this one," Mark deadpanned. "Next week it gets turned into offices."

"Fuck that."

"Yeah, it will be lost to greed. So you understand why we need to make the next twenty-four hours count."

Ward dropped the bag and walked over to the table with the laptop. "Who do you have lined up so far?"

"I'm starting off pretty vanilla. I've got five guys stopping by for blo and go. I figure sucking them off will get me warmed up."

"Kewl. I'll work the keypad and get the rest going while you service. But first . . ."

"What?"

Ward smiled as he unzipped his jeans and let them drop to the floor.

Mark nodded. Ward was the blue-collar type he craved, and he wasn't shy about taking care of his own needs. They'd get along fine.

Mark got on his knees and took Ward into his mouth. He buried his nose deep into the hair and inhaled. It smelled like an auto mechanic's garage mixed with Ivory soap. Could this guy really be a gearhead? Mark moaned at the idea. His mouth became too enthusiastic too quickly, and in moments he felt Ward burst.

"That's just a quick preview," Mark said. "Stick around and I'll give you the whole show."

Ward's legs were still shaking as he walked over to the laptop to begin screening and lining up more guys.

Word of the birthday party burned through The City's online world. As men left the warehouse, they went home to e-mail friends, and the number of solicitations for invites nearly overwhelmed Ward. Even with a little coke and a hit of *E* to take the edge off, it was hard to keep up.

Vanilla quickly turned to fucking, and fucking soon became

kink. Mark especially liked the electro-charged paddle, with a combination shock and sting. "Even getting spanked has gone high-tech," he joked. Sometimes he just watched, or kicked back to be pleasured. He allowed himself to be both the top and the bottom, but held back from climaxing to keep his enthusiasm intact.

Playful S&M segued into hard-core B&D. Mark worried he might become noticeably bruised from having his wrists cuffed so many times. Going into the weekend, he thought he would probably draw the line at scat play. Then a man showed up with a folding luggage rack stolen from a cheap motel, asking to do something called a "hot karl." He instructed Mark to sit on the cloth slats, while the man lay face up beneath with his mouth open. "I want to taste the depths of you," he said. Mark wondered if he could move his bowels after being fucked so many times. He felt obliged as a good host to try to give his guest what he wanted. He strained and pushed for a few moments until a generous deposit abated the man's hunger.

By Sunday afternoon and thirty-five party guests later, Mark wondered if there was anything worthwhile left. He'd had every crevice explored with both pleasure and pain, his senses stimulated to their tolerance, and sometimes a little beyond. Exhausted, he threw himself down onto the bed while the latest partier zipped up to leave.

"Ward," Mark said. "That might be my last. Even a pig like me can only take so many times at the trough."

"Hold on, bro. I just found someone you gotta meet." Ward clicked away at the keyboard in a flurry. "Yeah! I can't fucking believe it! It's The Tube!"

"The Tube? Who the fuck is The Tube?" The words barely made it out of his mouth as Mark drifted off into a healing snooze.

He woke when the doorbell rang. "Who is it now?"

"I told you," Ward said. "It's The Tube!"

"Man, I feel like a horse that's been rode hard and put away wet," Mark said in a mock Texas accent. "I'm not sure I can take another oversized dick . . ."

"All you have to do is watch, man. This is *the* hottest show in town. He charges, though, so I hope you don't mind. It's just five hundred bucks."

"For a front row seat at *the hottest show in town*?" Mark laughed. "Sure. Let him in."

Ward raced over to the door. "I'm surprised a guy like you hasn't heard of The Tube. A week or so ago he just appeared—like out of nowhere. It's supposed to be amazing. Everyone online is talking about it." Ward opened the door with the enthusiasm of a giddy child.

The man who walked in had a lean, athletic build. Young, Mark thought, but it was hard to tell exactly how old because his identity was concealed behind a black, leather ski mask, allowing for glimpses of only his eyes, nose, and mouth. A middle-aged woman dressed in a bright white nurse's uniform, complete with matching cap, followed with a large black doctor's bag. Her face was harsh, her expression humorless.

"Hey bro, this is The Tube. Tube, this is . . ." Ward stopped. "Man, I don't even know your name, except Birthday Boy."

"That's all you need to know," Mark smiled. "So, Tube, what is it you do?"

. Tube stood motionless. He appeared frozen by his first look at Mark's face. Then he calmly shed his beige, denim jacket, folding it carefully onto the desk. He looked over at the black leather massage table and gestured to the nurse. She placed the case on the floor and opened it, dutifully arranging its contents for use.

Mark propped his head up with pillows to watch Tube get undressed. Tube peeled off blue jeans and a pressed white T-shirt to reveal a naturally muscular body. Not overbuilt, but nicely proportioned for someone on the thin side, with a modest amount of neatly trimmed hair on his chest, none on his back. Tube stripped naked, but continued to wear a single black leather racing glove that matched his hood.

Tube got on the massage table and stretched out onto his back. The nurse put on latex gloves and bent over to whisper something. Mark couldn't hear what she said, but Tube slowly nodded in agreement to whatever it was. The nurse took a small procedure kit from the case. Mark sat up as the woman tore open the sealed plastic bag and removed a catheter.

She took a container of K-Y from her uniform pocket and applied a large glob to the stem of the clear piping. She rubbed a small amount onto Tube and gently inserted the hollow rod up his urethra. Tube began to moan as soon as it started to enter, his excitement visibly growing.

Mark moved to the edge of his bed for a closer look. The catheter was connected to a line that ran into a clear pouch. As soon as it was inserted all the way, the bag started to fill with bright yellow liquid. Tube let out a long sigh.

When the flow tapered off, the nurse removed the tainted pouch and attached a new one. It was twice as large and filled with saline. She lifted it above her head and stared intensely as the stream reversed, this time into Tube. His teeth clenched when it became clear his bladder could take no more. But the salty river continued. The nurse squeezed the bag to force the last cup inside, but kept the pouch high until Tube signaled her to retreat. She placed the bag on the floor as a torrent of fluid returned home. Throughout it all, Tube swooned, as if the discomfort was actually joy.

Taking out the catheter caused as much groaning as its insertion. Mark held his breath as he watched, wrenching as if he could feel the tearing of inner flesh as much as Tube. When the catheter finally came out all the way, Mark exhaled in relief and turned to Ward.

"I've never seen that before. Thanks, man." He placed his arm across Ward's shoulder.

"Birthday Boy, you haven't seen the show yet. That was just the opening act."

The nurse took another plastic-wrapped object from the case, this one much longer. Her face remained expressionless as she tore off the protective casing to reveal yet another type of tube. It looked vaguely familiar to Mark, as if he had seen it on television somewhere.

The nurse moved around to the back of Tube's head. He eagerly opened his mouth wide. She placed her left hand on his forehead and jerked it back, opening the airway. With acute concentration on her face, she took one end of the pipe and began to stick it down Tube's throat.

"Oh, god, no!" Mark yelled. Both the nurse and Tube darted their eyes at Mark in glares of disappointment.

"It's OK, man," Ward assured. "He's totally into this. The nurse knows what she's doing. Don't worry! Just watch."

"What the fuck?" Mark whispered to Ward.

"It's called bagging," Ward quietly explained. "Like in emergency rooms. When people stop breathing on their own, a tube and bag pump air into their lungs. It keeps 'em alive."

"But this guy is *conscious*." Mark felt nauseous. "He can *feel* that. I think I'm going to be sick."

"Krunk, huh?" Ward grinned.

The nurse looked back down at her work. After maneuvering for a few moments, she was inside. Tube kept his eyes open the entire time, watching even as she attached the large inflating bag. She clenched it in her hand, pumping air into his lungs. With each compression, Tube squinted.

Mark felt a small amount of vomit come up into his mouth. He discreetly swallowed it back down.

After five minutes of bagging, the equipment came out.

Again, the nurse whispered something to Tube. Once more he nodded his head in agreement.

The nurse took from the black case the largest hypodermic needle Mark had ever seen, something he imagined was for elephants, not people. The nurse drew fresh saline into the syringe until it was filled.

Mark cringed.

The needle went into Tube's scrotum. The liquid soon followed. Tube's testicles swelled to the size of grapefruits. After the needle came out, the nurse turned away and walked over to the corner of the Persian rug and lit a cigarette. She took a cell phone out of her pocket and powered it up, making an invasive beeping sound. Mark looked over incredulously. *She just stuck a needle in this guy's nuts, and now she's casually checking her fucking voice mail messages?*

With his swollen testicles bobbing like water balloons, Tube stroked and pleasured himself for his audience. Mark stared and wondered. He'd spent his life collecting experiences, provoking them even, hoping they'd add up to some type of enlightenment. Now here was this Tube *freak*, a man merged with medical equipment for gratification. Had Tube found the answer? A place of true, complete, satiated pleasure? It was too hard for Mark to tell since he couldn't see the face beneath the leather mask. No, this couldn't be it, he reasoned. This guy Tube was searching just as much as Mark. Another step in the journey. Mark smiled. Now that he'd seen it, he wouldn't have to take this detour himself. Like the roulette sex party, the proximity was enough for him to learn all he needed.

"Freaky, huh?" Ward whispered. "Fucked up . . . even for SoMa."

"No shit," Mark sighed back.

"It's called tubing—a fetish way beyond anything done before. You really have to be in a special place to do that, if you know what I mean."

"Do you know this guy Tube? What's his deal? Who is he?"

"No one knows his real name. Word is he's some dot-com debris. Figures, right?"

"Well, they're used to getting screwed," Mark smirked.

Tube rolled off the table onto wobbly legs. Mark got off the bed and walked over to offer to help, but Tube grabbed his arm and pushed it away. "No, thank you." Mark thought he recognized the voice. Was that a trace of anger he heard? He couldn't be sure with so few words.

Then Tube gestured to the table.

"What?" Mark asked. "You want *me* to get on the table?"

Tube slowly nodded his head.

"I'm not doing that shit. No offense, but that's your freak. I'm just here to watch. I could never do that."

Tube shook his head. He held the hand encased in the leather glove up in front of his masked face. With the dramatic flair of a magician, he took the other hand and tugged on each of the fingers, loosening the black leather until with one swoop the whole thing came off. Underneath was a latex surgical glove.

"Oh, I get it," Mark said. He knew what the single glove meant. "You want to fist me."

Tube nodded.

Mark stared at the hand. He'd never tried fisting before, at least not as the bottom. The idea had intrigued him for quite some time. Porsche and Devina had once asked if they could do it to him as part of their dominance game, but he didn't trust women to know what to do. The Tube seemed to be an expert at sticking things in himself. Who better to guide him through this new experience? After all the pounding his ass had taken in the past day, Mark figured his muscles could never be more stretched and ready.

"Fuck. Why not?" Mark finally conceded. "After all, it is my birthday."

Mark climbed on the massage table and got on all fours. Tube reached down into his black bag and retrieved a white, plastic jar of lubricant. The cream felt cold at first, but Tube's fingers were gentle and soon the motions brought a type of soothing sensation to Mark's sore opening. He'd had too much rough sex, and now the fingers and lube offered a healing touch.

Mark moaned. Tube knew exactly how to get all his fingers in without causing any pain. It was like a game of advance and retreat. As each limit was pushed, the fingers came out, and the surge subsided. More was immediately replaced with less. Mark soon lost track of how many fingers were inside him. Only when he felt the sensation of knuckles rapidly rotating back and forth across his prostate did Mark realize that Tube's whole hand was already inside.

As the knuckles brushed with bumps of bliss, the hand simultaneously thrust further inside. The combination of sensations overwhelmed Mark's body. He shuddered, lost control, and climaxed onto the table. Tube had never touched him—only from inside. At the moment of release Mark let loose a howl, a sound he didn't recognize as something that could have come from his own mouth. Tube pulled out his hand. Mark collapsed onto the pool of his own fluids.

His body completely spent, he opened his eyes slowly. The first thing he saw was the nurse. She was still on the phone.

The nurse clicked the cell phone closed and walked over to nonchalantly pack all the supplies back in the black bag, including Tube's jeans, which clearly would not fit now. Instead, Tube slipped on loose sweatpants, carefully lifting them over his engorged state. As the soft cotton on the waistband brushed the swollen area, Tube winced.

Mark edged himself off the massage table and crept over to the faux French desk. Every step felt as if he were weighted down with hundreds of pounds on his back. He'd never before been so completely drained. He opened a drawer and took out a wad of cash to pay the nurse, throwing in an extra hundred as a tip. The nurse and Tube walked out of the warehouse as quietly as they entered.

Mark tossed himself onto the bed. This time he was finally finished. *Happy Birthday to me . . .*

Outside at his car Tube peeled off the leather hood. Drenched in sweat, his brown hair was matted down into a fetid helmet. The soul patch under his chin felt damp. After he touched it, his fingers smelled like a dog left out in the rain. He carefully counted the money. Six one hundred dollar bills. He peeled off one and handed it to the nurse, then stuffed the rest into the glove compartment. The box was crammed with a nest of cash from other gigs. At least six thousand dollars in just his first week. *The hottest show in town.* He liked how men now *paid* for him. Just to watch. It was an incredible feeling of power and control.

He thought them fools for paying so much money for only a glimpse of what had now become so natural to him. It all started with the high colonics. That addiction was the gateway that made booty bumps so easy to take . . . and now this. His body seemed made for it. *Man mates with machinery.* Hospital technology created to save human lives now subverted for sexual pleasure. Andrew came up with the idea after the piss enema. "You're a natural," he said. The medical procedures fetish was the latest extreme. He figured people would pay to see it, and he just happened to know a nurse looking to make a few bucks on the side.

And so Tube was born. He walked the tightrope between pain and ecstasy. Audiences could never be sure which side he was on. That was the thrill of it.

Only The Tube knew the truth. He *was* the line. The raphe. That place in between two points. Pain and pleasure. Gay and straight. Happy and not. He fit somewhere in the middle, not allowed to comfortably exist at either end. Being The Tube was just one more example of that. It wasn't his first exploration of what existed on the line. He knew it wouldn't be his last. Destiny would never allow him to settle on either side.

Baptiste. Julie. Who needs them?

Happy Birthday, Mark Hazodo.

I hate that guy.

"You get the pictures with the phone?" Raphe asked the nurse.

"Yup. Already uploaded them to your e-mail. We gonna be taking pictures at all the gigs from now on?"

"No, just this one. This guy was special."

30

Raphe sat down at his computer and signed on to his anonymous Hotmail account. Forty new messages in just the past hour. He scanned the subject lines to see that most were fan mail. One was from Mark Hazodo, the third so far this week:

YOU FREAK. I WILL FUCKING KILL YOU WHEN I FIND OUT WHO YOU ARE! AND I WILL FIND OUT. YOU HAVE NO IDEA WHO I AM.

First it was lawyers. Now death threats. And in all capital letters no less, the internet equivalent of shouting. The guy must be hysterical, Raphe thought. He remembered that night in Mark's loft when he was held down on the bed and brutally taken. No choice. No condom. Complete panic. *That* was a real death threat. The words Raphe looked at on the screen now were only harmless static.

Raphe once believed internet fame was especially fleeting. Not just because of his days working on the frontier of dotcom, where so much was built up and then suddenly gone. He'd seen even successful web sites come and go swiftly—people tired of everything so quickly in search of the next big thrill.

Each day a new limit was pushed on the net, then immediately abandoned as boring.

Yet the traffic for AnalBizz.com kept growing. It was only fitting Raphe picked that name, since it was the thing that got him fired from dot-com in the first place. Not surprisingly, the domain name was still available. Now Raphe owned it.

The video of Mark Hazodo in a compromising position had become a huge hit in cubicle culture, the internet explorations of people bored at work. Within a week of the launch of Anal-Bizz, traffic to the site exploded, with most of the hits coming from offices in the video gaming world. The nurse had done an excellent job recording the fifteen-second video clip on her cell phone. Raphe took the sequence and put it into a continuous loop, which made the title *NeverEnd, My Ass!* all the more appropriate.

Once the cult of nerdy NeverEnd gamers heard about the site, the traffic went from phenomenal to server-crashing. Some lifted the footage to create their own animations cut to the beat of pop songs. The number of hits soon surpassed *The Star Wars Kid* and threatened to break the record set by Paris Hilton's X-rated home video. Raphe wondered if Mark Hazodo's minor celebrity in the tech world was what fueled the attention. It was a small subculture, but they were all online and likely jealous of Mark's success. Ability and hate are a powerful combination.

The fury of interest even led the *New York Times* to run a vague piece about the remarkable popularity of a "ubiquitous and execrable internet film alleged to be of a young videogame entrepreneur." There were editorials in newspapers and magazines about whether the web had finally gone too far. All the negative press only spawned a burst of new hits on the web site. No one in the mainstream media dared to publish the actual name AnalBizz.com, though that didn't seem to prevent people from finding it.

An army of attorneys working for Mark Hazodo's company threatened the web site hosting service with lawsuits, but Raphe had been careful to go offshore where US courts have no jurisdiction. It was all just saber rattling. Raphe knew if Mark actually pursued a suit, it would only draw attention to the fact that it really was him in the video—confirmation that might ruin his company's plans for getting on the stock market someday. It would look bad to have a guy selling videogames to children publicly admit he likes to have a fist stuck up his ass.

Raphe scrolled through the other e-mails until he hit one with a subject line that read:

Book Deal?

It was from a publisher who claimed she'd made a fortune peddling the autobiography of a porn star. She wondered if there was a book in all of this. She included her private cell phone number and an invitation to call anytime, day or night.

A book? Raphe's heart pounded. After all the years he'd struggled to find something to write about, was this his chance? Raphe tugged on his soul patch and grinned.

He got up from his desk and walked over to the window. From the panoramic view of his bedroom he watched the cars bumper-to-bumper on the Bay Bridge. He looked downtown where he could make out the tiny figures of people scurrying about the financial district. He thought of their routine lives, and how they'd be stunned to find out what was really happening just beneath the surface of their beautiful jewel of a city. So many of the amazing secret worlds he'd seen existed in plain sight, for those who knew where to look. Who better to write the story than someone who'd lived it?

An author! The images of what he'd write flashed through Raphe's mind with remarkable clarity. Mark Hazodo was only a small part of the tale. Raphe pledged to tell it all, from Dr. Kaplan, to the stabbing, to The Tube. It would make a great story—

a real shocker. After so many years of false starts, his fingers now burned to type. The words would fly.

Of course, to write he'd have to scale back on Tina. She messed with his head too much to concentrate on a book. He might even be forced to kick her out of his life for good. He thought fondly of her. She'd helped him through a rough patch, but like all the others she would never work as a long-term relationship.

He'd still do his act as The Tube. It was a freak show, Raphe knew, but that's how he felt about himself these days. The raphe—the freak—the guy who doesn't quite fit anywhere. He was beginning to understand that about himself and accept his fate. The act couldn't last forever, but being The Tube turned out to be the best job he'd ever had. A turning point. The popularity of The Tube also said something about this time and place. He'd have to chew on that a bit more to sort it all out.

Besides, as The Tube, Raphe was finally making enough now to cover his mortgage, his bills—this incredible view!—and the rest of his life in SoMa.

His home.

Author's Note

When I first moved to San Francisco, I was deep into my career in journalism. Like so many in my profession, I was pretty jaded. I'd seen it all. I knew it all. Just ask me, I'd tell you.

Nothing prepared me for living in SoMa. South of Market wasn't like the quaint San Francisco of tourist fame. It was raw and filled with extremes. As I grew to know the people, I'd listen to their tales.

I turned what I learned into short stories. In journalism, we're obligated to stick to the facts as a way to reach the truth. I chose to write these stories as fiction, since I felt the underlying meaning was more important than real names and facts that might embarrass individuals.

Eventually, I wondered if others might find these stories as insightful as I did. In 1999, I launched SoMa Literary Review, www.somalit.com, with my friend and collaborator Jon Stuber. I wrote every story for that first edition under a variety of pen names. The premiere struck a nerve. Submissions began coming in. Other writers had observation about SoMa and San Francisco they wanted to share.

So how much of *SoMa* is true?

All of it. And none of it.

It's fiction based on real events and places. All of the charac-

ters are fictionalized composites of real people. Most of the settings actually exist, and many of the types of events described in
this book have happened at those places. There really is a BART
fetish group with more than three thousand registered members. It's true I knew a banker who had a separate life as a drag
persona. The Power Exchange and Bondage-a-Go-Go are real
and have thrived for years. And yes, men and women hook up
for sex via the room rental classified ads on craigslist.org. I per-
sonally know of four people who have done this, three straight
and one gay.

On the other hand, there is no 225 Folsom Street. It didn't
seem fair to make an actual place appear to be the headquarters
for a criminal enterprise. There is also no state agency called the
Internal Department of Labor and Employment, although some
might argue that several deserve the acronym IDLE.

However, what is absolutely true in *SoMa* is San Francisco's
depiction as an "open city." Perhaps the only one in America.
Just about anything goes here. People arrive with a clean slate.
They are allowed and encouraged to be whoever they really are,
and indulge their desires. What people do with that freedom,
and the paths they choose, is a reflection of our time.

My intention in writing *SoMa* was to provoke readers to
think about that. What would you do if you were truly free?

Aren't you?

Acknowledgments

Thank you to the countless people whose real life stories provided the material for this book.

Writing a book filled with shocking content is bound to offend, but I've been extraordinarily fortunate to be surrounded by fellow writers who gave me the feedback and support I needed to complete *SoMa*. The Writers' Bloc group has been there from the very beginning, with Steven Bodzin, Melodie Bowsher, Camincha, Michael Chorost, Paul Freedman, Bruce Genaro, David Gleeson, Ken Grosserode, Arlene Heitner, Jeff Kingman, Heidi Machen, Shana Mahaffey, Joe Quirk, Maria Strom, Alika Tenaka, Rob Tocalino, and Heather Wagner.

My thanks also to the famed San Francisco Writers Workshop led by Tamim Ansary. Talented writers like Erika Mailman and dozens of others help me every week. My daily retreat for writing is a co-op of authors called the Sanchez Grotto Annex, created by Doug Wilkins. There's no better place to work.

At an early stage of the book, a group of readers located throughout the United States agreed to give *SoMa* a dispassionate critique. Hours of phone calls and in-person interviews followed, with some folks clearly rattled by what they'd read. Those conversations were incredibly valuable, and each person influenced the ultimate direction of this book. Many were complete strangers, yet they generously gave me their time and insight. Thanks to Eric Allen, Ryan Barrett, Jerry Bolton, Mark Casey, Julie Cavellini, Pam Conroy, Libby Dodd, Maj-Britt Hansen, Dr. Karin Hastik, Mariesa Kemble, Rose Lamoureux, Sarah Lugaric, Anne Marie Luger, and Rob Rosen.

Many thanks to editor in chief John Scognamiglio and Justin Hocking at Kensington. Your support has been a joy, and you provoked me to make *SoMa* a better book. I couldn't ask for anything more.

Although I'm sure they'd prefer I'd written a nice, cozy mystery, I've always had the love and encouragement of my family. That means more than we ever express to one another.

Jon, I couldn't have done this without you.

Jerry, I wouldn't want to do this without you.

SoMa

Kemble Scott

ABOUT THIS GUIDE

The suggested questions are included to
enhance your group's reading of
Kemble Scott's *SoMa*

DISCUSSION QUESTIONS

1. There are several examples of extreme behavior in *SoMa*. Which, if any, was the most disturbing, outrageous or shocking to you? Why?

2. Raphe, Lauren, and Mark are all in their mid-twenties. What drives people so young to engage in this type of behavior?

3. Raphe lives in a type of sexual gray zone. He doesn't fit comfortably in either the straight or gay worlds. Discuss the complexities of sexual orientation. At what age did you first understand your own sexuality? What made Raphe the way he is? Choice? Environment? Genetics? Fate?

4. Julie describes San Francisco as an "open society where everyone who comes here gets a clean slate to be whatever they want." Is that what allows the characters to behave the way they do? Is the type of behavior depicted in *SoMa* limited to big cities?

5. The story is set in the time immediately following the dot-com crash that crippled the economy of San Francisco. Beyond the loss of his job and financial troubles, how does the economic collapse affect the psyche of Raphe?

6. At nearly every moment of despair or questioning, Raphe turns to technology for help or guidance. His answers often come from the internet. What is the author saying about the role technology plays in lives today?

7. Baptiste appears to be the poster child for hedonism, but later we learn he really wants a long-term monogamous relationship. These two ideas seem to be in conflict. Are they? Is it possible to want both things? Is it possible to have both? Explain.

8. Lauren is repeatedly drawn to men who are unattainable. She spurns other men who are attracted to her. Why does she behave this way? What is the root cause of her behavior? What will it take for Lauren to have a successful long-term relationship?

9. Several times the issue of "fate" comes into play, especially for Raphe when he learns the secret of his name. Do you believe in fate? Are our lives predetermined for us?

10. Raphe, Lauren, and Mark each have life philosophies that guide their actions. They are loose metaphors for three ancient belief systems. Identify those philosophies and match them with the characters. Why did the author decide to model the characters this way? What comment is being made?

PLEASE TURN THE PAGE FOR A VERY SPECIAL
INTERVIEW WITH KEMBLE SCOTT!

**Many events in *SoMa* are apparently based on actual oc-
currences. How did you come across such a multitude
of bizarre stories?**

These days, bizarre stories seem to find *me*.

I'm very curious—if I hear an interesting story, I ask questions. That's the journalist in me. People love to talk about
themselves, and they'll share the most amazing details. I carry
around a little notebook and the first chance I get, I scribble
down everything I can remember to use later.

That doesn't mean I believe these tales. People also love to
fib and exaggerate. So I'll do my own research to confirm a
story, sometimes going to see for myself. That's what happened
with the BARTM4M scene in *SoMa*. I'd heard the story a
dozen times from a guy who rode the commuter train every
day. He couldn't stop talking about it! It sounded too outrageous
to be true, but I wrote a version of the story based on what he
described. The first draft was terrible. I'd never taken the commuter train before, so I struggled with the details. What did the
station look like? How did it smell? I didn't even know the color
of the seats on the train. The next afternoon I went for a ride.
Sure enough, on my very first trip I witnessed the fetish first
hand, so to speak.

Now that I've developed a reputation for these twisted tales
on my web site, people routinely seek me out to tell me their
strangest stories. Just the other day I heard about the most
bizarre new behavior involving iPods.

**Raphe is a character who has been let down by the either/
or, strictly binary dot-com world. Rather than seeing
everything in black and white, his new existence forces
him to accept many of life's gray areas. Yet, many of our**

**contemporary leaders claim to live by moral and reli-
gious absolutes (and seek to impose those absolutes on
others). Why did you write a novel that lives so much
"in the gray," and why do you think so many Americans
are uncomfortable with ambiguity?**

Alvin Toffler was mostly right with his predictions in 1970
in *Future Shock*. We now live in that anticipated age of "information overload." But instead of rejecting tech and retreating to
agrarian compounds, many people are shutting down in a different way. They've turned off their brains.

It's easy to see why it's happening. People are bombarded
with media and messages to the point where it's too much to
process, so they accept easy answers. They embrace ridiculous
notions like Red States and Blue States. The truth is, the United
States isn't really divided into Red and Blue. If you apply those
color codes, everyone turns out to be a shade of purple.

When the world is dumbed down to simple black/white,
yes/no choices, it makes life easier to perceive of. The problem,
of course, is that such simplistic, dogmatic thinking is usually
wrong and inherently dangerous. The character of Lauren in
SoMa represents this fundamentalist type of thinking. If a guy
isn't with her, he must be against her. You're on her side, or
you're her enemy. Or to quote someone else, "You're with us or
with the terrorists." As Lauren learns the hard way, dismissing
the world's shades of gray can lead to a heap of trouble.

People are complex, and so are the issues they face. Raphe
struggles with the discovery that he's an individual, not fitting
into the ready-made definitions of society. *SoMa* tackles this
gray zone through its exploration of sexuality, but it's analogous
to much of life in the new millennium.

You have an impressive ability to write both gay and straight sex scenes. I'm hard pressed to think of many other writers who can do this. Can you name a few, and discuss whether or not they had an influence on you?

The problem with writing sexy sex scenes is describing the male organ. Let's face it, all the words we have in English sound silly. I was once asked to review an anthology of short stories that were supposed to be sexy. I ended up making a list of the stupid phrases the writers used: *honker, pisser, poker, monster, putter, scepter, piston, schlong,* and *meat tube.* The editor refused to print my list. It was too dirty for the newspaper.

The master of writing about sexy sex without using dirty or silly words was Anaïs Nin back in the 1940s. Her work is beautiful and provocative, no matter if the scene is straight, gay, or godknowswhat. She wrote about it all, but you won't find a single *meat tube* in her prose.

On my wall I have a framed original letter from Anaïs written in 1970 to writer Maurice Rosenbaum. In it she complains about how she is "misquoted, disliked and misunderstood" in the media.

So while I treasure the artifact, and I am inspired by her work to be careful with my language, the letter is also a frequent reminder to me of what can happen to authors who write about sex.

Craigslist.org features prominently in *SoMa's* plot. It's a community site that allows strangers to easily share goods, ideas, and services. Yet, many of the "dot-com bust" characters in *SoMa* use it simply to find anonymous sex. As a writer, do you feel technology serves to isolate people more than it connects them?

There's a funny expression I quote in *SoMa* about online dating: "The odds are good, but the goods are odd."

I use craigslist.org as the ultimate temple of technology in *SoMa*, and eventually all the characters end up praying in that church. Sometimes they receive divine intervention. Sometimes they get burned. The internet is a devilish trickster.

The blessing of technology is how it allows people to find each other and bond in ways that were unfathomable not so long ago. A person struggling with cancer in Istanbul can get advice from a survivor in Anaheim. Adoptees are reunited with brothers and sisters they never knew they had. You can sell that Ikea couch you hate to someone who's always wanted one just like it.

And yes, you can possibly find your perfect love match. If you seek a "Diesel Dyke Harley-riding Save-the-Whales Log Cabin Republican redhead (no weirdos please)," then the internet gives you the chance to find her. In fact, you can find hundreds who fit that description.

That's the conundrum. You can hook up in an instant with your ideal and have an unfathomable number of liaisons, all facilitated by web sites like craigslist. Does quantity create substance in human relationships? Or does it simply make it easier to know more people at a superficial level?

It depends on your definition of what constitutes a meaningful human connection.

It's logical to believe there's a better chance of understanding someone if you're with them for a long time. But then how do you explain couples who have been together twenty years, then wake up one morning, look at each other and say, "I have no idea who you are."

You have to wonder how many people are capable of making meaningful connections with others, internet or not. At least with web sites like craigslist, you can try to screen.

In recent advertising campaigns, books, and films, American pop culture seems to increasingly embrace the "man's man"—the strong, beer-drinking, strictly heterosexual male who refuses to show the slightest shred of femininity. On the other hand, *SoMa*'s hero experiments with bisexuality and leads somewhat of a "metrosexual" lifestyle (though he hates this term). Is Raphe a relic of the 1990's or the man of the future?

For better or worse, the term "metrosexual" has become shorthand to describe a type of guy. He dates women, plays sports, *and* uses hair product. He's heard of both Prada and ESPN SportsCenter, *and* uses deodorant. The previous incarnation of man, known as Cro-Magnonsexual, was not able to multi-task in this way.

Okay, so metrosexuality has become a punch line. That's why Raphe holds his nose at the expression. But make no mistake, metrosexuality is a real step in the evolution of guys, kind of like an awkward adolescent phase that will lead to New Millennium Man.

Take a look at the upcoming generation of guys. They grew up watching *Will & Grace* on primetime TV, so they aren't ignorant and shocked that gay people exist. Today's teen boys were weaned on episodes of MTV's *Cribs,* so they don't associate being knowledgeable about fashion or design as feminine behavior. The hyper-masculine role models, like sports stars, have turned out to be hugely disappointing and not worth emulating.

It's going to be harder to implant bigotry and old stereotypes of male behavior on this next generation. It will be fascinating to watch how they turn out.

Raphe is representative of New Millennium Man in many ways. He doesn't possess any fey mannerisms, and to those who want to possess him—Lauren, Baptiste, and Julie—he's the ideal guy's guy. Raphe himself is surprised to discover that he's more complicated than he ever believed. I suspect that will be the fate of many New Millennium Men.

Raphe attempts to work on his own writing during his job at the scam post office. Have you ever stolen time from a "B-job" to write?

When I started writing fiction, my work in journalism had me constantly flying around the country. One year I spent more than 200 days away from home. That's a lot of time spent on airplanes and in airports. I began to look forward to those dreary aisle seats and the undisturbed writing time they afforded me. The first drafts of *SoMa* happened at 30,000 feet.

What else can you tell us about your actual writing process?

I'm constantly writing—especially when I'm away from a keyboard or pen.

I'll see something and daydream a fantastic story around it. I rewrite in my head the conversation I just had with someone, making my fictional dialogue far more wittier and meaningful than it actually was. I guess we've all done things like that.

However, my mind is also writing in the background, when it's not in my conscious thoughts.

I'll typically sit and write the first draft of an entire chapter in one sitting, without taking a break. That can take anywhere from three to six hours. When I'm in that zone, I lose all track of time. Then I hit a wall, so I stop. I'll banish the whole thing from my mind, not thinking about it at all. The next day, or even a week later, I'll sit down and start again, with whatever obstacle I faced now miraculously resolved. I hadn't been dwelling on it, but somehow my brain fixed the problem, computing silently in the background. That's the best way for me to explain it.

I treat writing as a career, which is why I have an office in the San Francisco's writers co-op called the Sanchez Grotto Annex. It's home to several authors. We split the rent and share ideas. But even though writing has the work ethic and trappings of a job, it's never been a chore. I know people who struggle with every word. For me, those first drafts are a joy. They seem to flow from my fingers almost effortlessly. Which doesn't mean they're perfect. I then rewrite continuously. I workshop my drafts and make changes if I'm not getting the response I intended.

When you work in journalism, you quickly become very comfortable with feedback and editing. I stopped being offended by the need to rewrite after my first day in a newsroom. I'm lucky I learned that lesson early in my career. After all, I'm writing to be read by others. Making sure I'm connecting with readers is a crucial part of my process.

You're very active in the San Francisco literary scene. Can you tell us more about your web site and e-mail list, and talk about how working on these projects has affected your writing?

San Francisco has such a rich literary history, from Jack London to Amy Tan. Today there's a community of writers here that's comparable to what it must have been like for artists a hundred years ago in Paris. You can find Pulitzer Prize winner Michael Chabon offering advice to would-be novelists, or Dave Eggers mentoring inner-city kids. Heck, you can bump into Lemony Snicket out walking his dog! There are endless ways to connect with other writers, whether they are famous or still un-published. It can be remarkably inspiring.

I dove into the scene when I launched the online e-zine *SoMa Literary Review* back in 1999 as an outlet for my fiction. That first issue featured stories all written by me, under a variety of pen names. Almost immediately I began receiving submissions from other writers, and a real literary journal was born. Today we receive about two million hits per year and we've been thrilled to discover and publish many wonderful new San Francisco voices.

We recently launched a free weekly e-mail newsletter that lists all the author and book events happening in the area. It's astonishing how many great authors are available to meet and chat up.

I've met some amazing writers this way, and I've been able to ask them questions about their process, challenges and successes. Sure, some people are intimidating. But most are open and down-to-earth and offer insight that can be quite validating.

You absolutely need validation as a writer. Being part of a writing community can provide that. You can't succeed if you have a constant chorus in your head, or in your life, that beats you down. Cheerleaders are just as vital as an editor's red pen.

Were you inspired by any other particular novels or writers while working on *SoMa*?

You can't write about San Francisco and not be influenced by Armistead Maupin. His wonderful *Tales of the City* books captured The City at a crucial moment in history. It's amazing to read those books today and see how much of the San Francisco he described decades ago still exists today.

In their time, the *Tales* books and the newspaper column